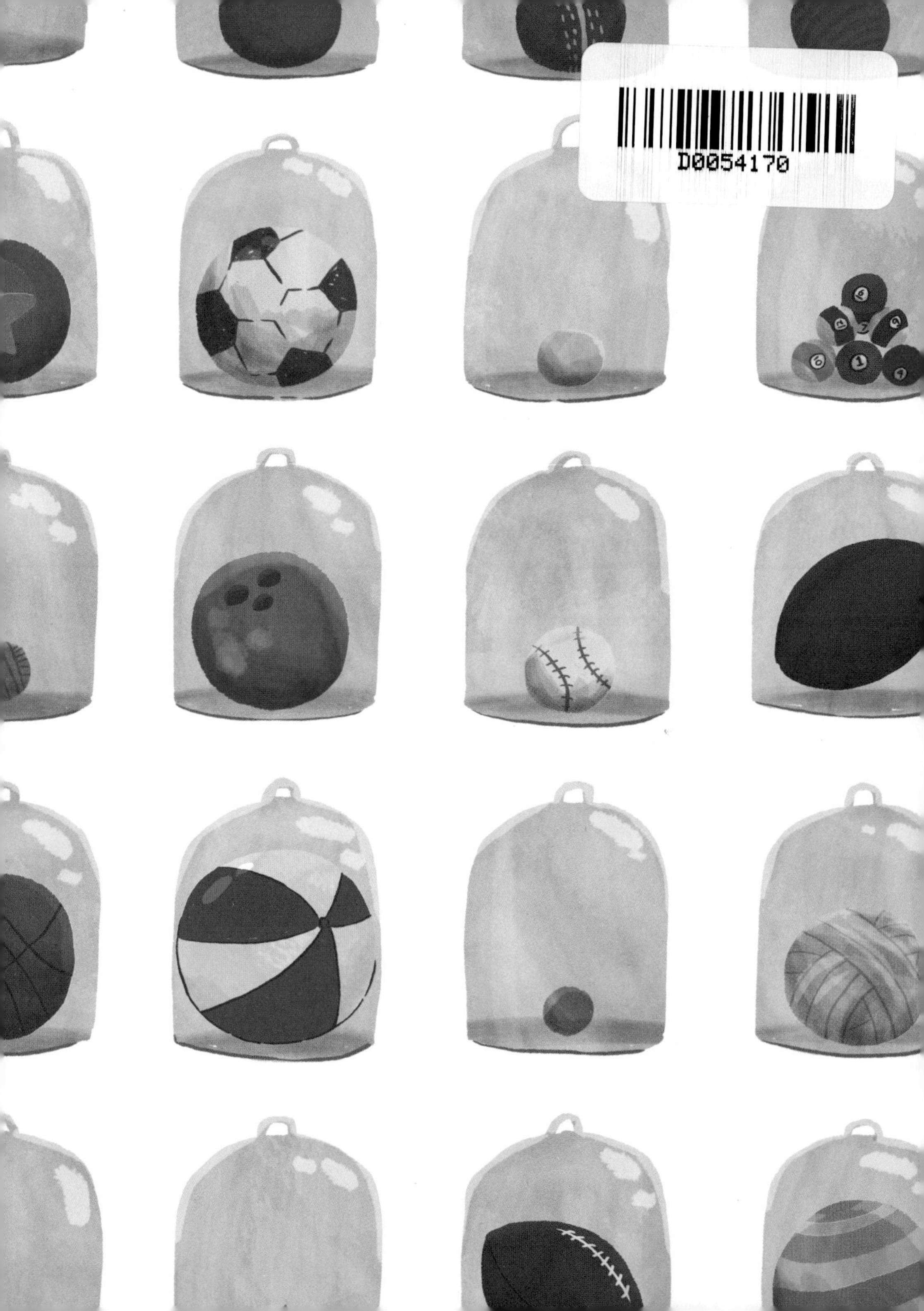

Blue, Barry & Pancakes

Barry & Pancakes

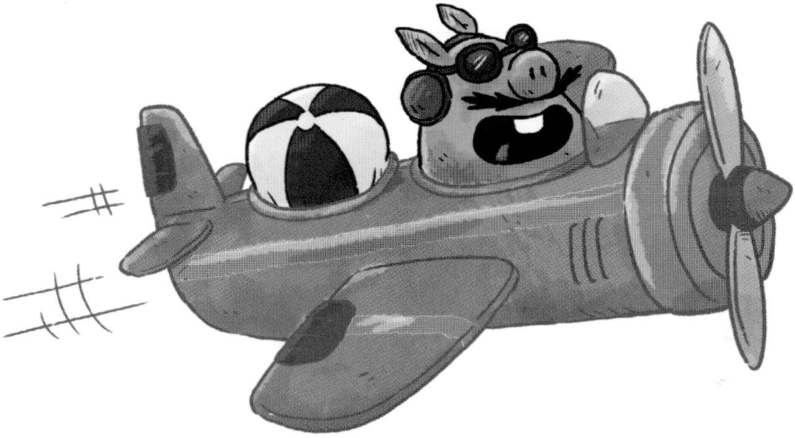

by
Dan & Jason

:01
First Second
New York

FOR:

Harrison and Vivian —J.P.

Eloise and Winona —D.A.

First Second

Published by First Second
First Second is an imprint of Roaring Brook Press,
a division of Holtzbrinck Publishing Holdings Limited Partnership
120 Broadway, New York, NY 10271
firstsecondbooks.com
mackids.com

Library of Congress Control Number: 2020911192

Our books may be purchased in bulk for promotional, educational, or business use.
Please contact your local bookseller or the Macmillan Corporate and
Premium Sales Department at (800) 221-7945 ext. 5442 or by email at
MacmillanSpecialMarkets@macmillan.com.

FIRST EDITION

First edition, 2021
Edited by Calista Brill and Alex Lu
Cover design by Sunny Lee
Interior book design by Sunny Lee
Printed in China by RR Donnelley Asia Printing Solutions Ltd.,
Dongguan City, Guangdong Province

This book was drawn mostly on a Wacom Cintiq and iPad Pro. Dan & Jason write, draw, color, and letter together in Photoshop and Procreate. The font is a unique Blue, Barry, and Pancakes typeset created specifically for this book.

ISBN 978-1-250-25555-6
10 9 8 7 6 5 4 3 2 1

Don't miss your next favorite book from First Second! For the latest
updates go to firstsecondnewsletter.com and sign up for our enewsletter.

BY ART WE LIVE

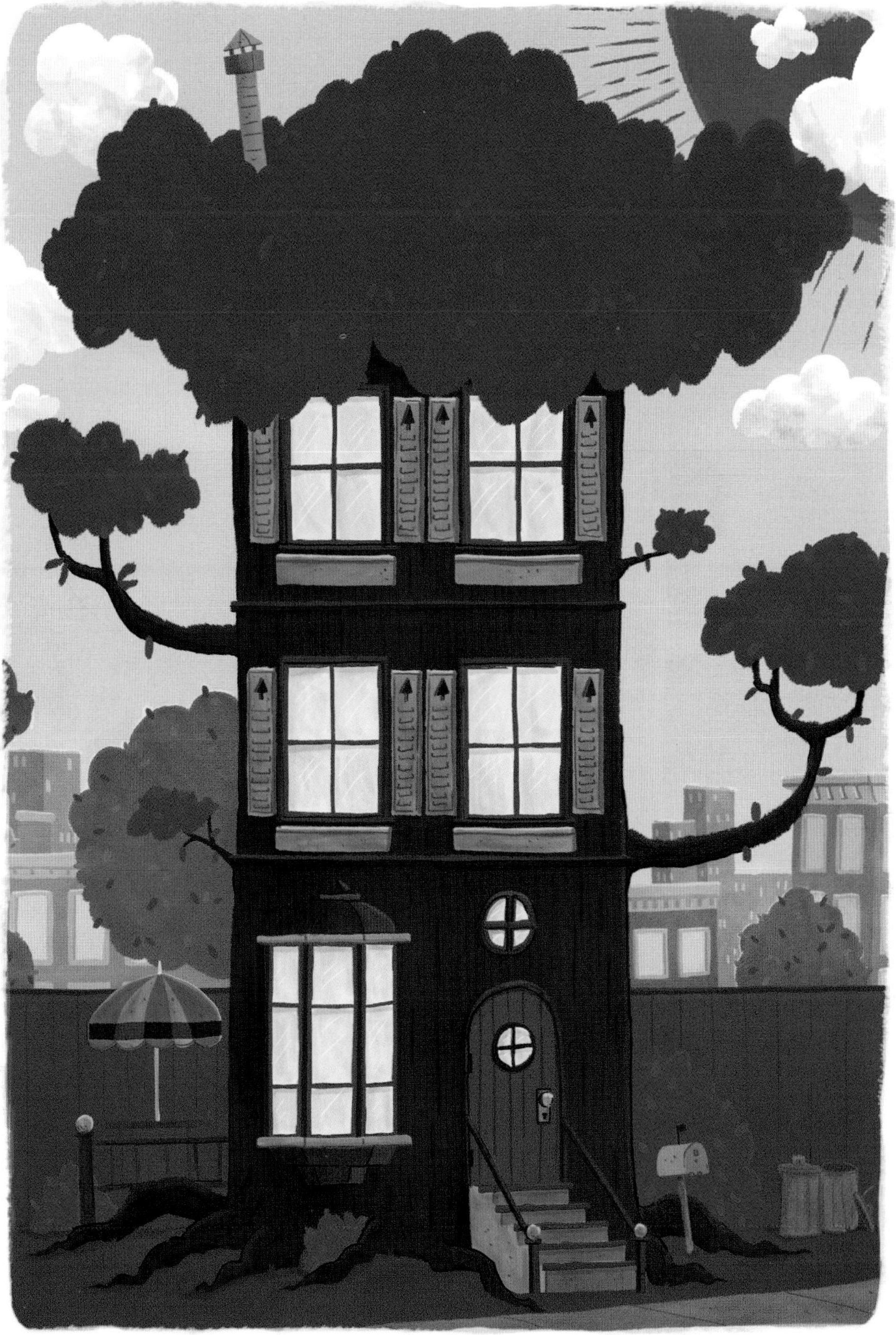

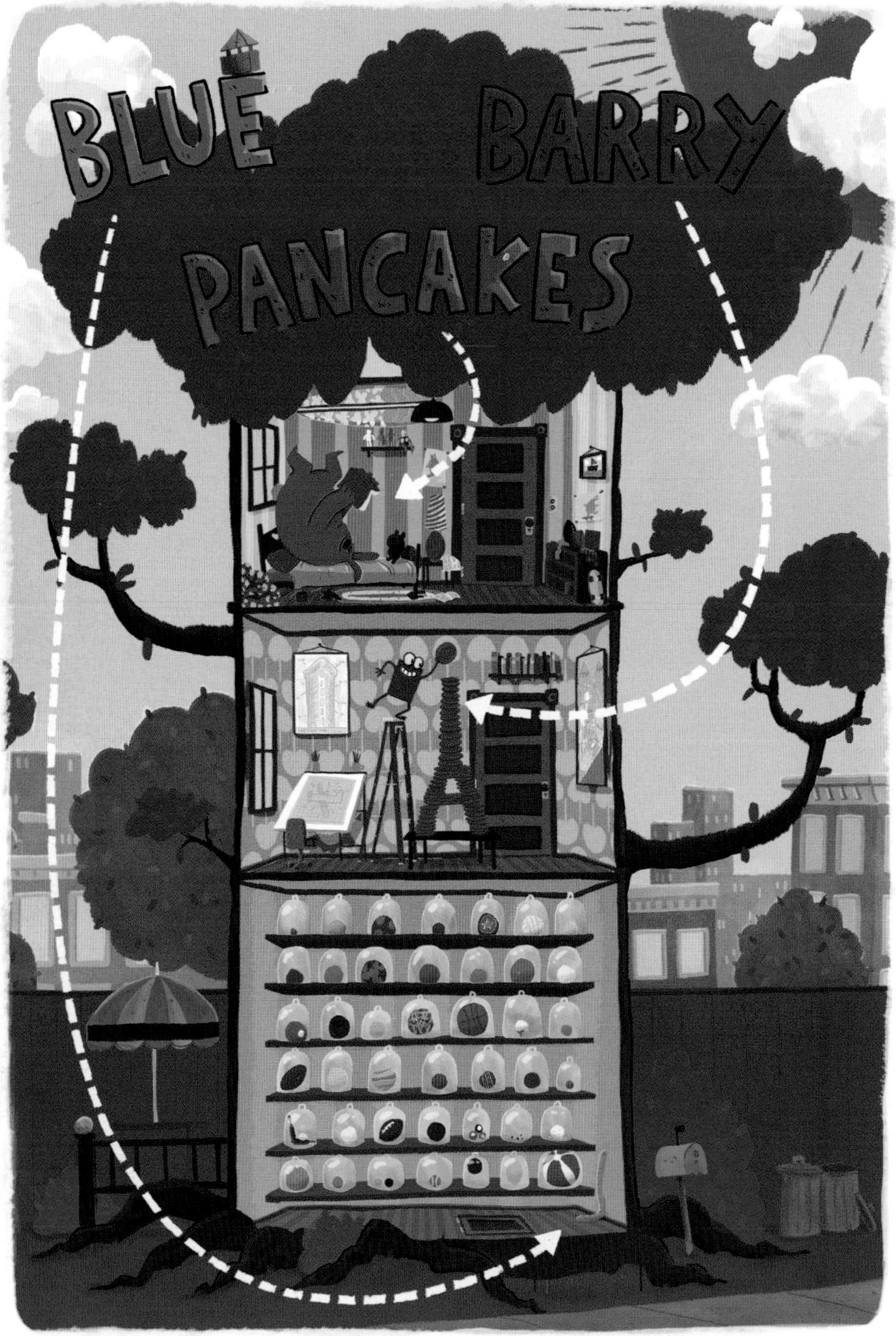
BLUE
BARRY
PANCAKES

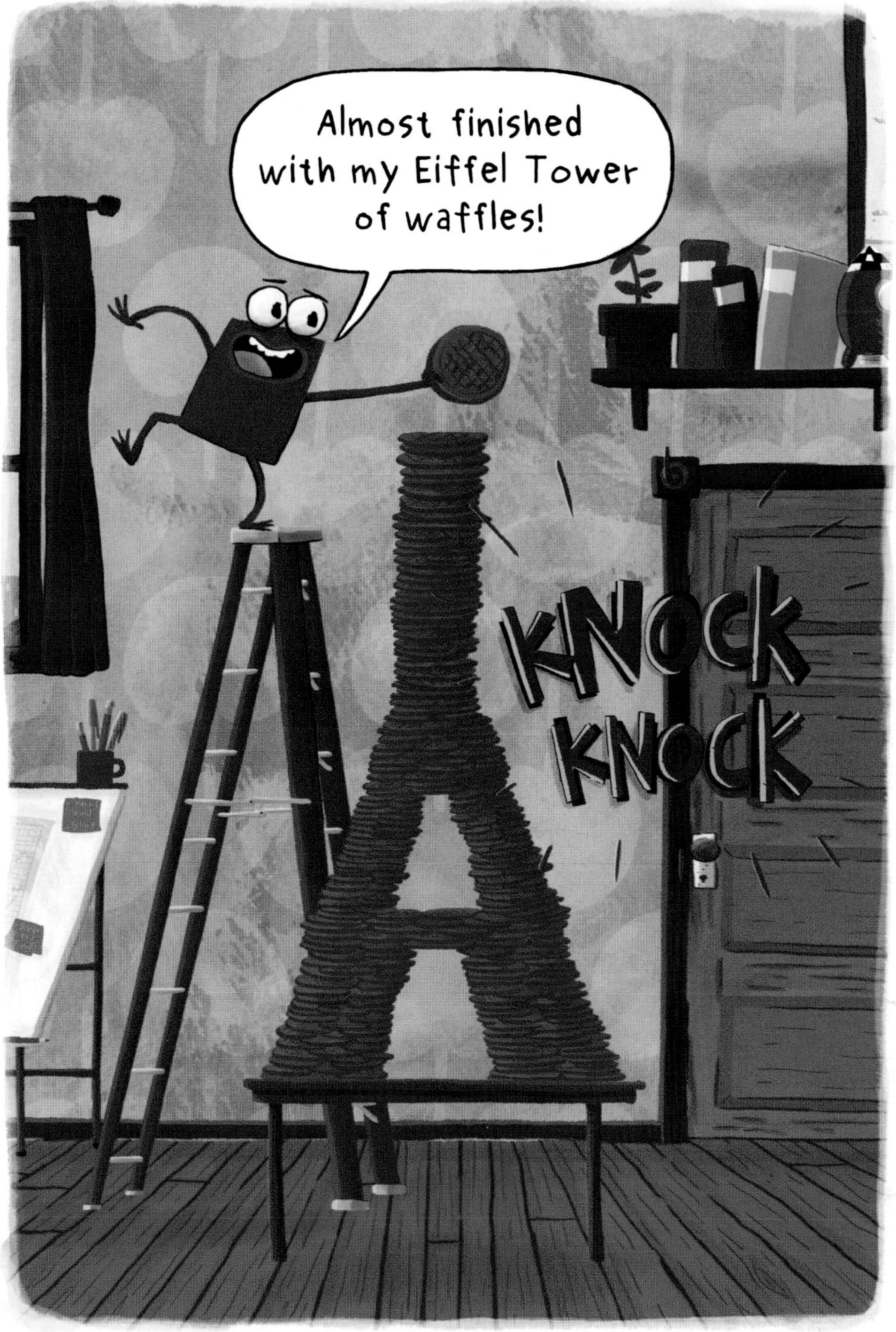
Almost finished with my Eiffel Tower of waffles!
KNOCK KNOCK

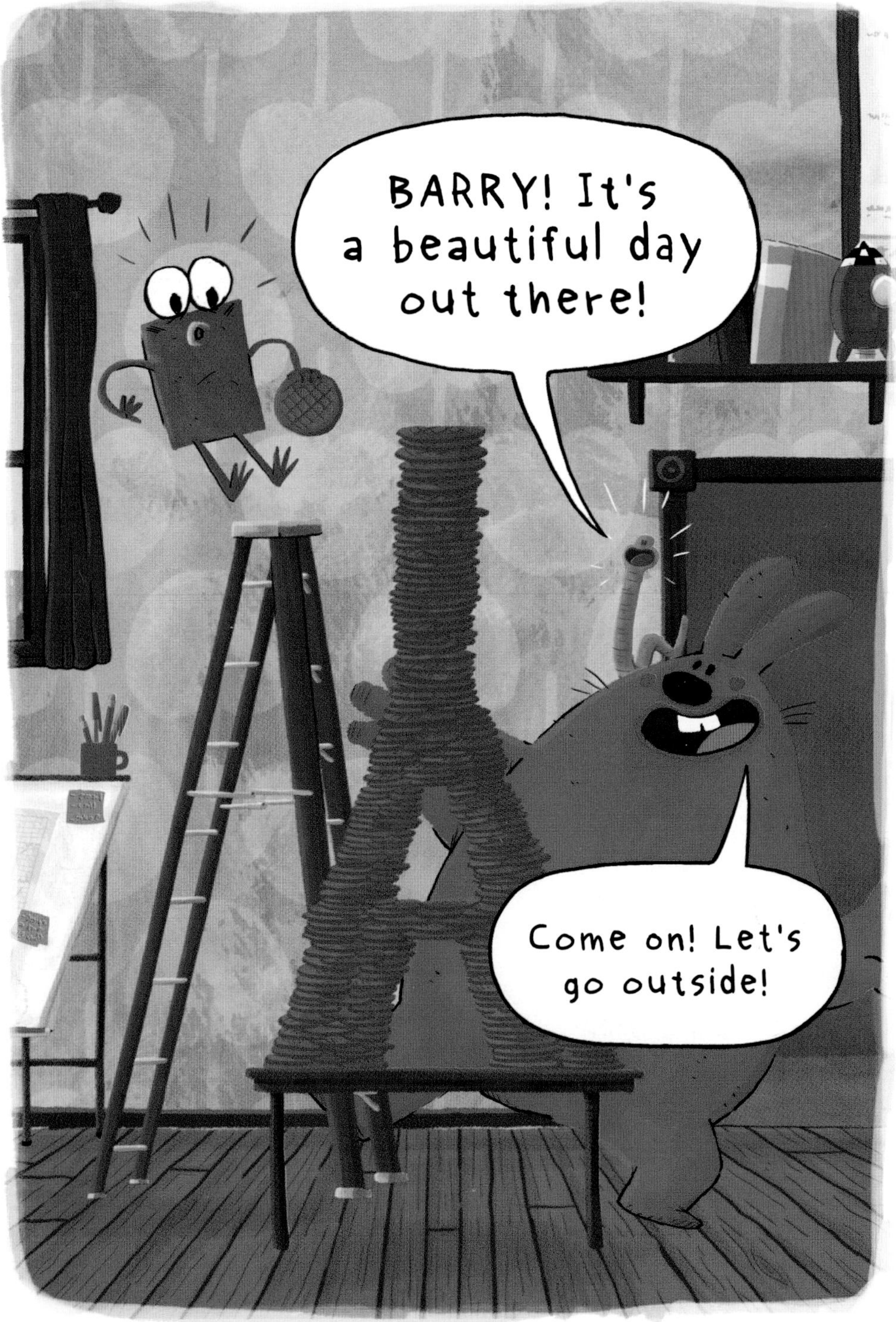
BARRY! It's a beautiful day out there!
Come on! Let's go outside!

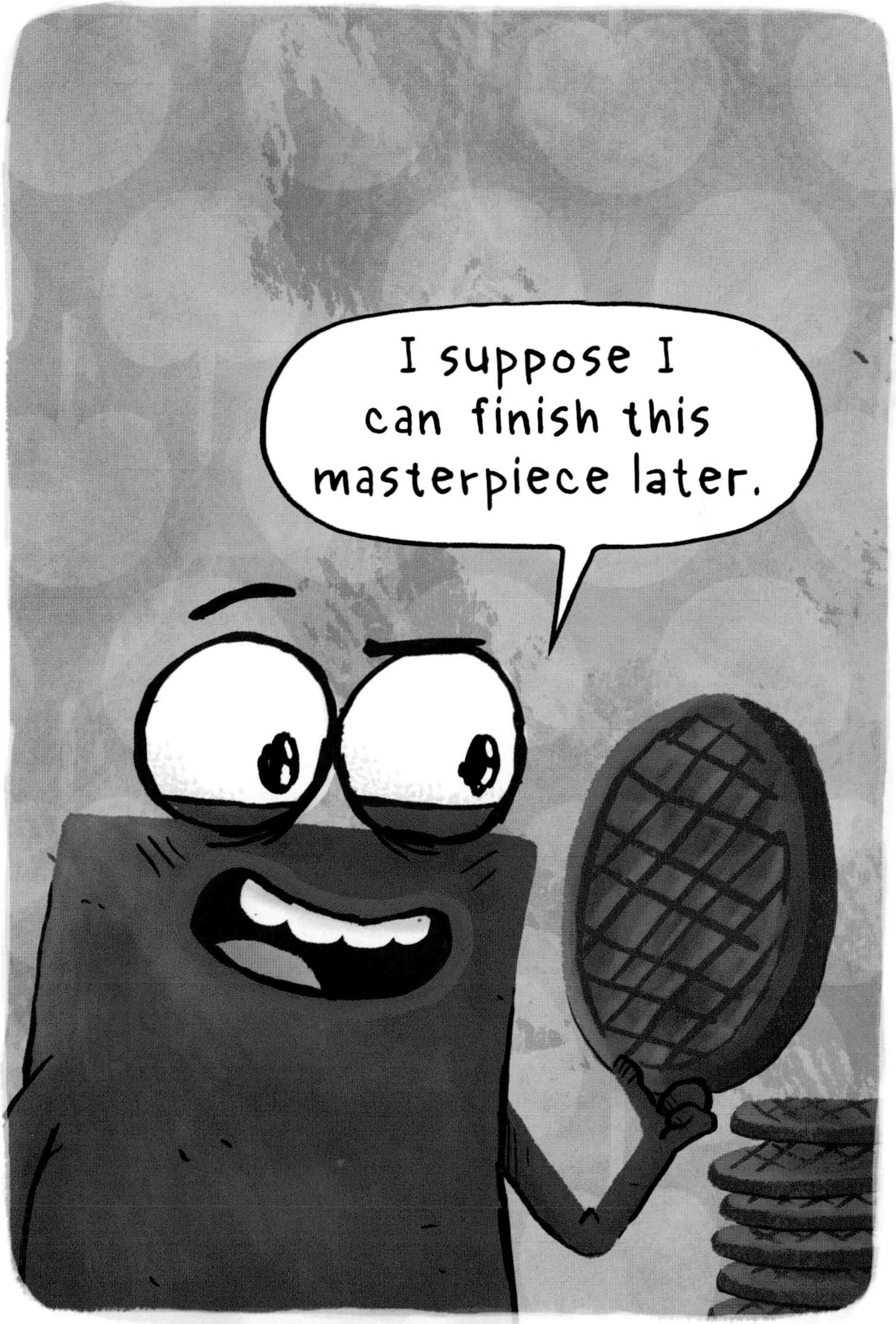
I suppose I can finish this masterpiece later.

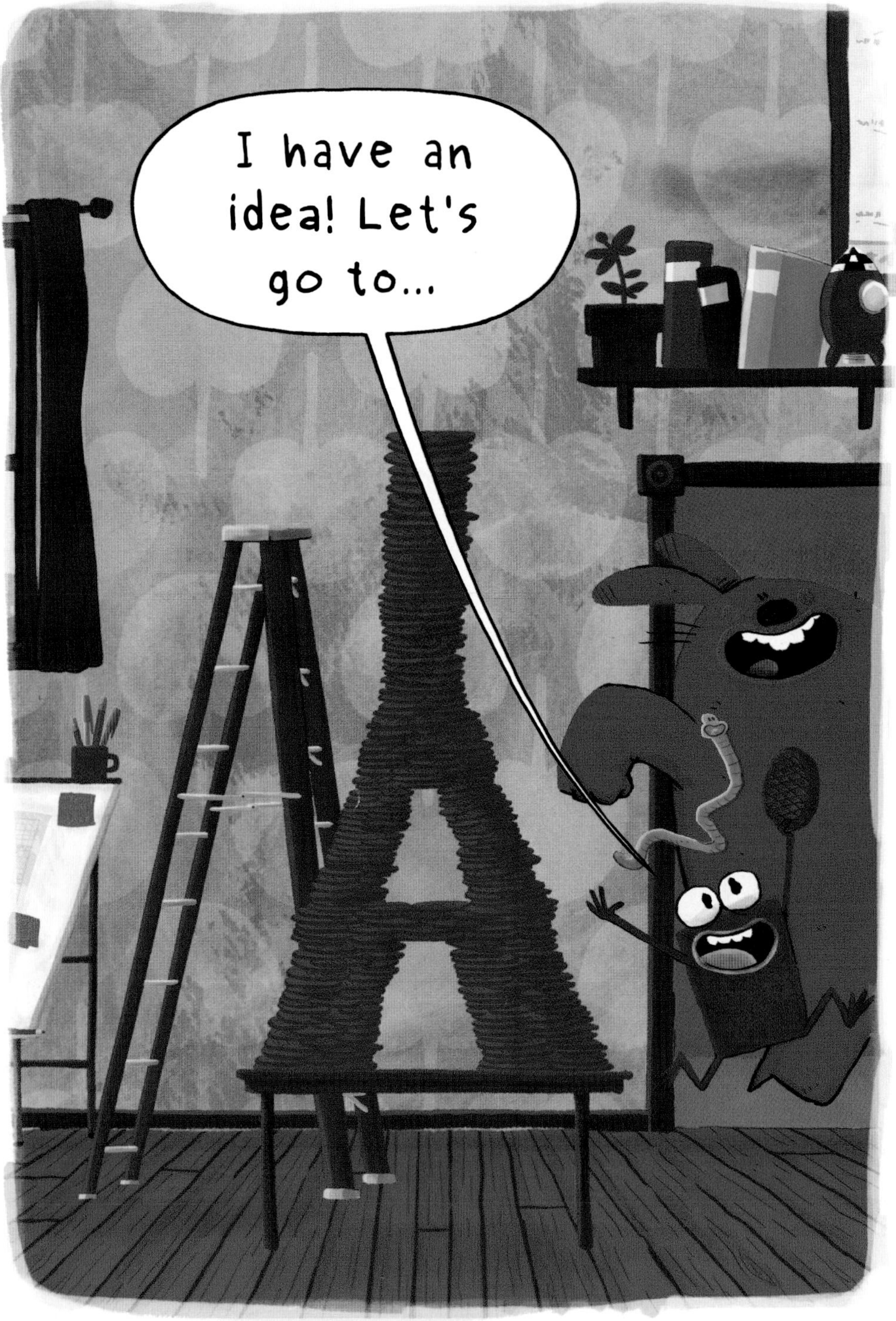
I have an idea! Let's go to...

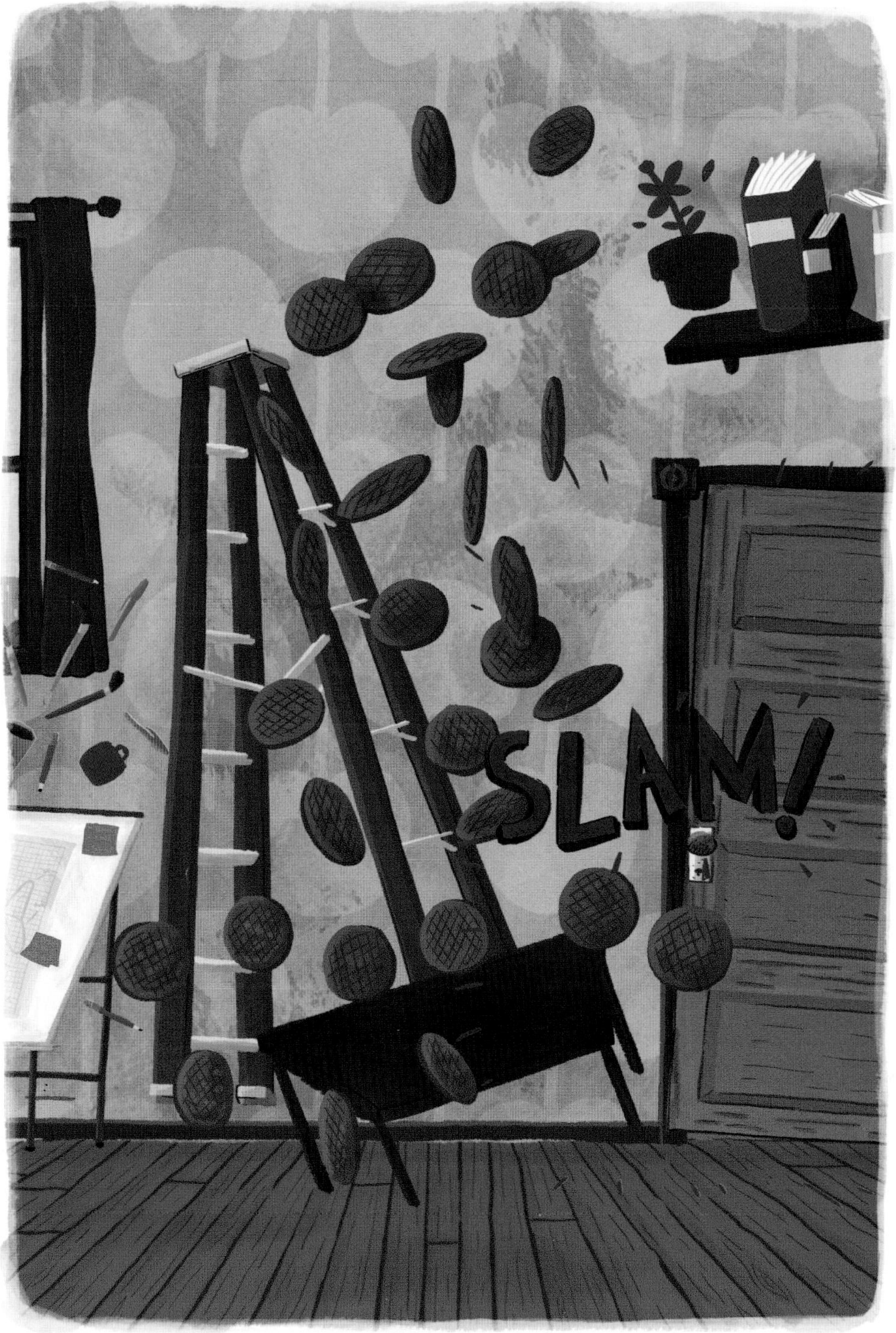
SLAM!

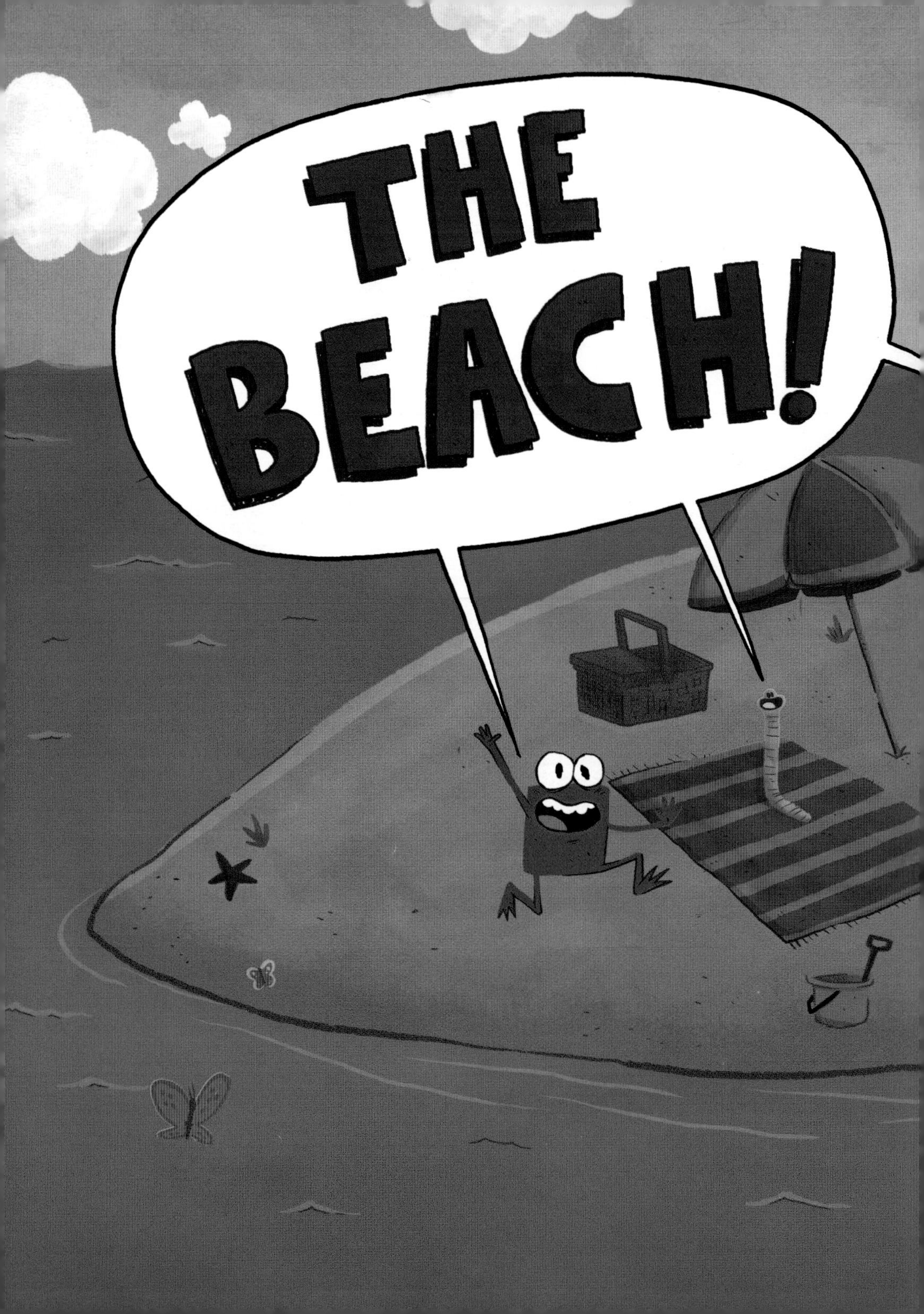
THE BEACH!

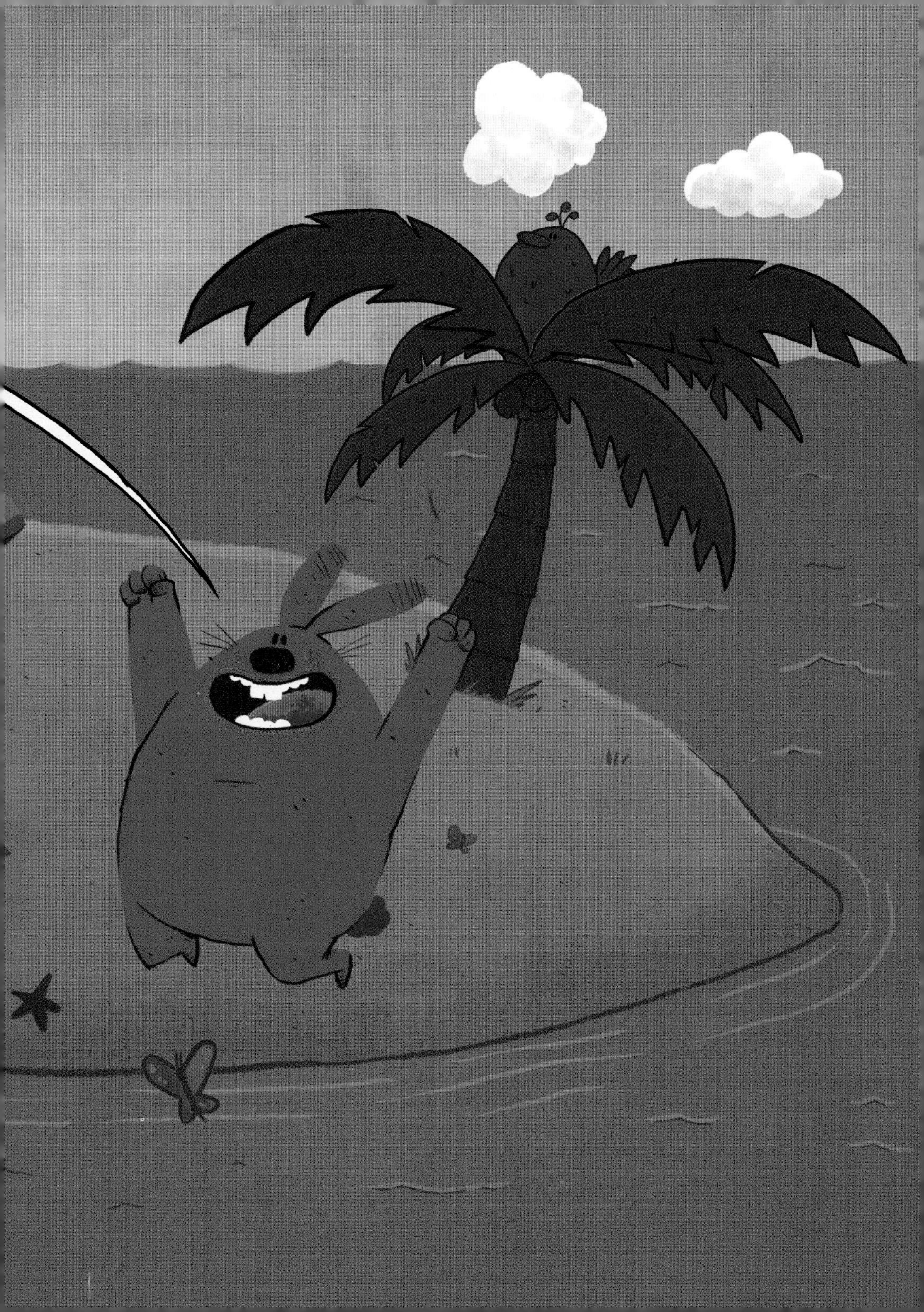

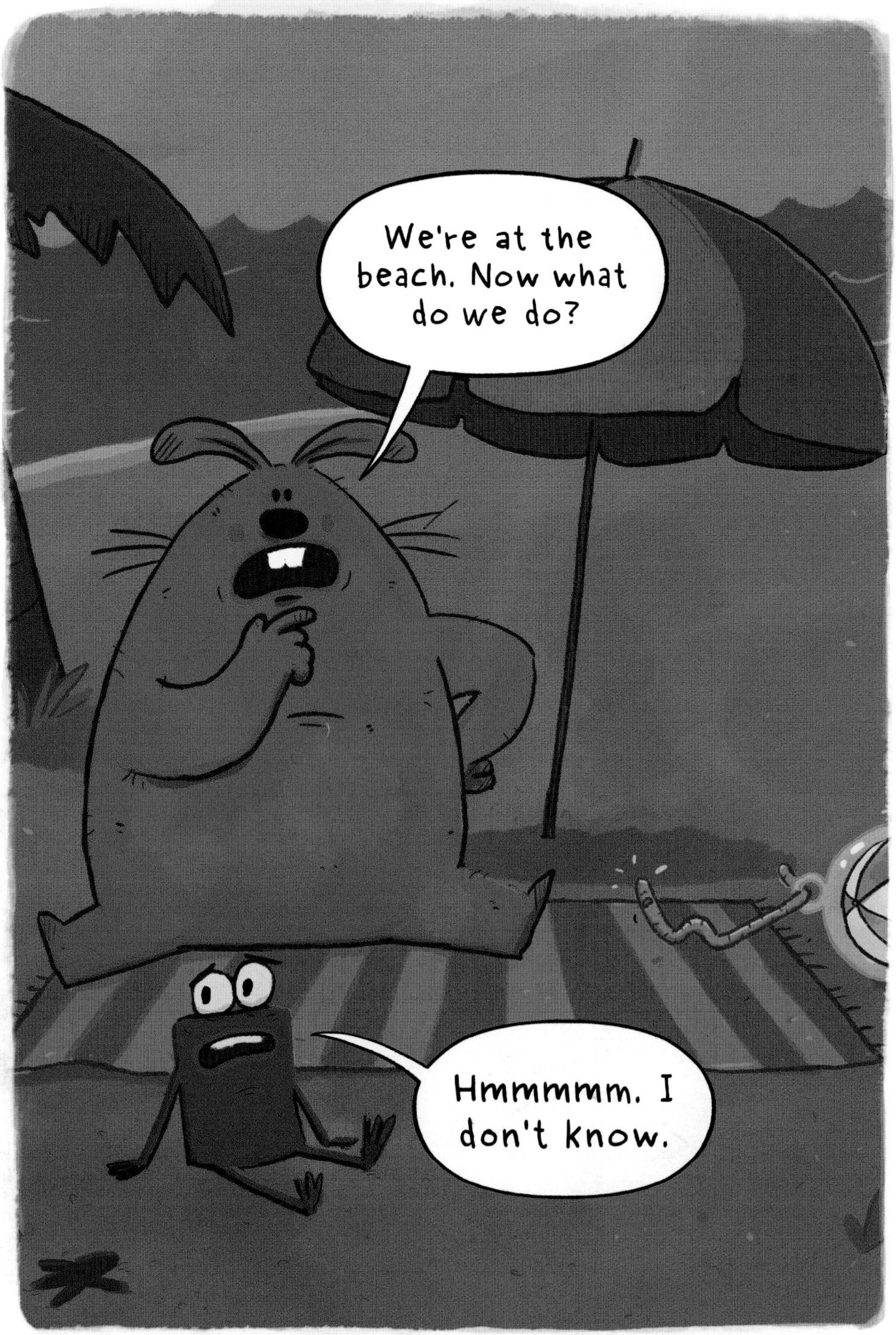
We're at the beach. Now what do we do?
Hmmmmm. I don't know.

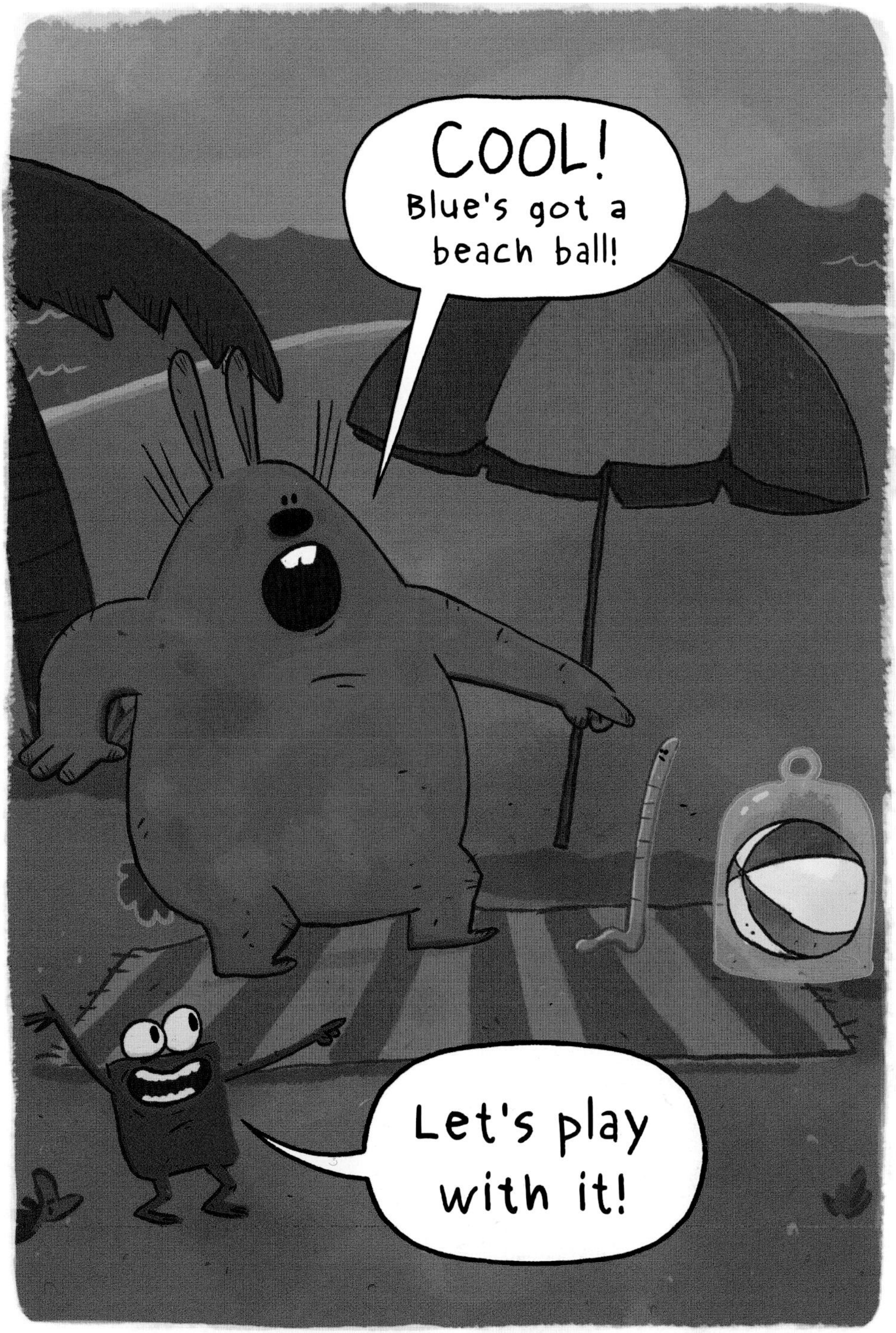
COOL! Blue's got a beach ball!
Let's play with it!

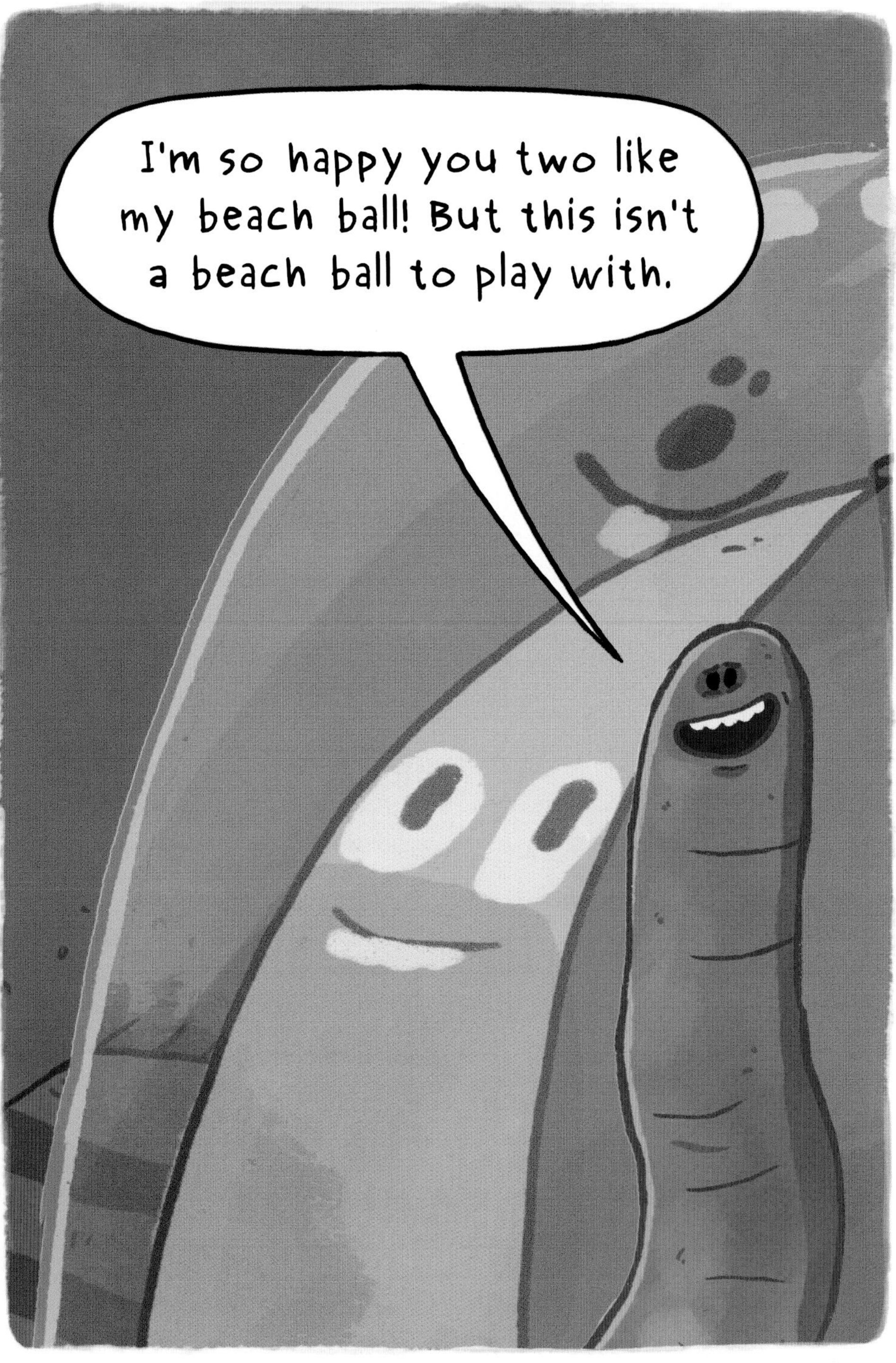
I'm so happy you two like my beach ball! But this isn't a beach ball to play with.

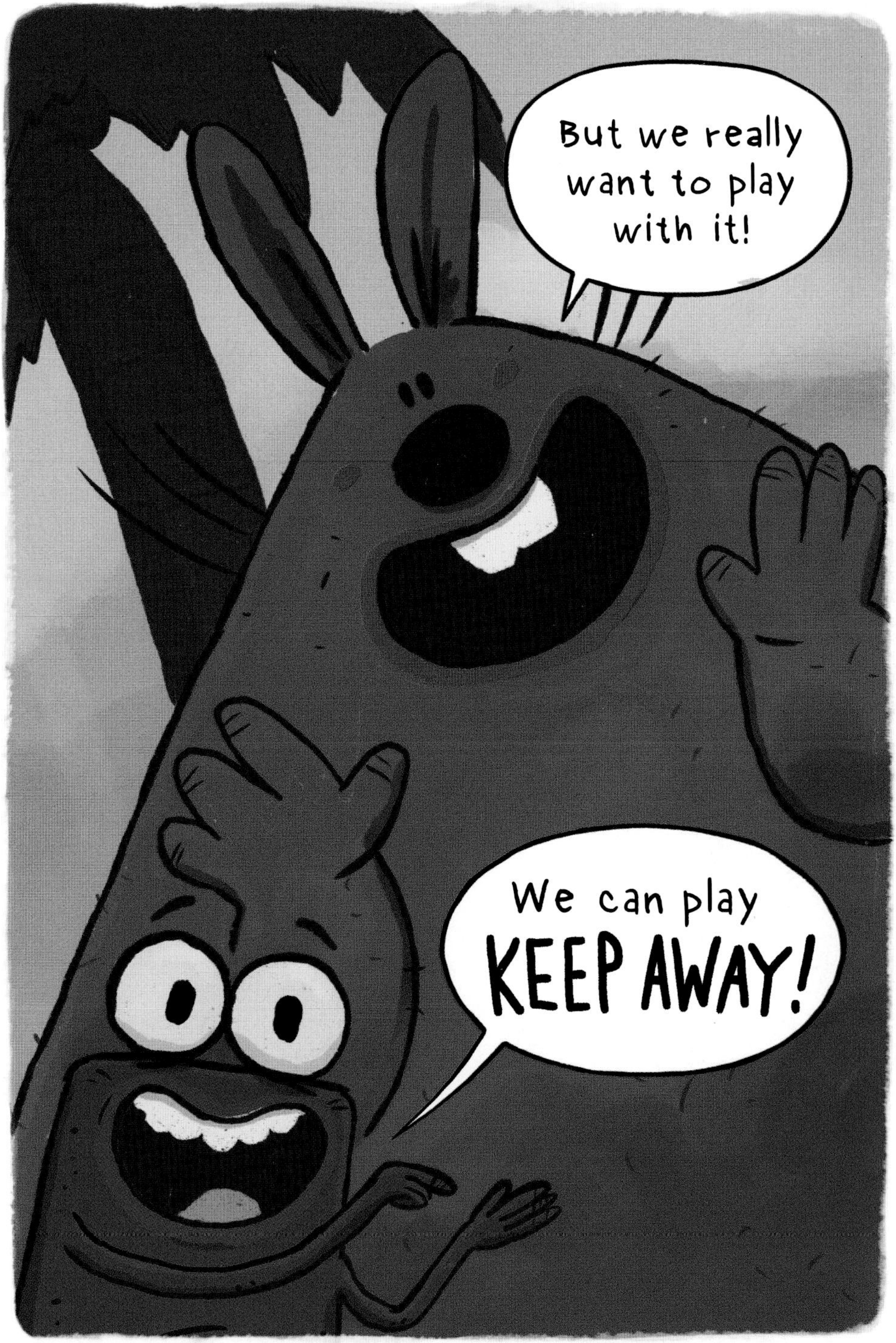
But we really want to play with it!
We can play KEEP AWAY!

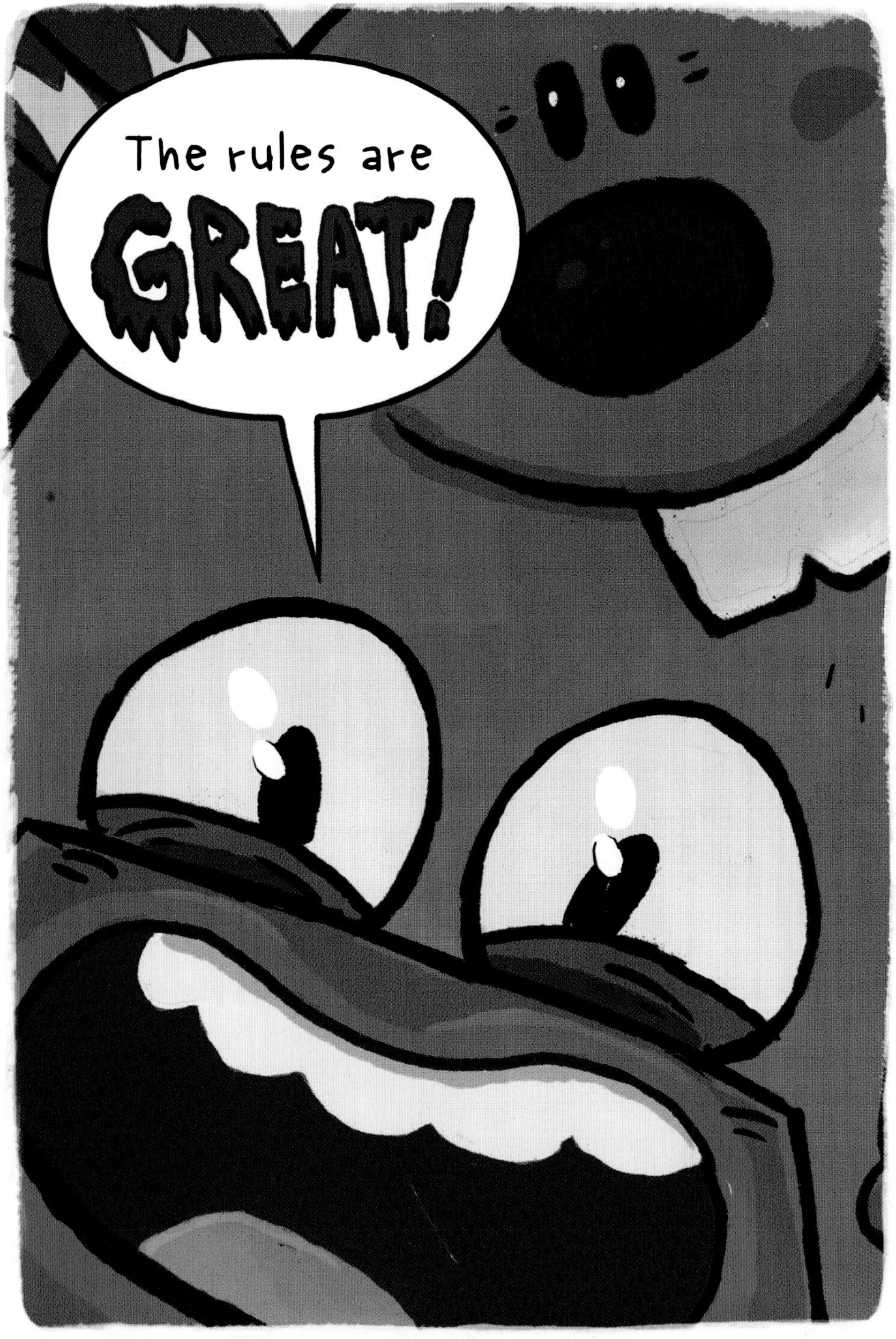
The rules are GREAT!

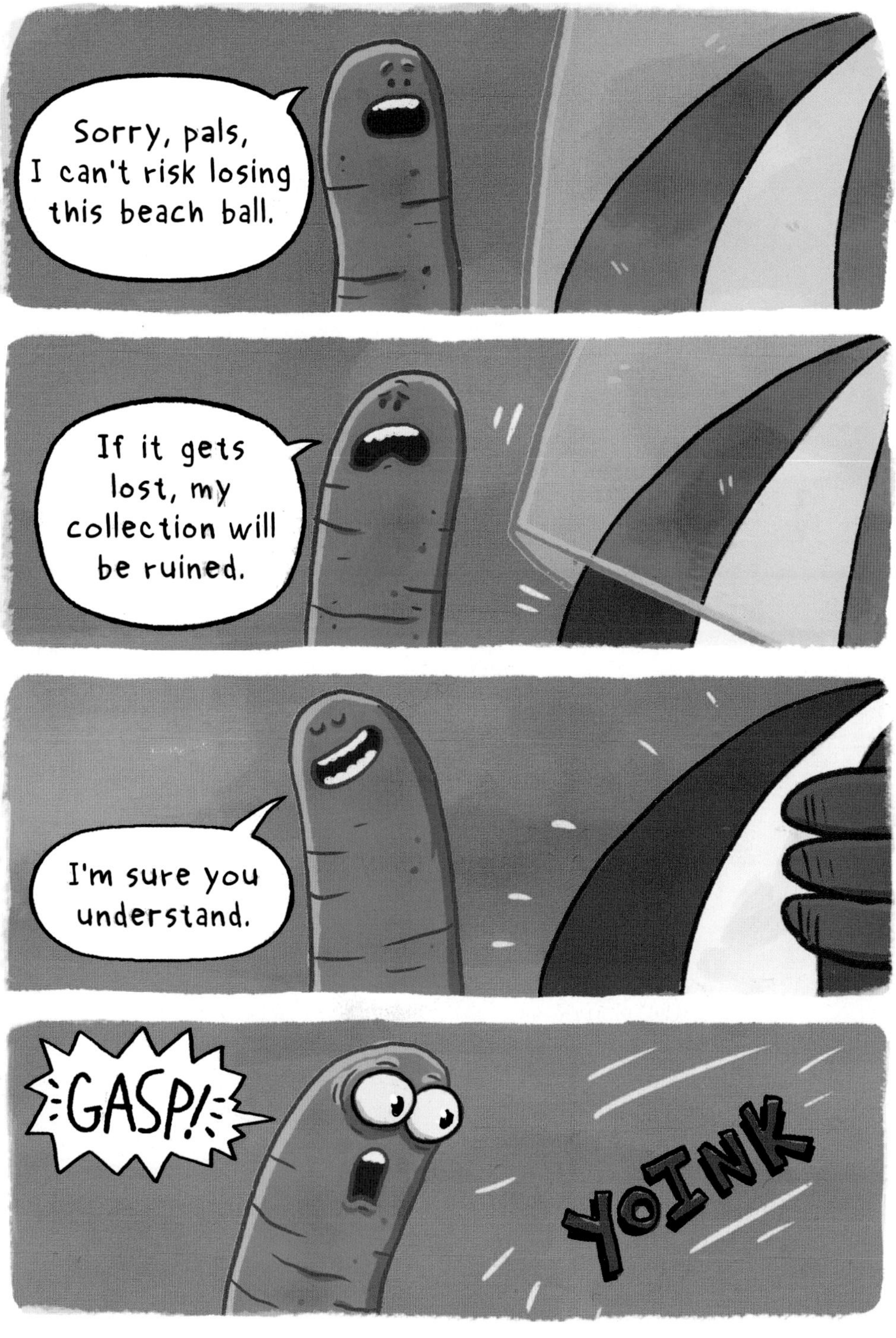
Sorry, pals, I can't risk losing this beach ball.
If it gets lost, my collection will be ruined.
I'm sure you understand.
GASP!
YOINK

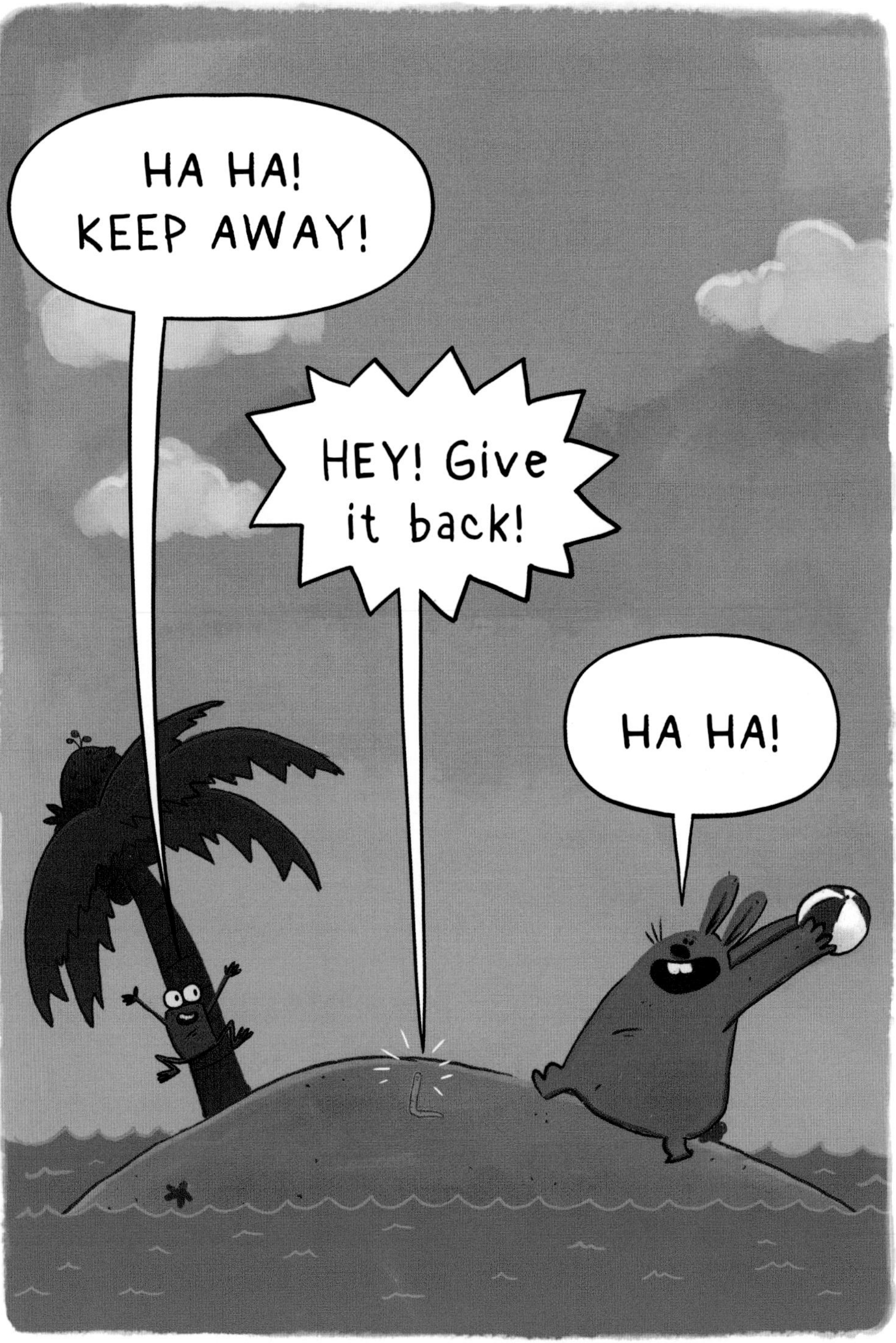
HA HA! KEEP AWAY!
HEY! Give it back!
HA HA!

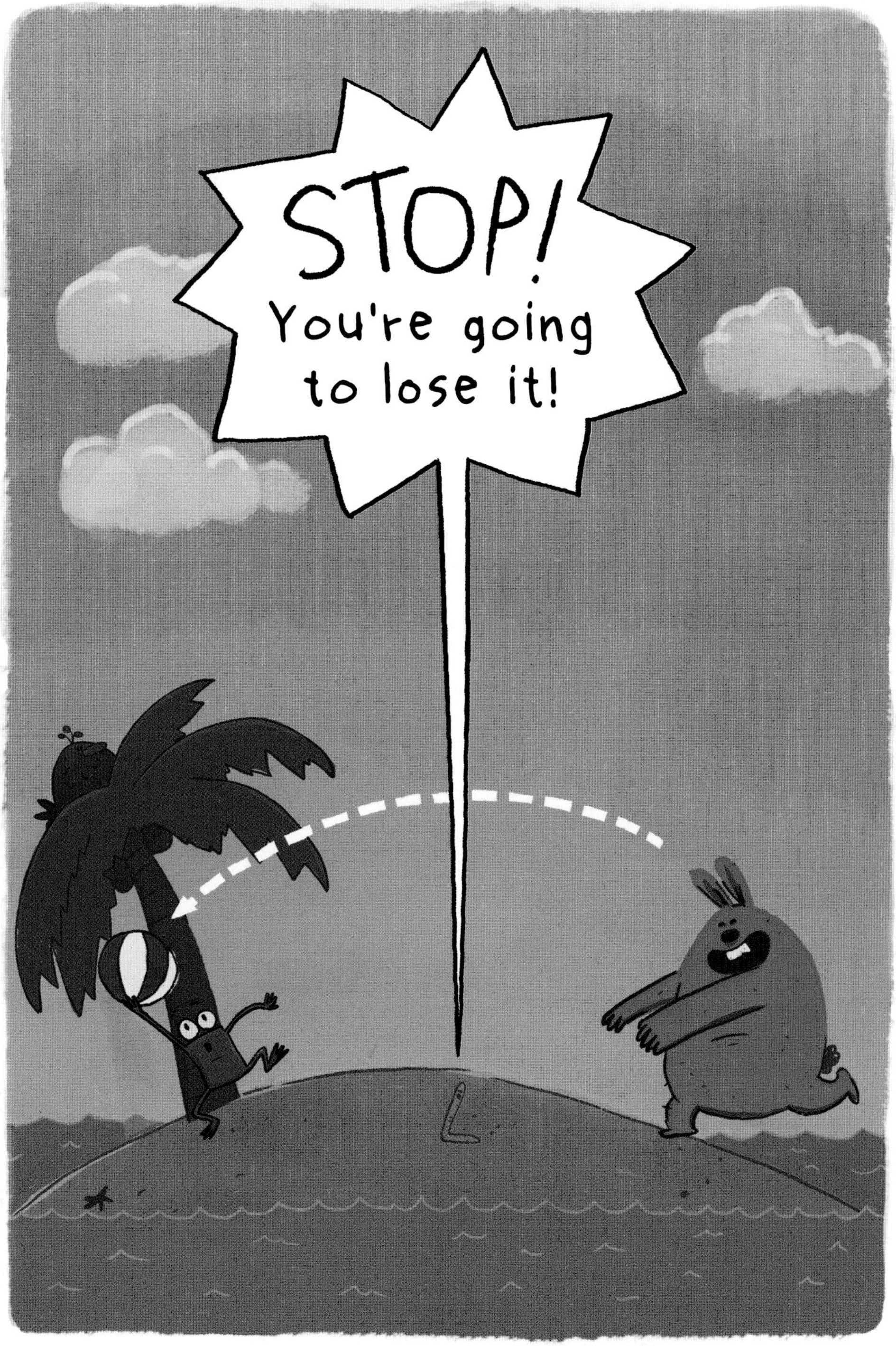
STOP!
You're going to lose it!

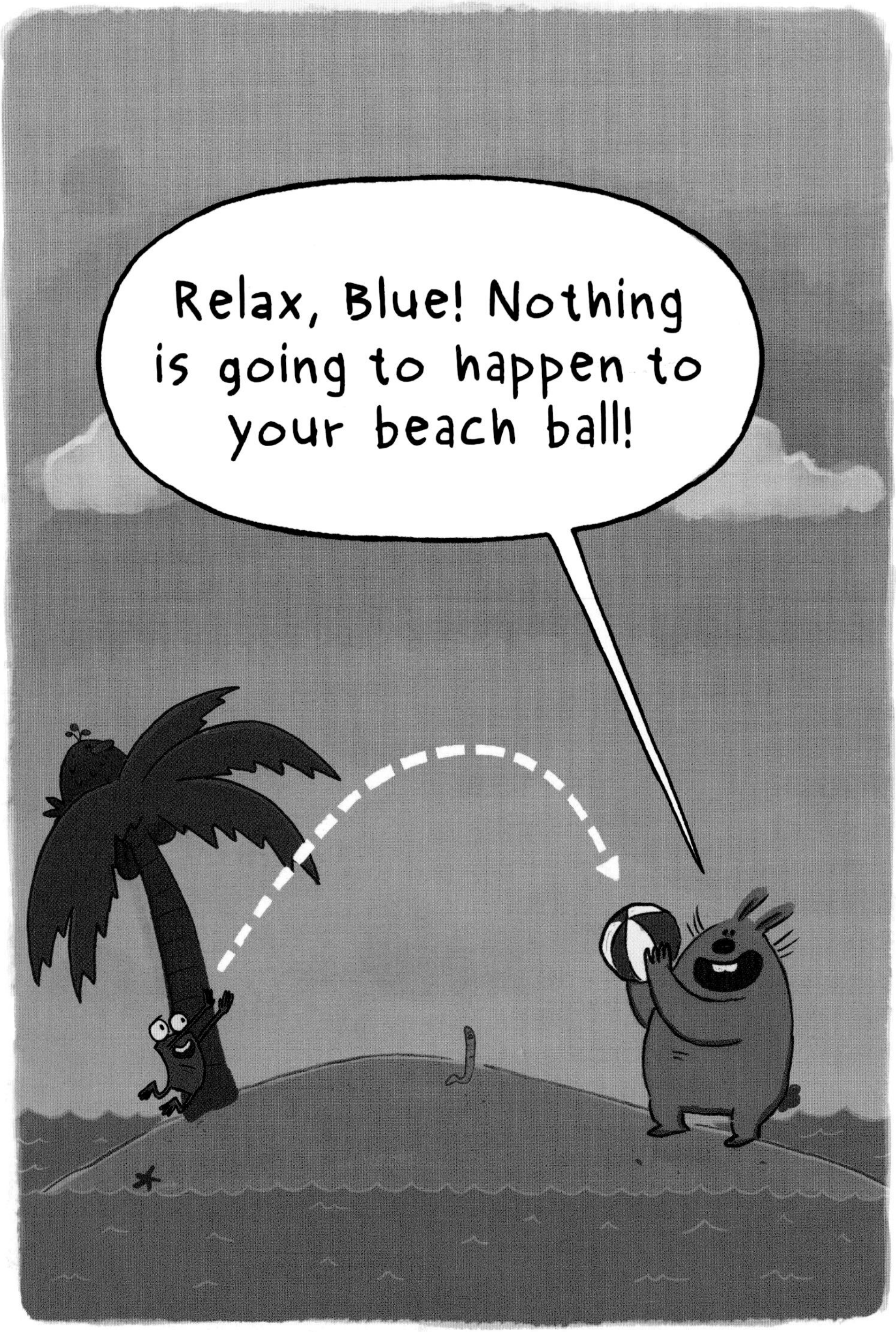
Relax, Blue! Nothing is going to happen to your beach ball!

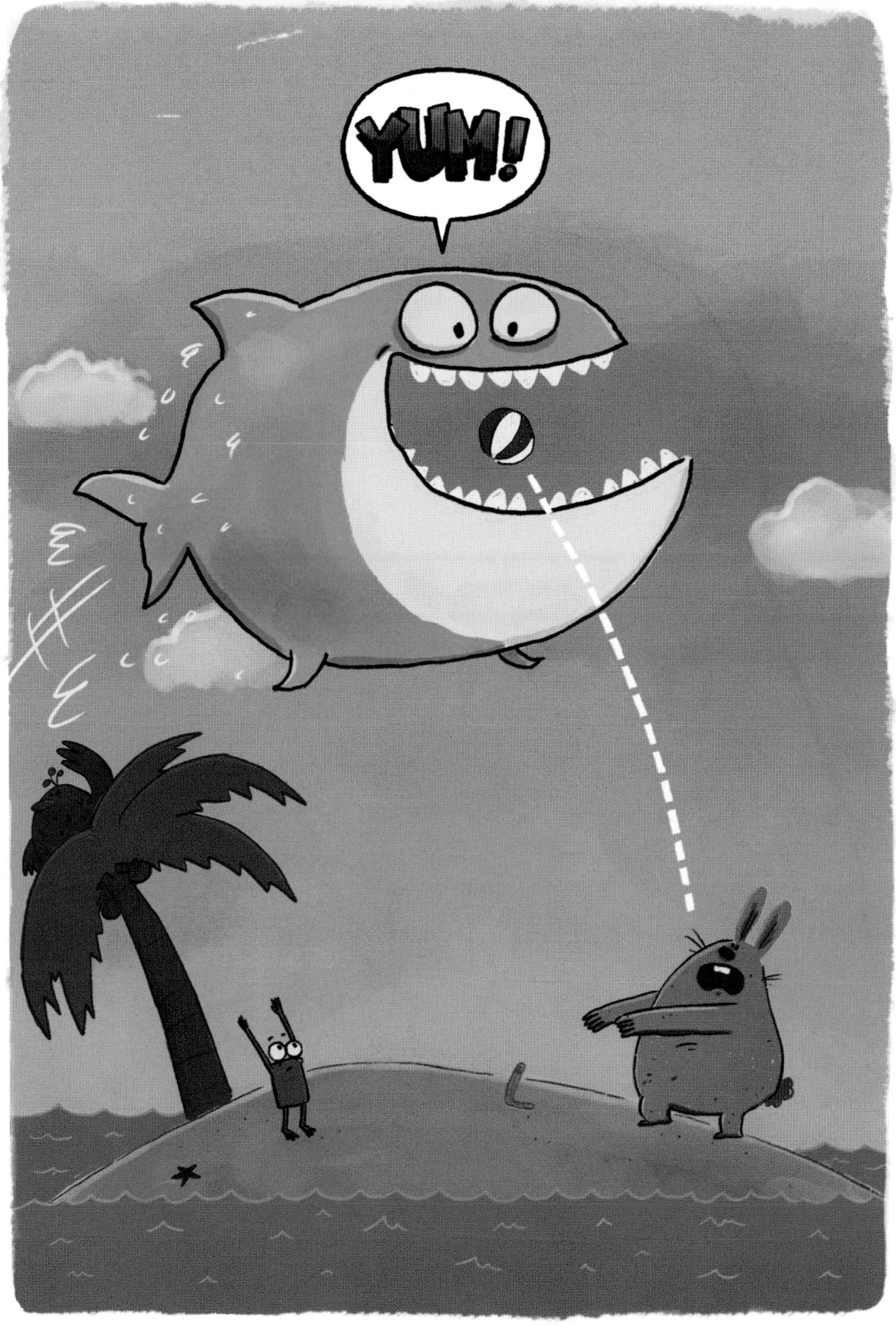
YUM!

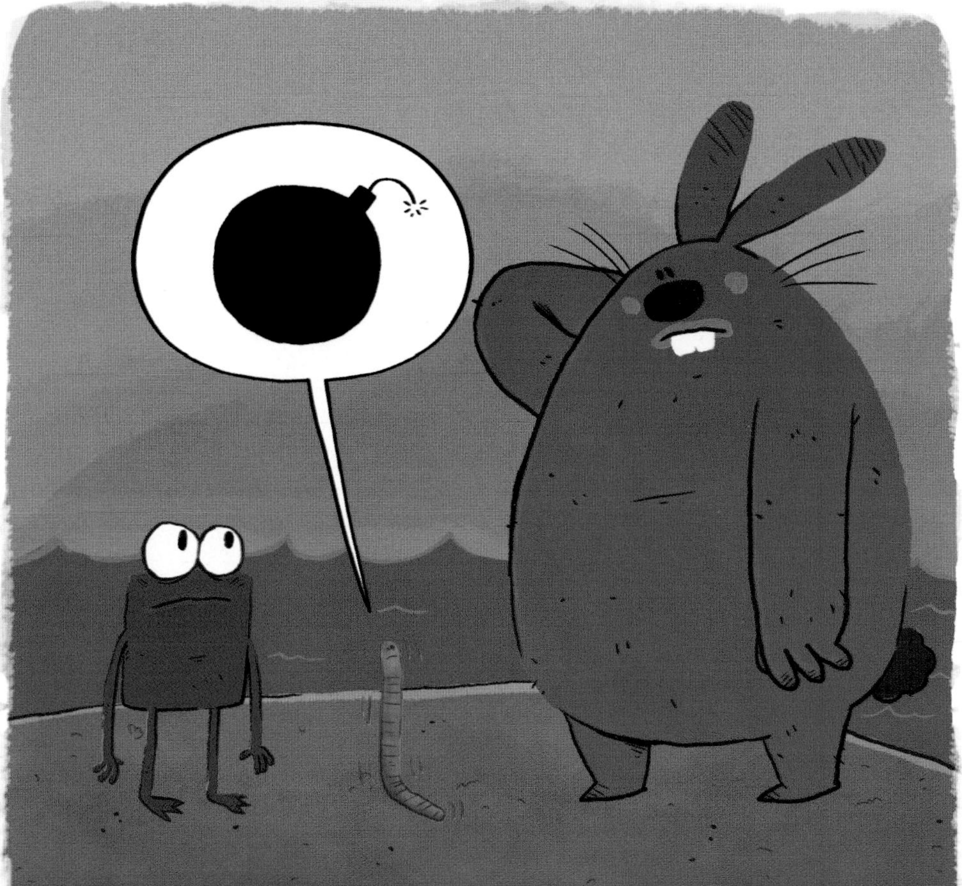

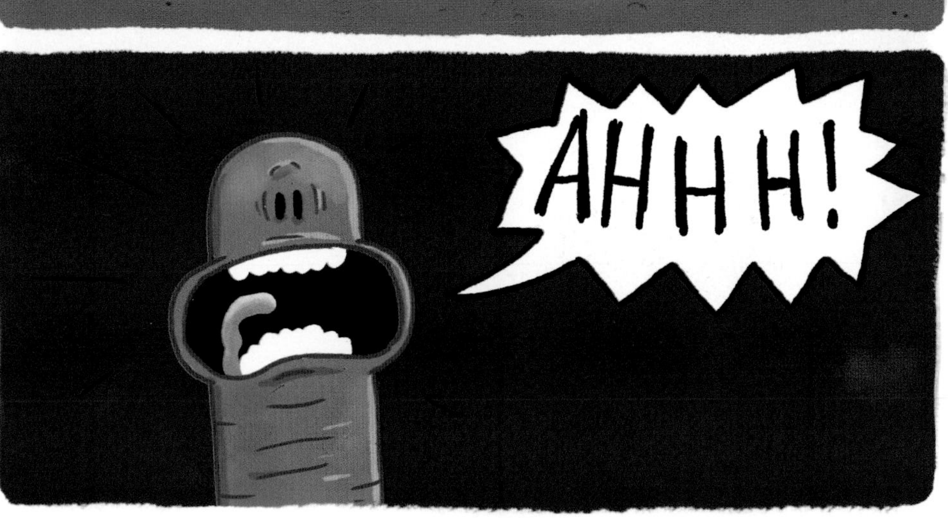
AHHH!

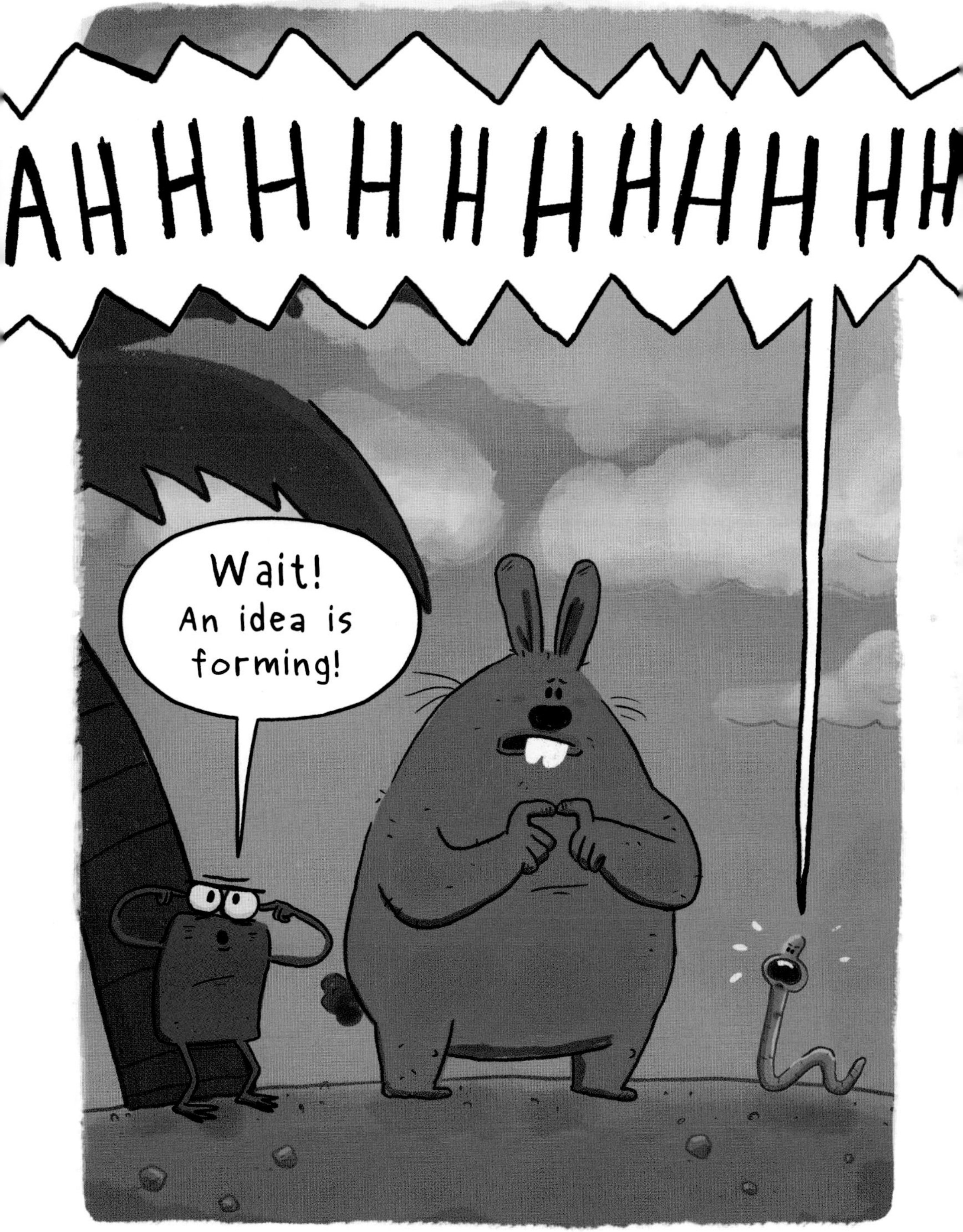
AHHHHHHHHHHH
Wait! An idea is forming!

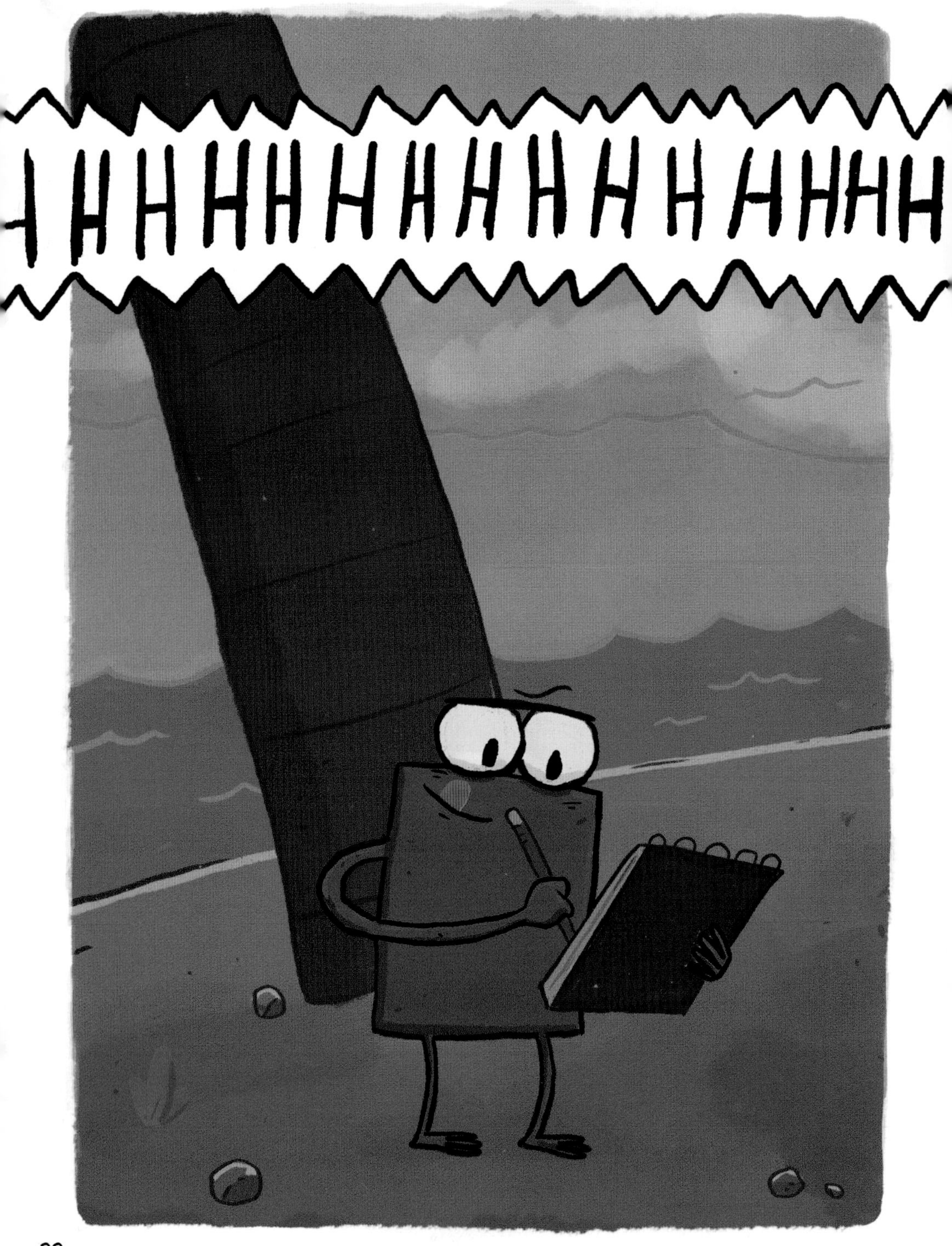
HHHHHHHHHHHHHH

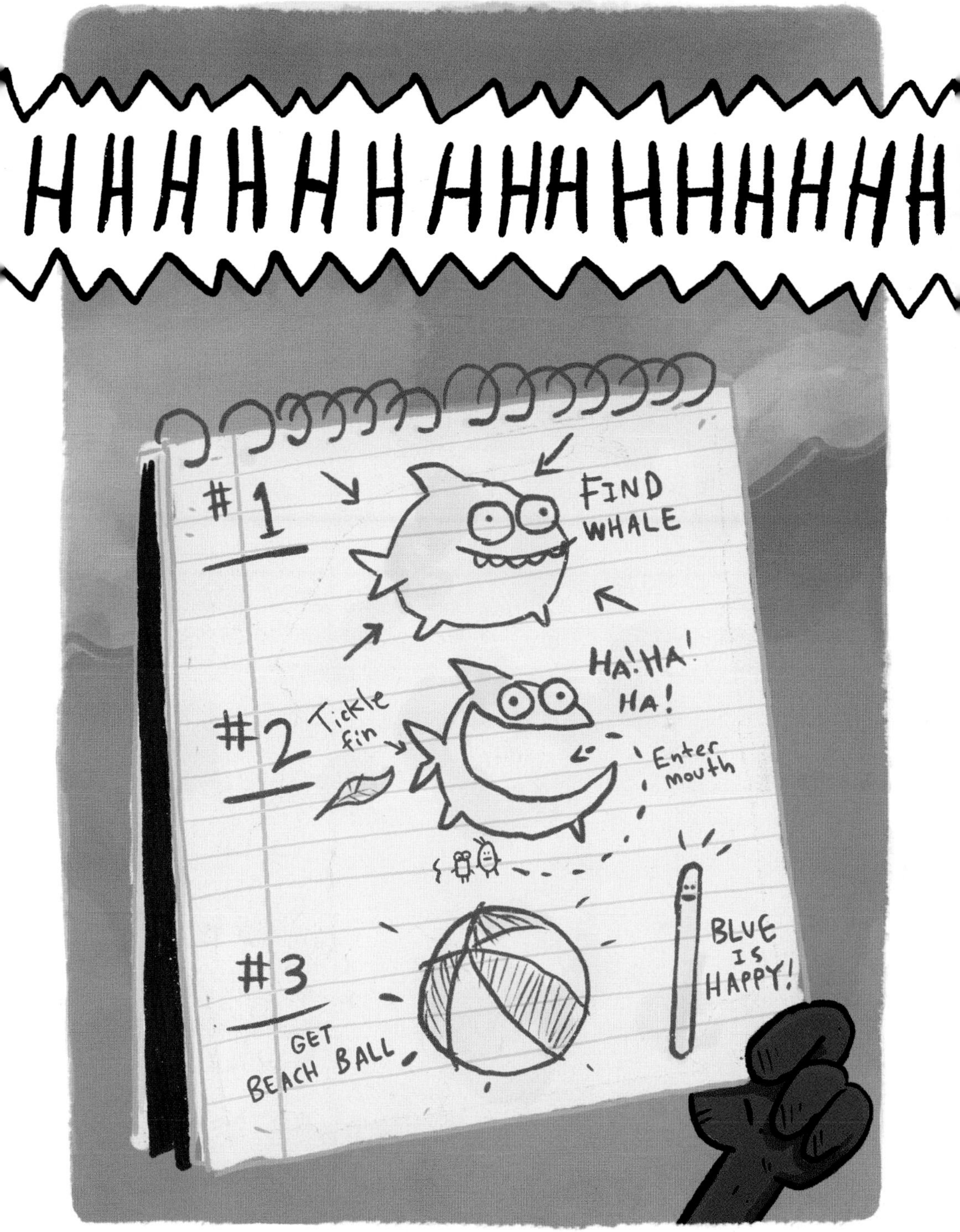

HHHHHHHHHHHHHHHHH
#1
FIND WHALE
#2
Tickle fin
HA! HA! HA!
Enter mouth
#3
GET BEACH BALL
BLUE IS HAPPY!

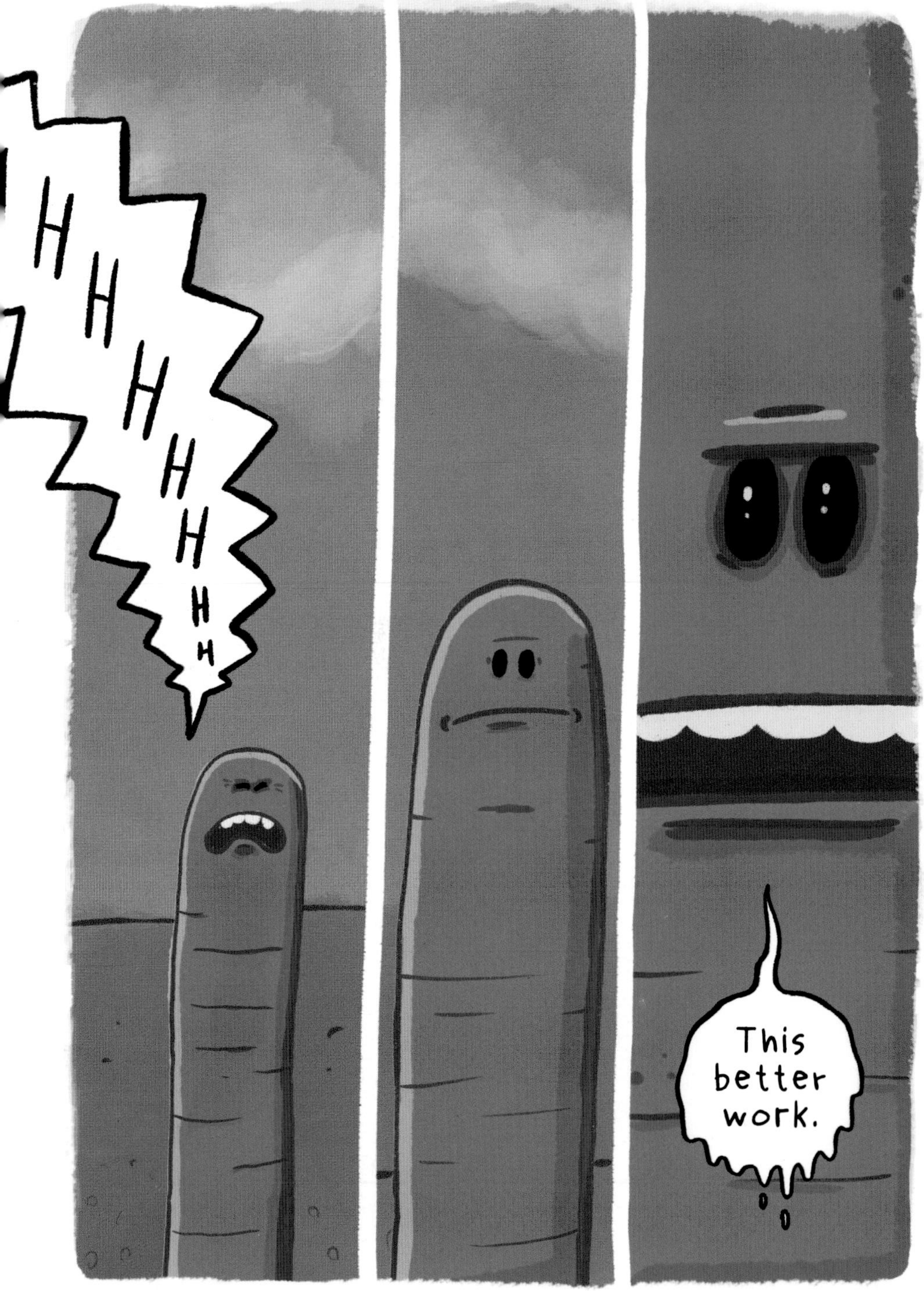
HHHHHHHH
This better work.

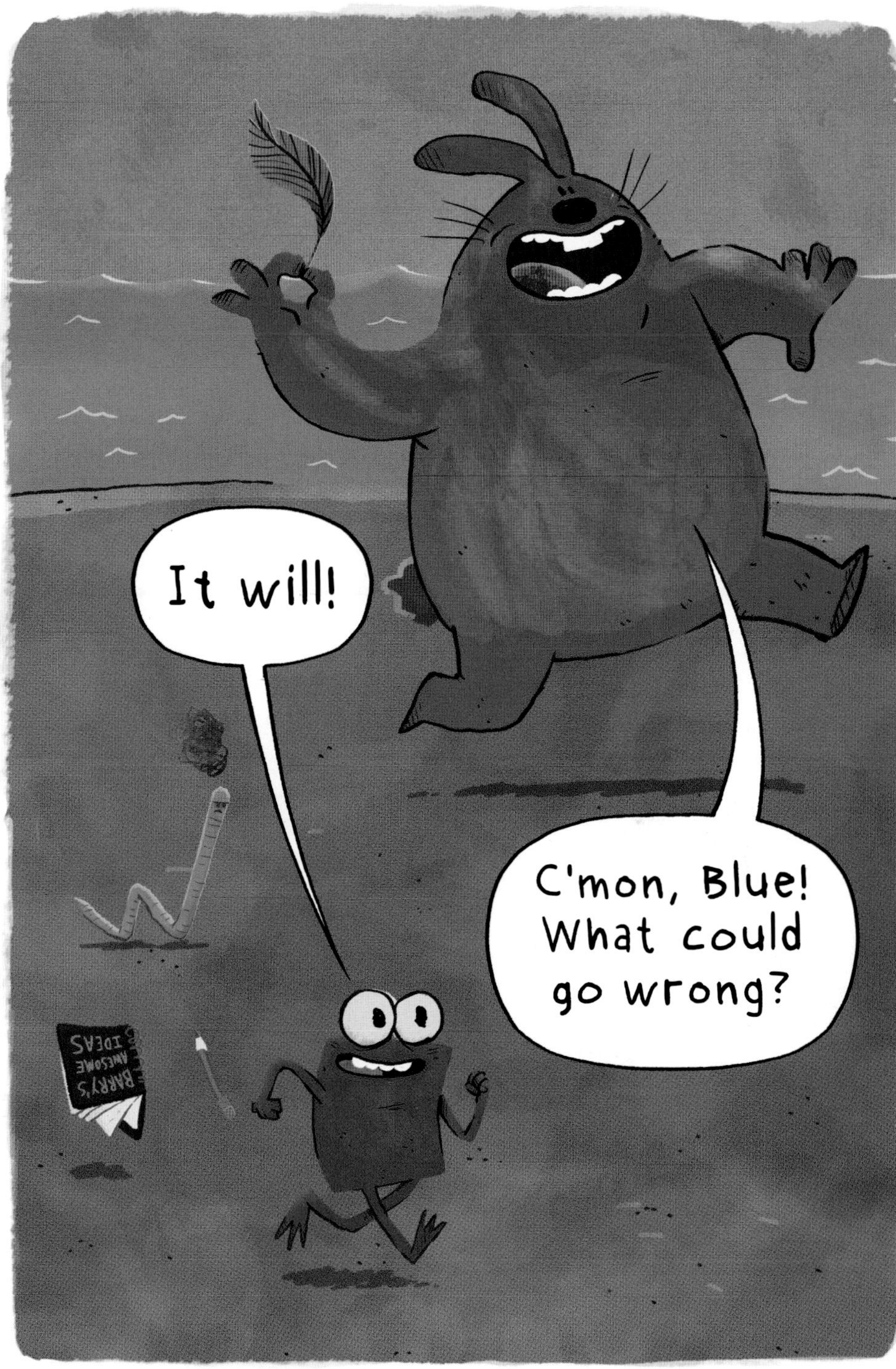
It will!
C'mon, Blue! What could go wrong?
BARRY'S AWESOME IDEAS

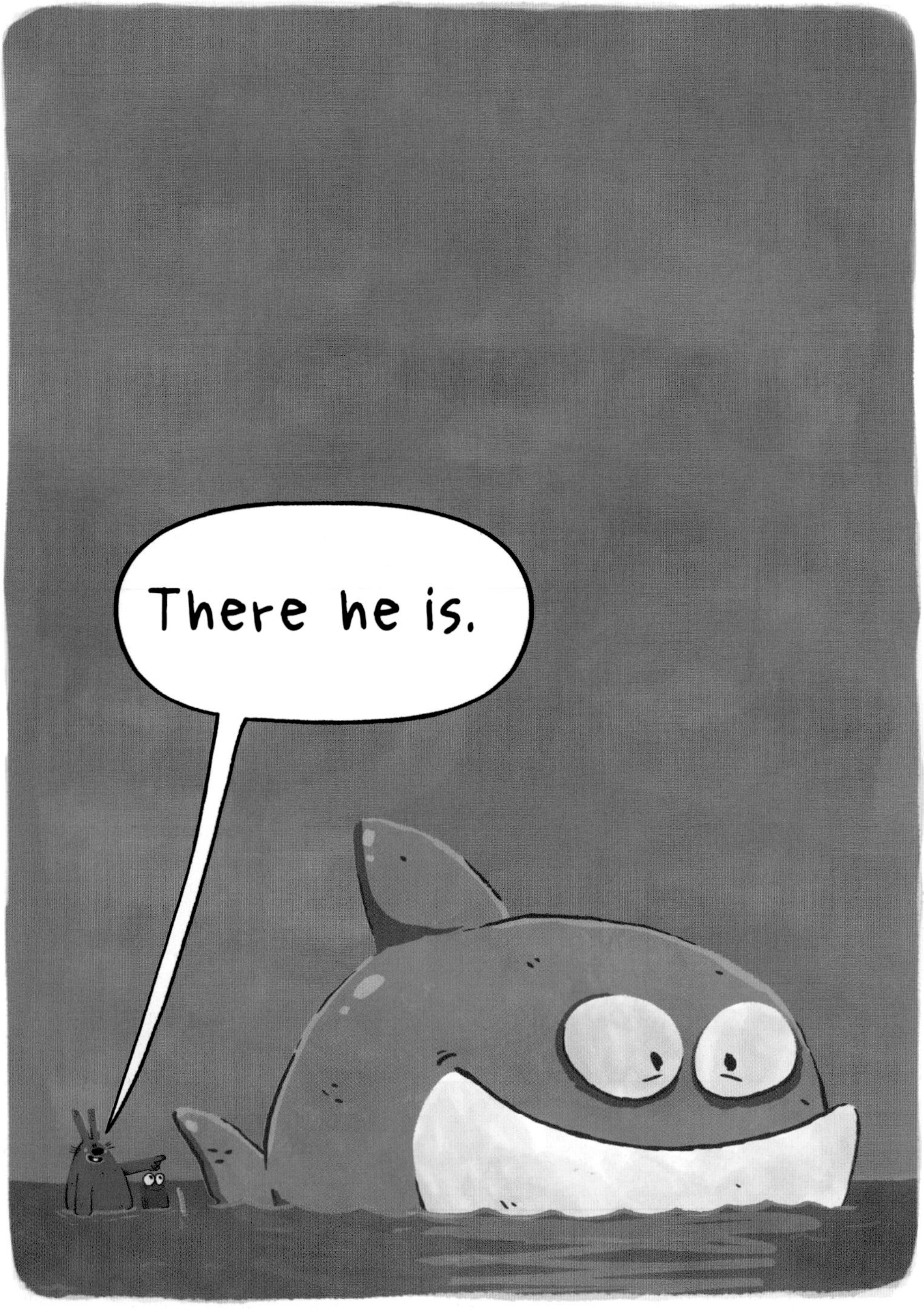
There he is.

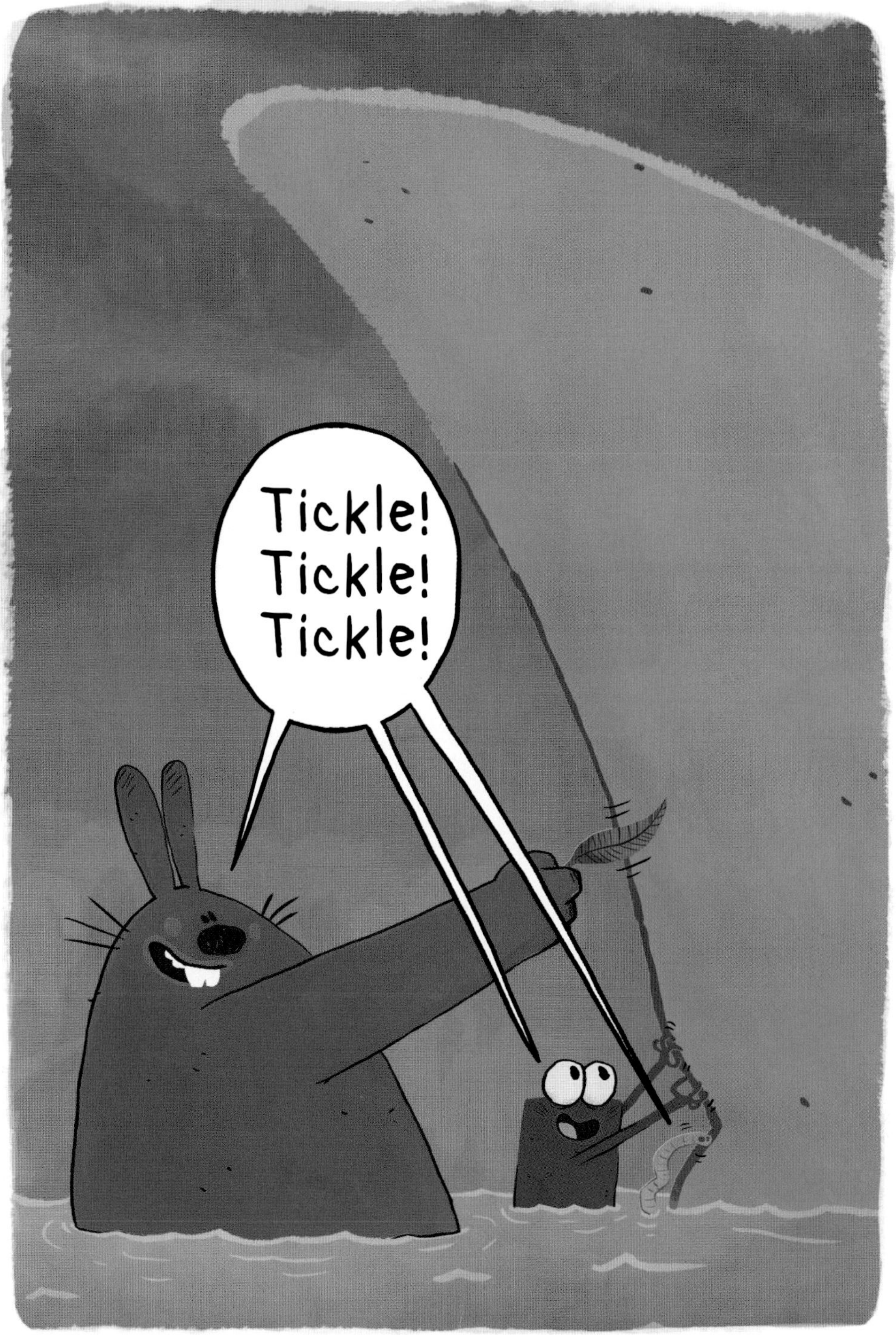
Tickle! Tickle! Tickle!

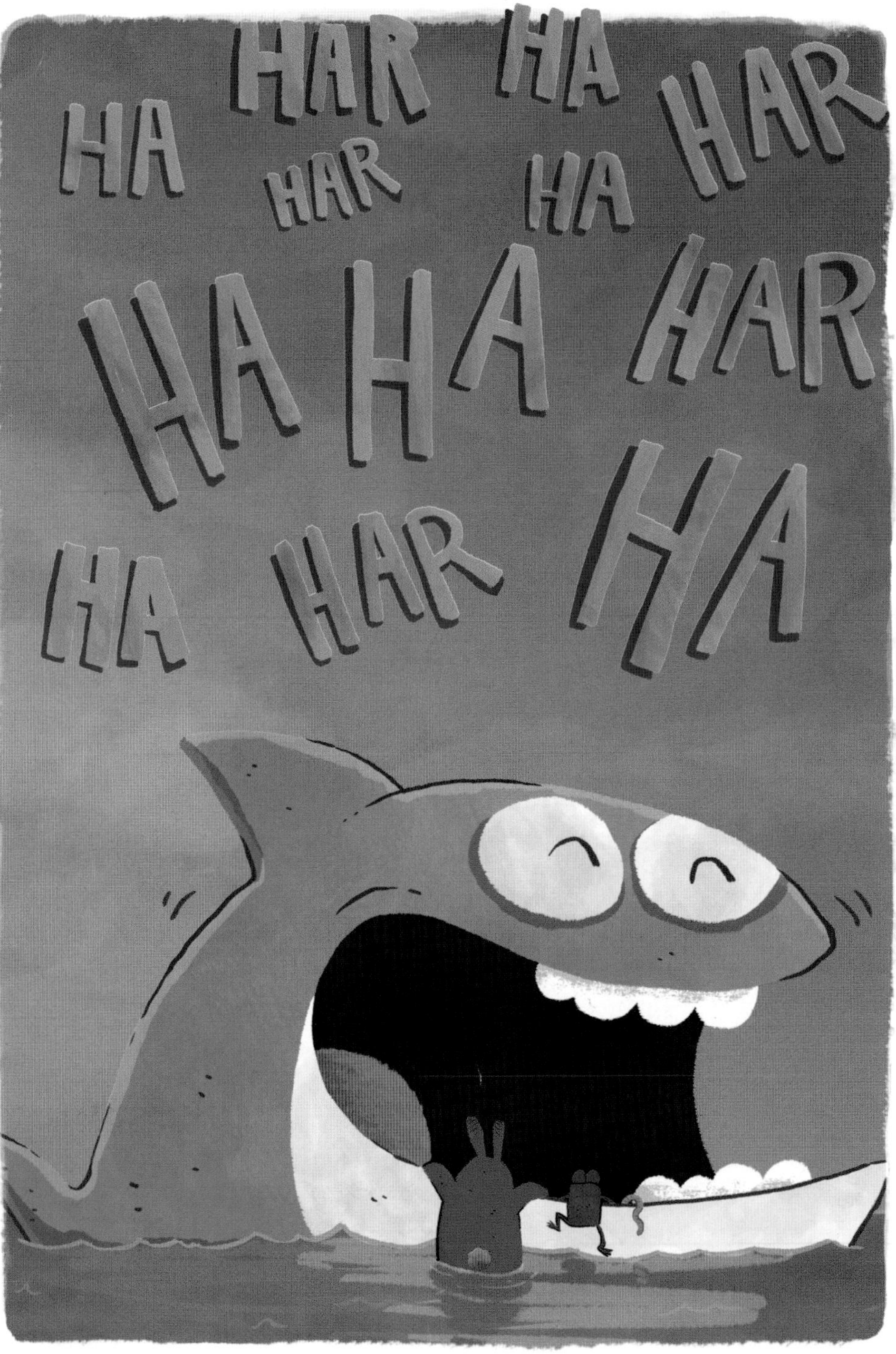
HA
HAR
HA
HAR
HA
HAR
HA
HA
HAR
HA
HAR
HA

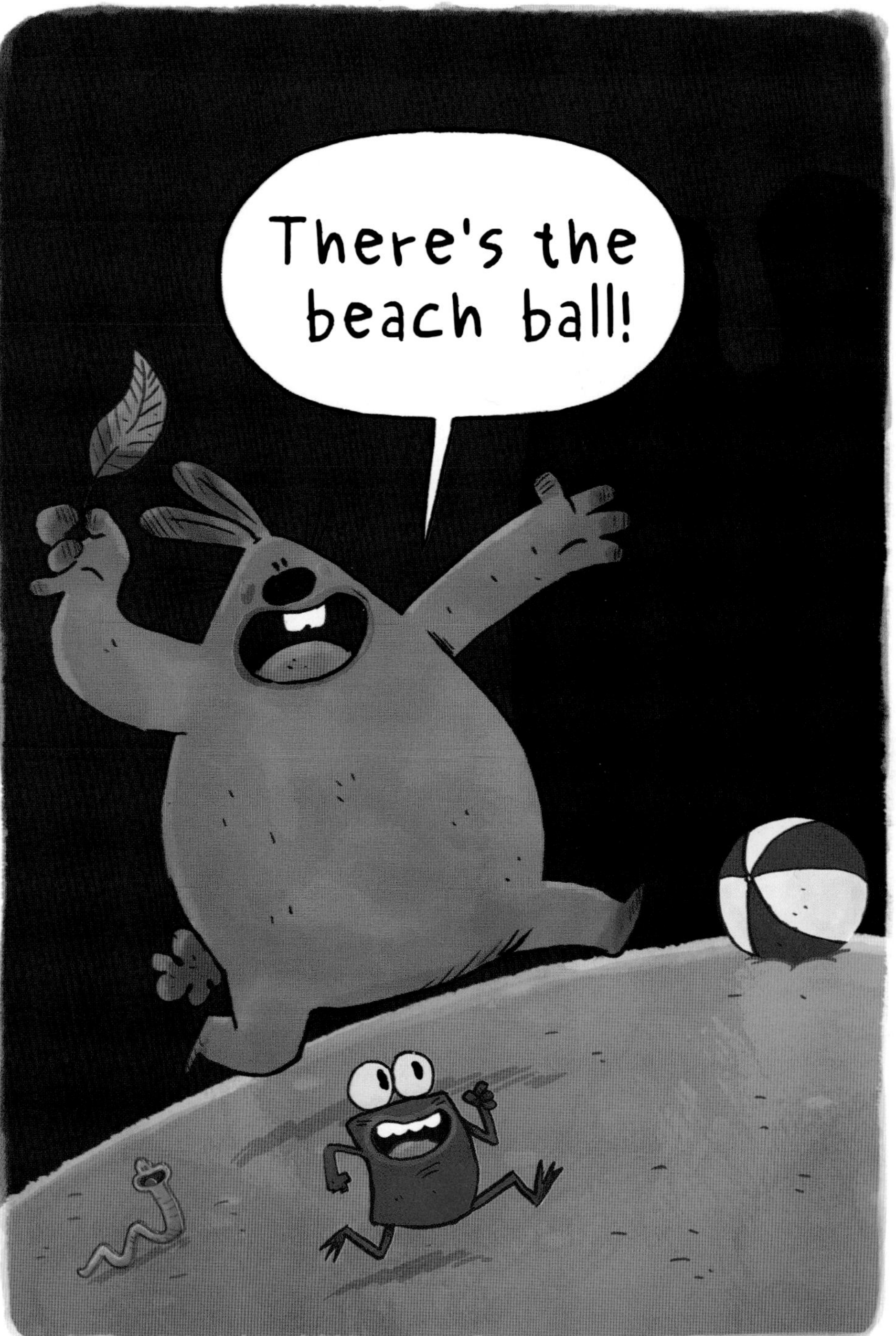
There's the beach ball!

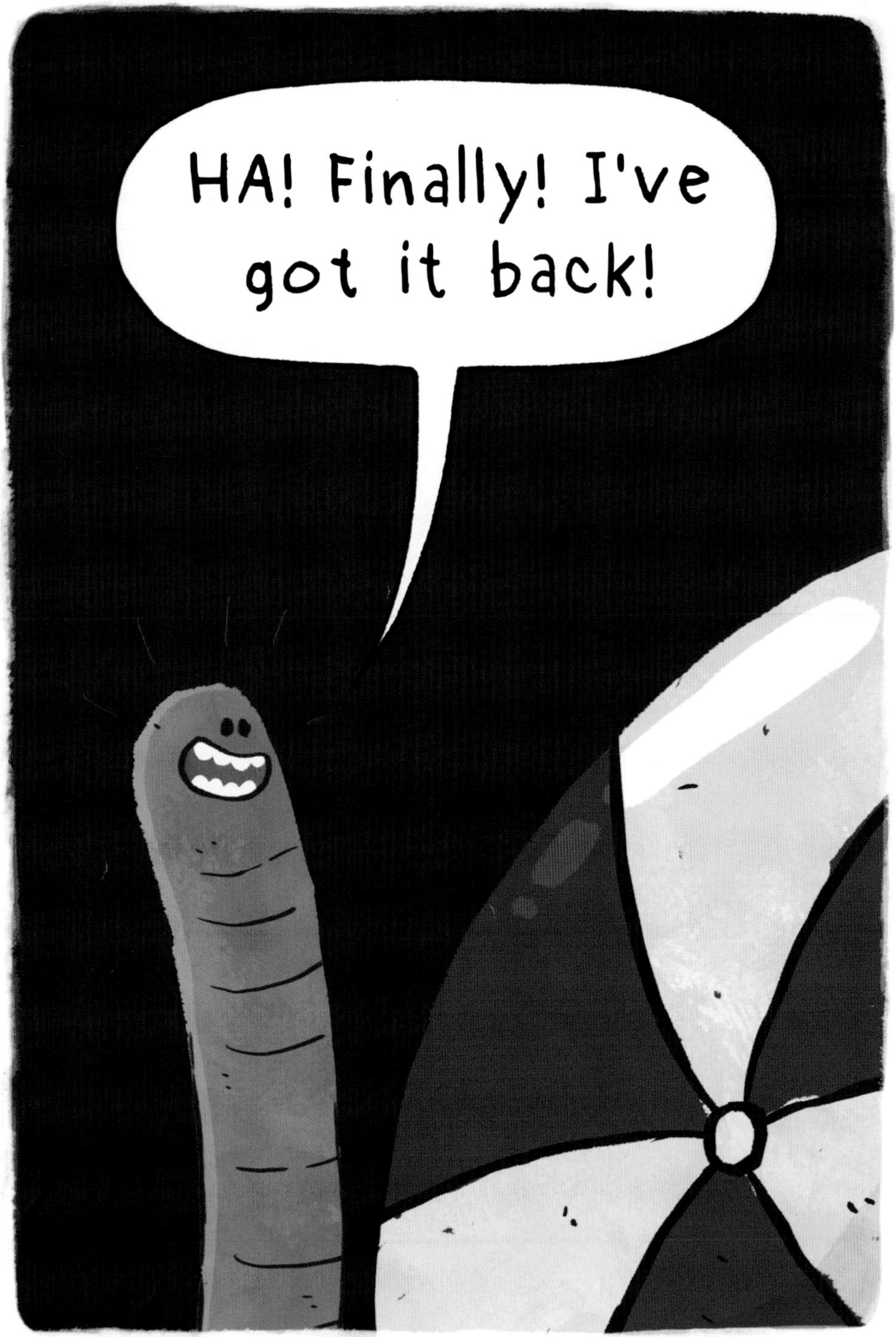
HA! Finally! I've got it back!

When I tickle this uvula, everything shakes.

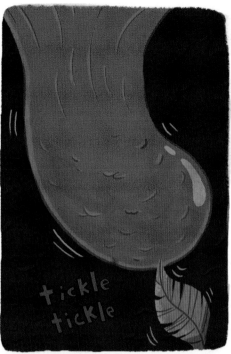

tickle tickle

PANCAKES, STOP DOING THAT!!!

HA HA HA!

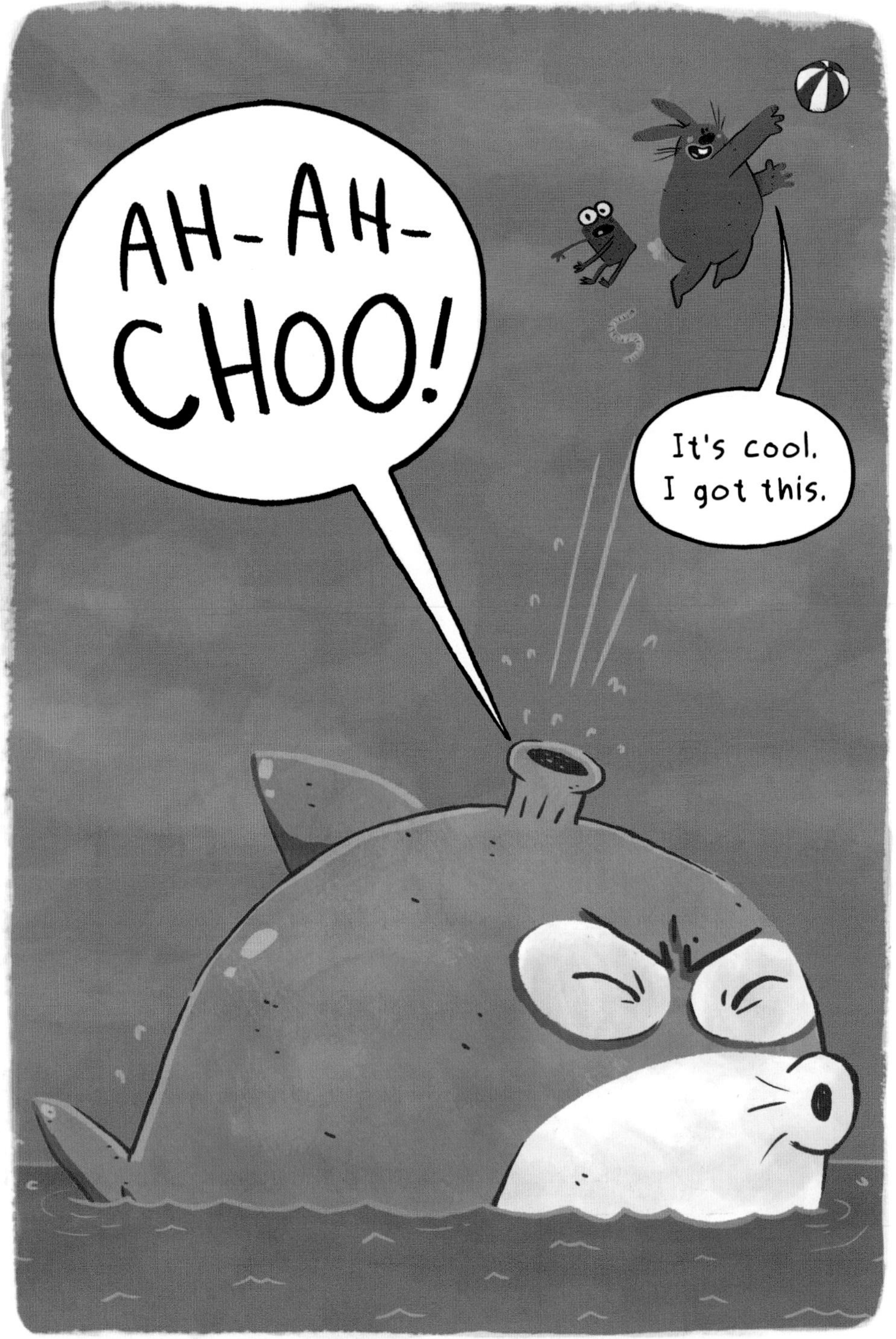
AH-AH-CHOO!
It's cool. I got this.

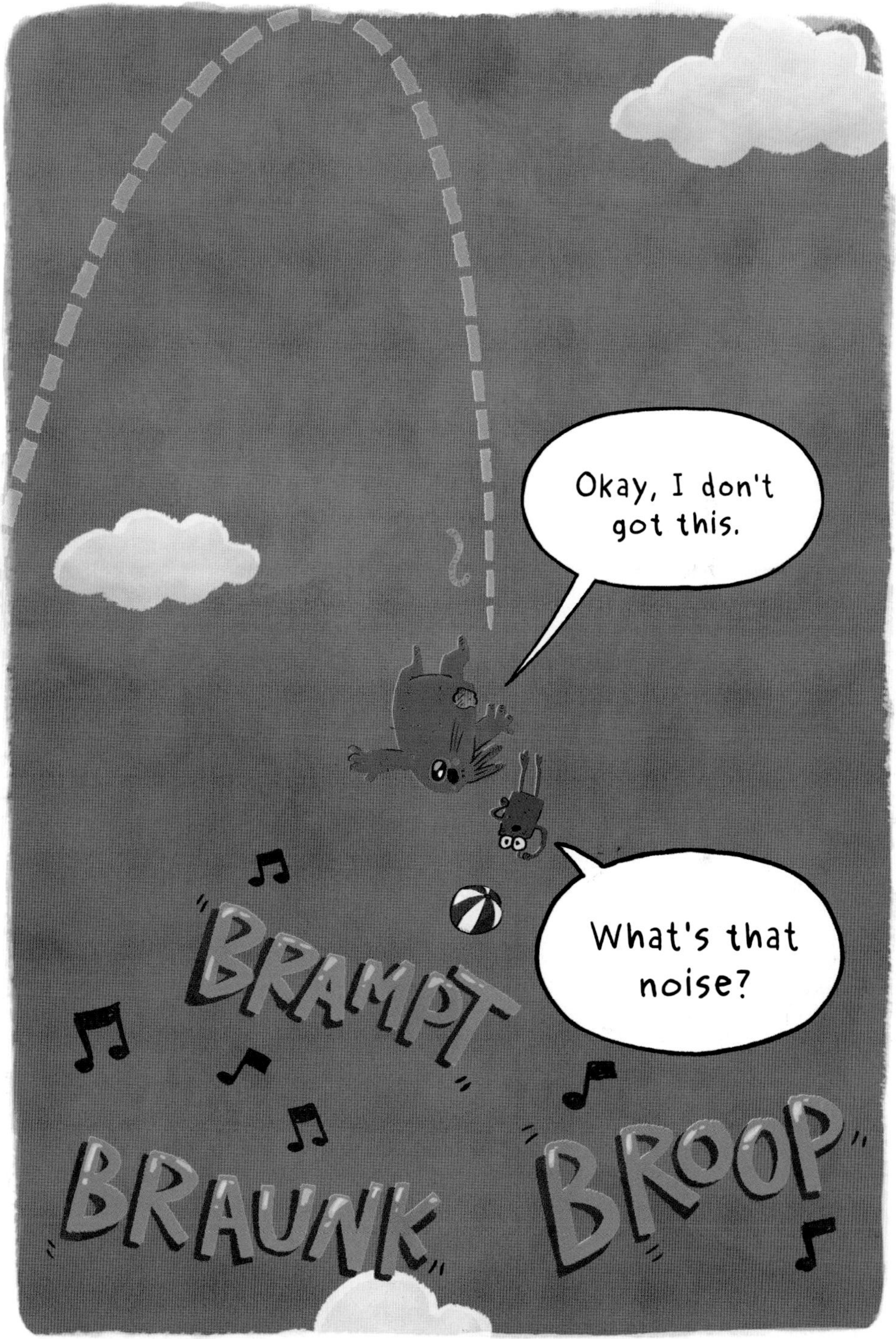

Okay, I don't got this.
What's that noise?
"BRAMPT"
"BRAUNK"
"BROOP"

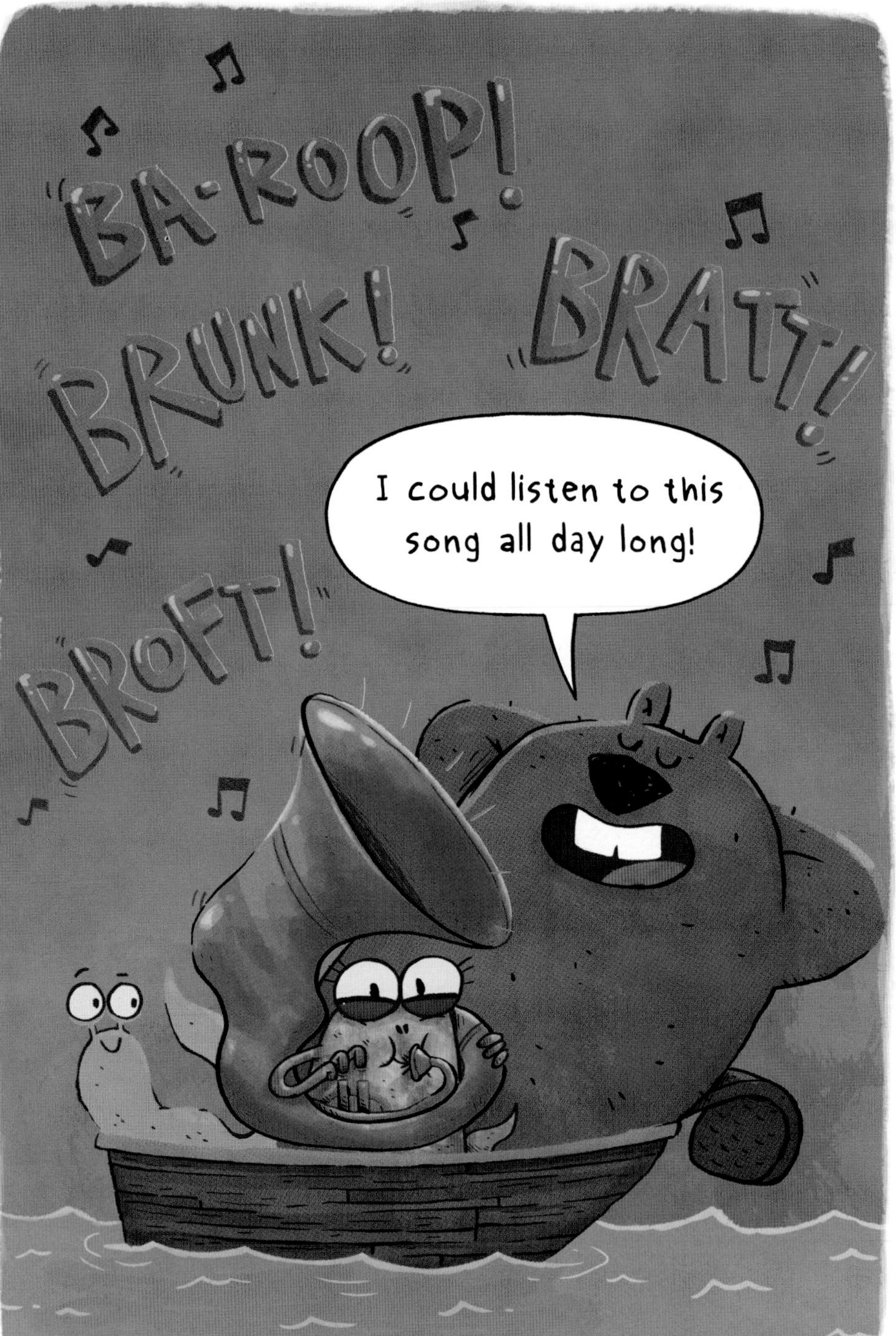
BA-ROOP!
BRUNK!
BRATT!
BROFT!
I could listen to this song all day long!

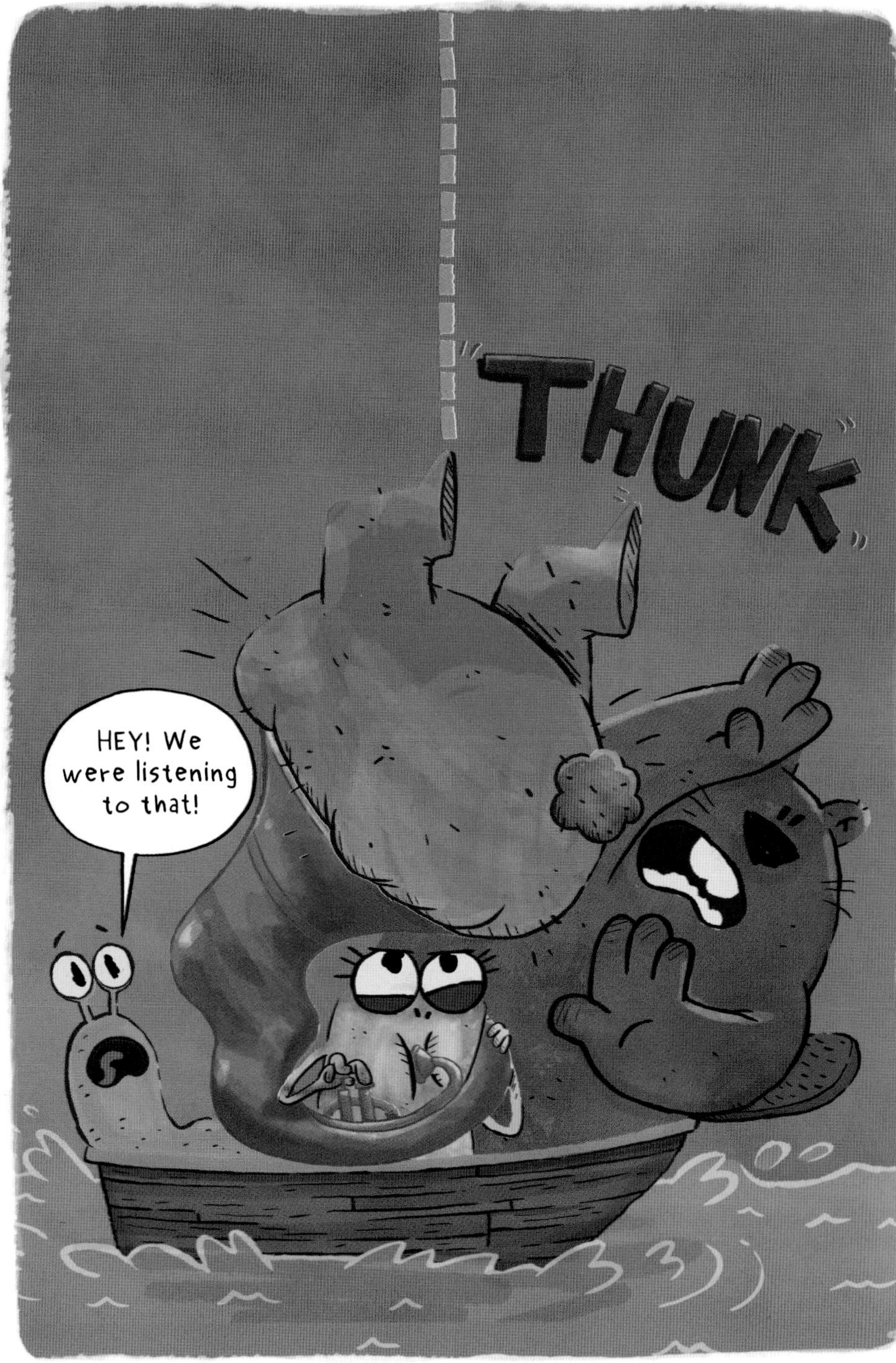
THUNK
HEY! We were listening to that!

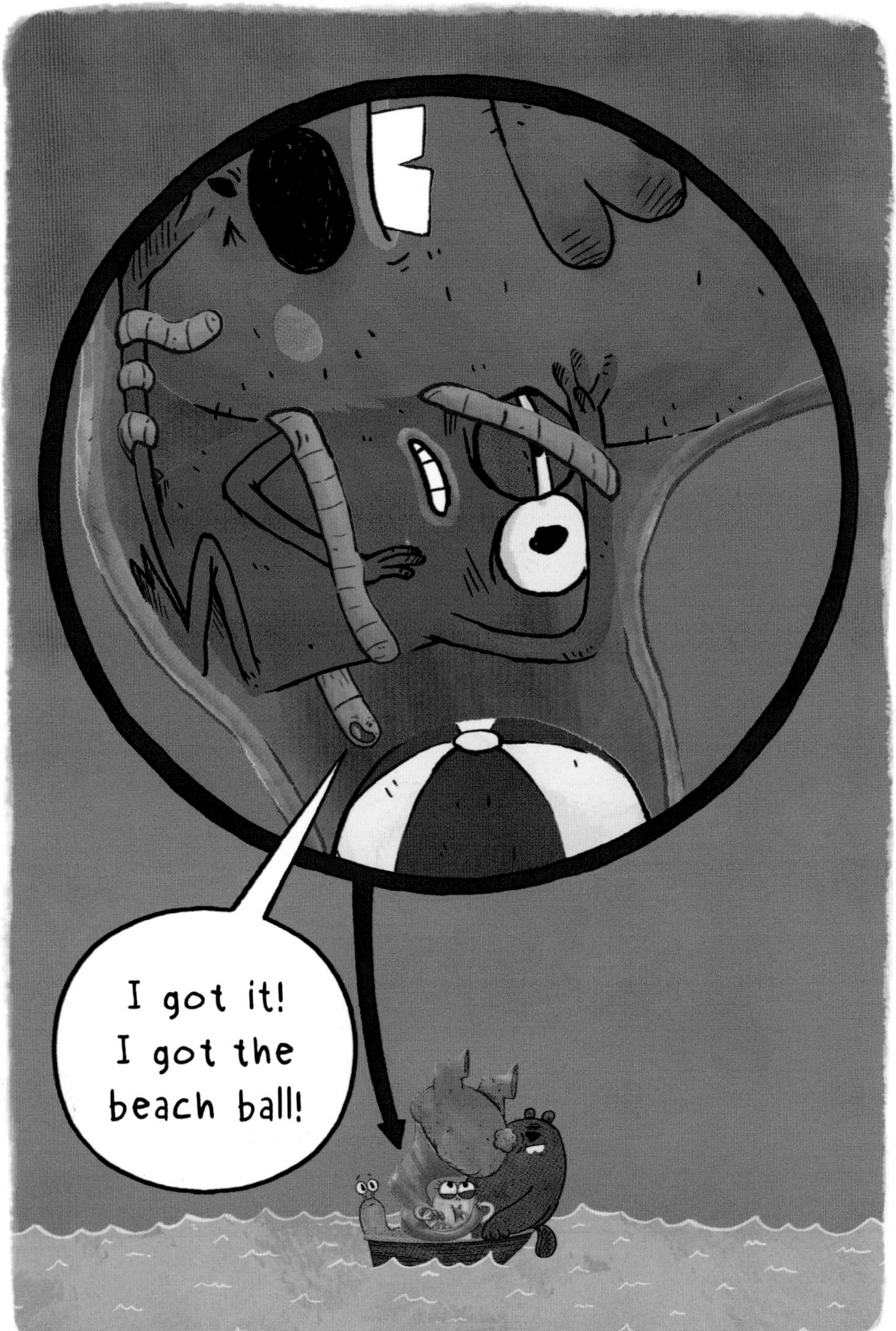
I got it! I got the beach ball!

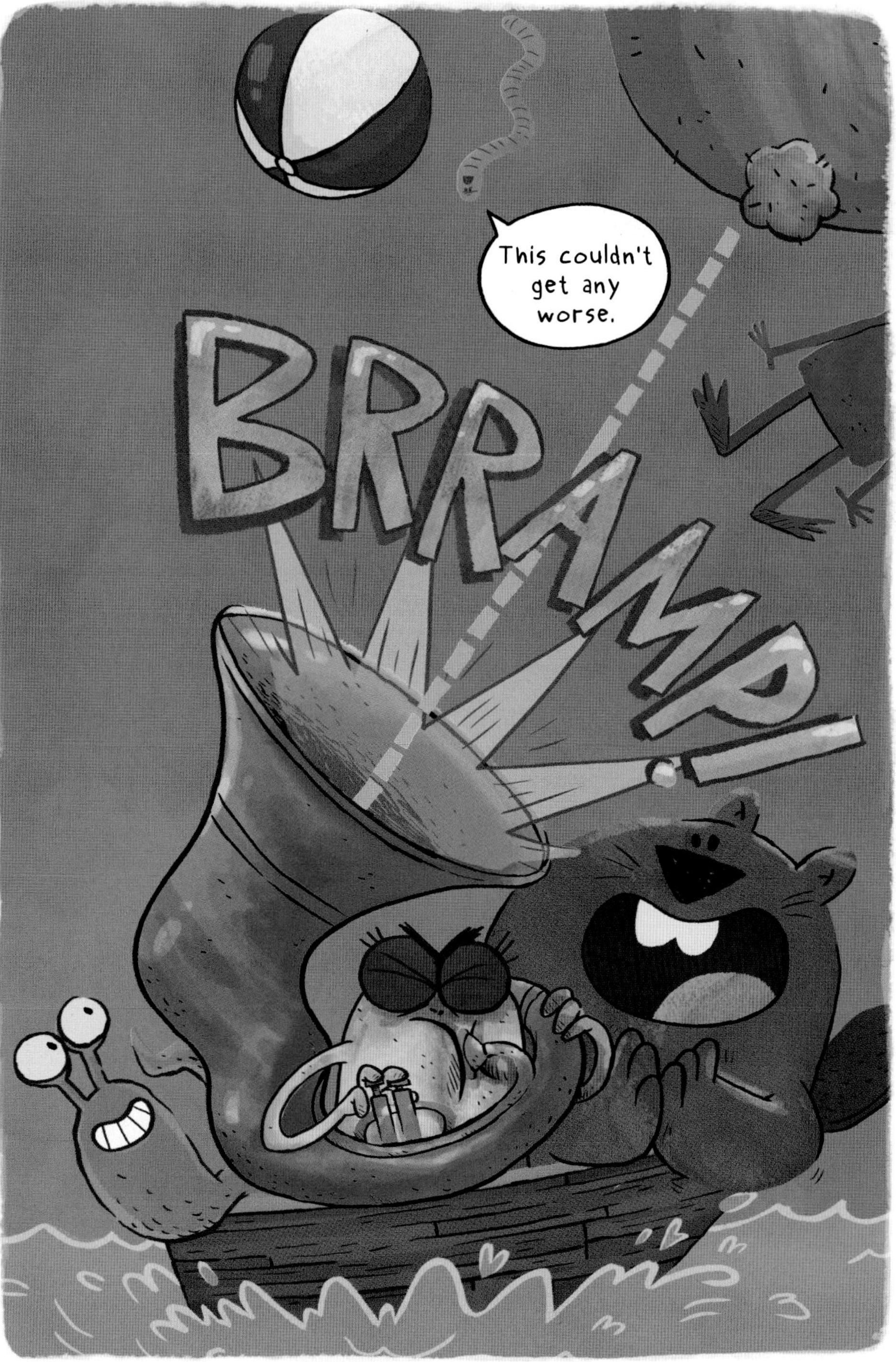
This couldn't get any worse.
BRRAMP!

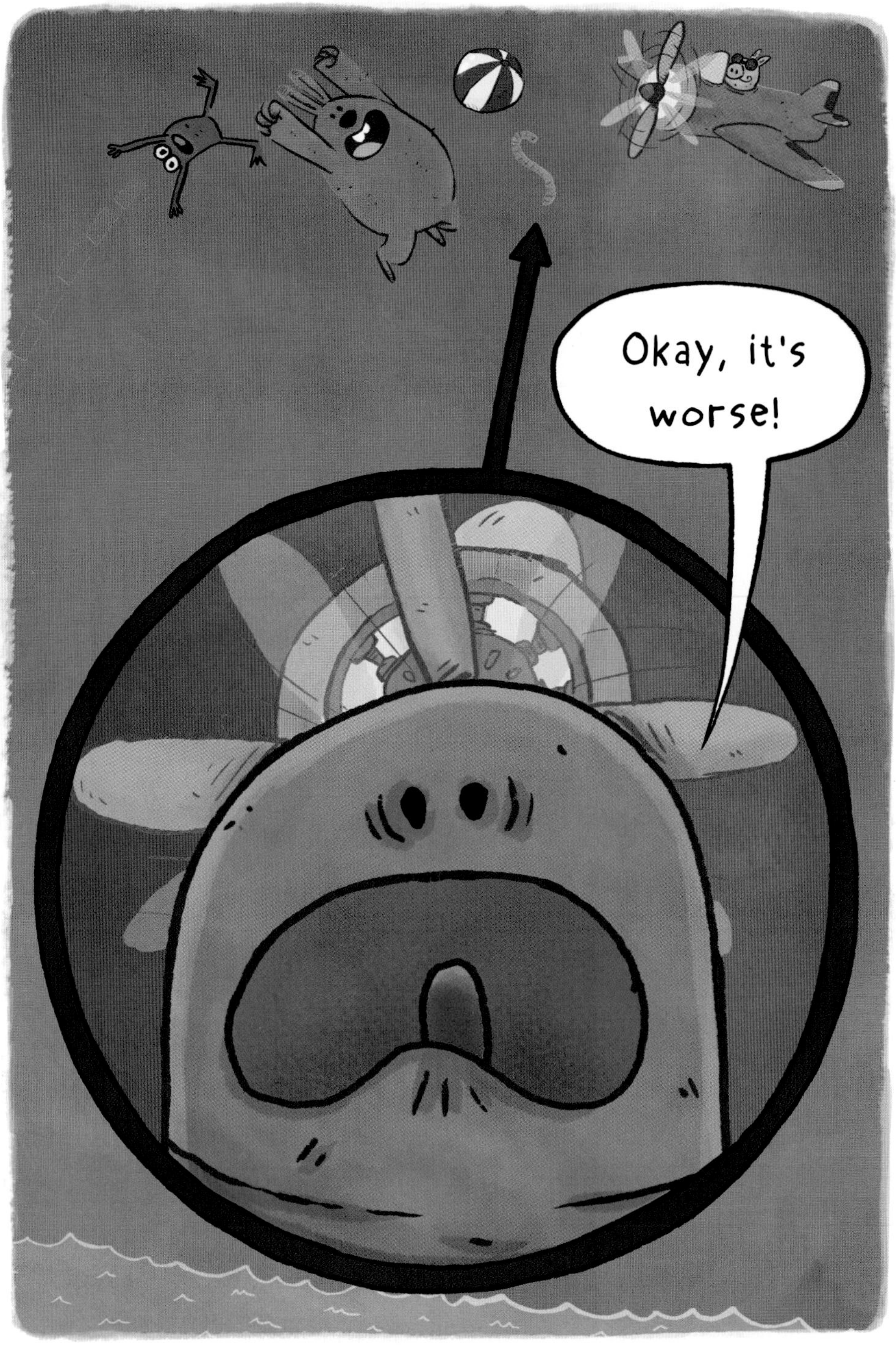
Okay, it's worse!

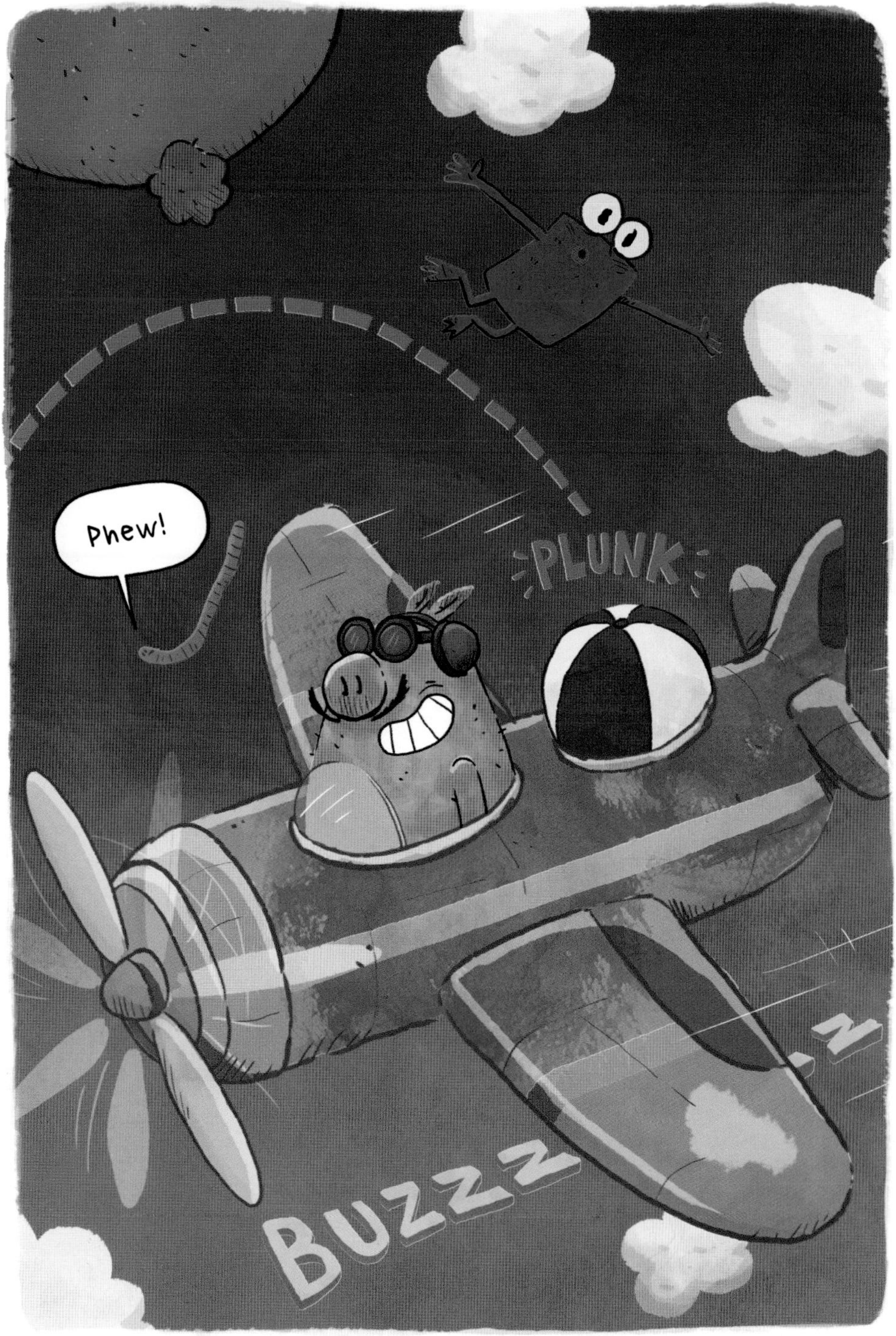

Phew!
PLUNK
BUZZZ

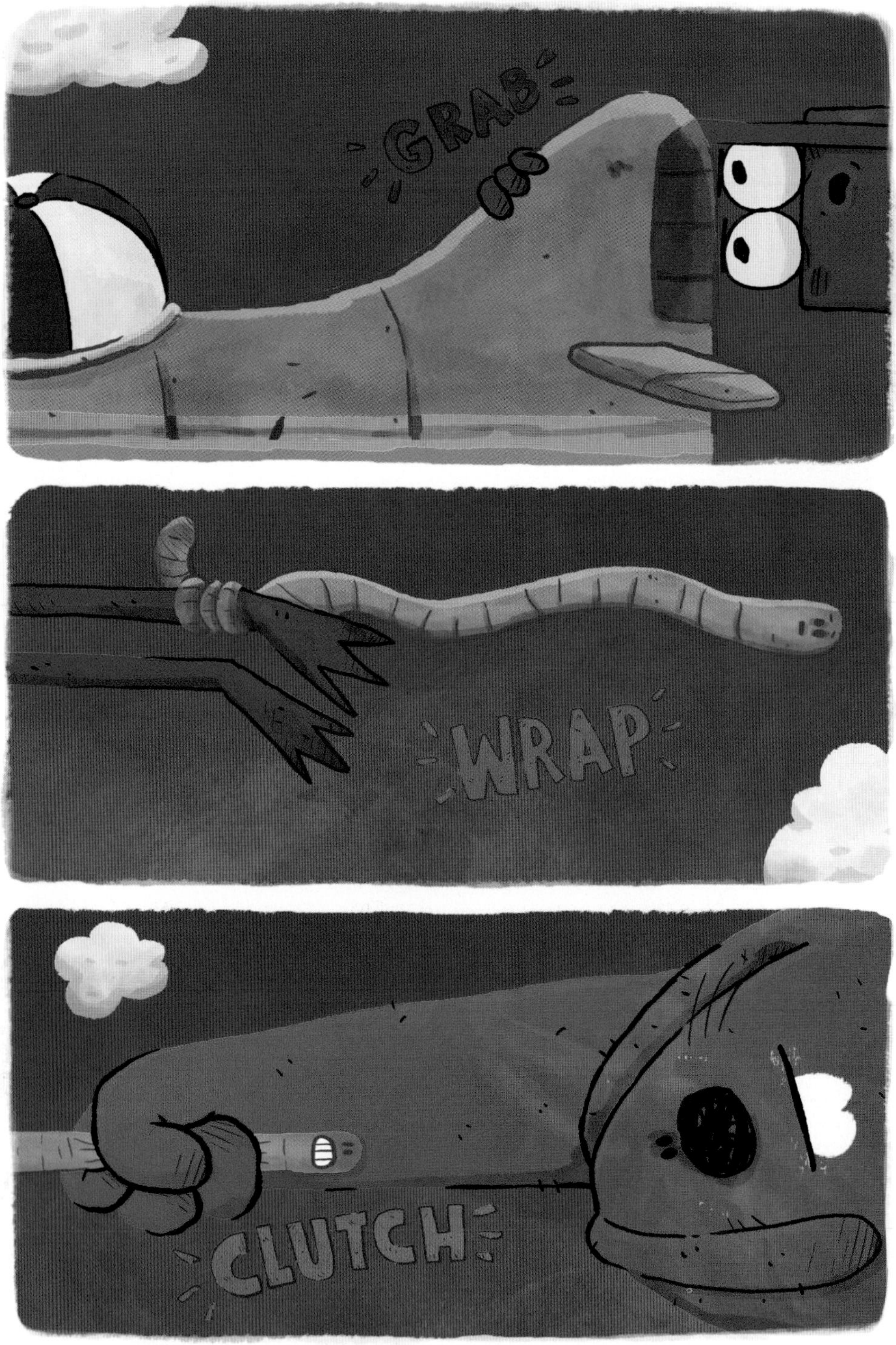
GRAB
WRAP
CLUTCH

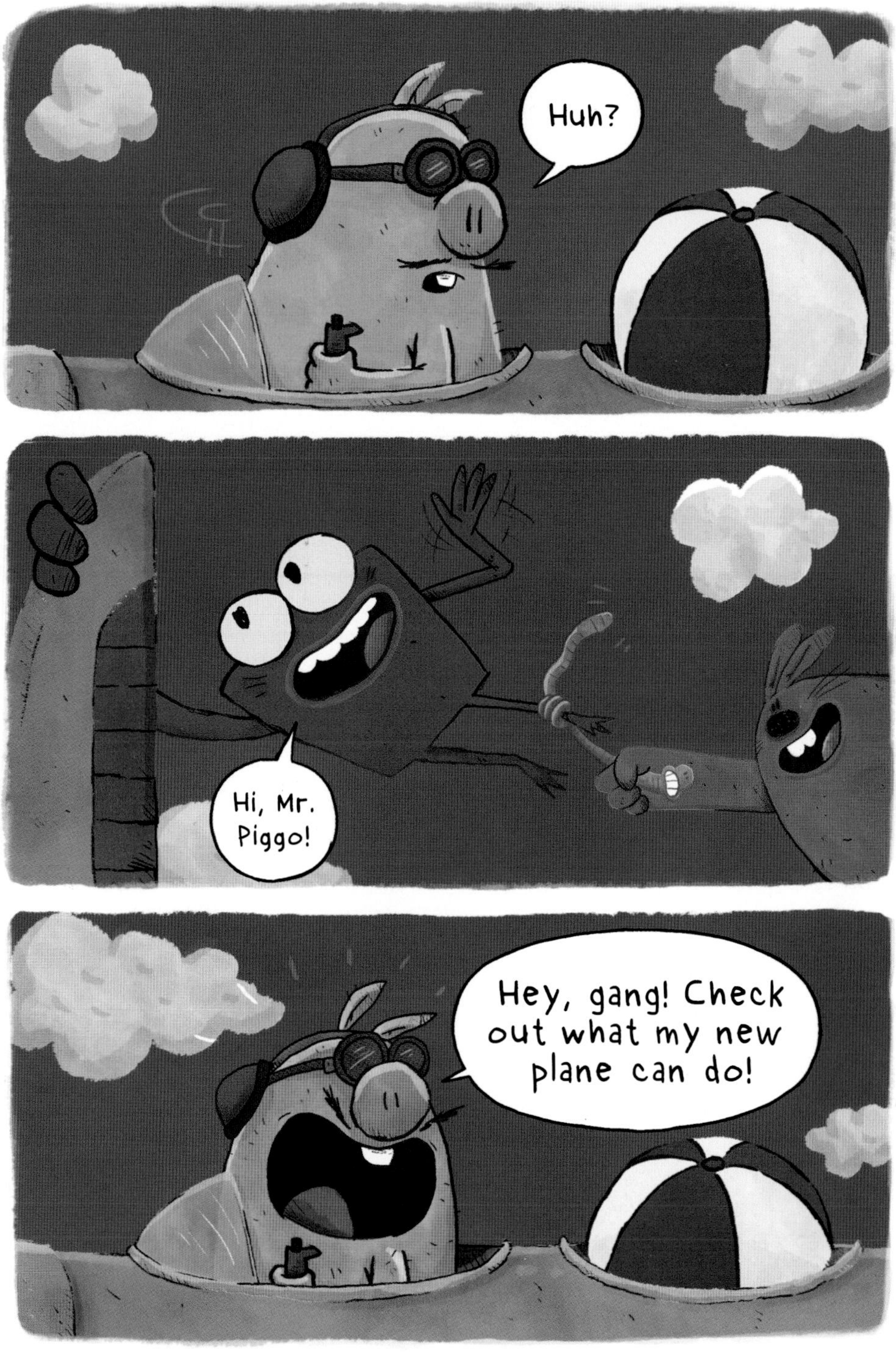
Huh?
Hi, Mr. Piggo!
Hey, gang! Check out what my new plane can do!

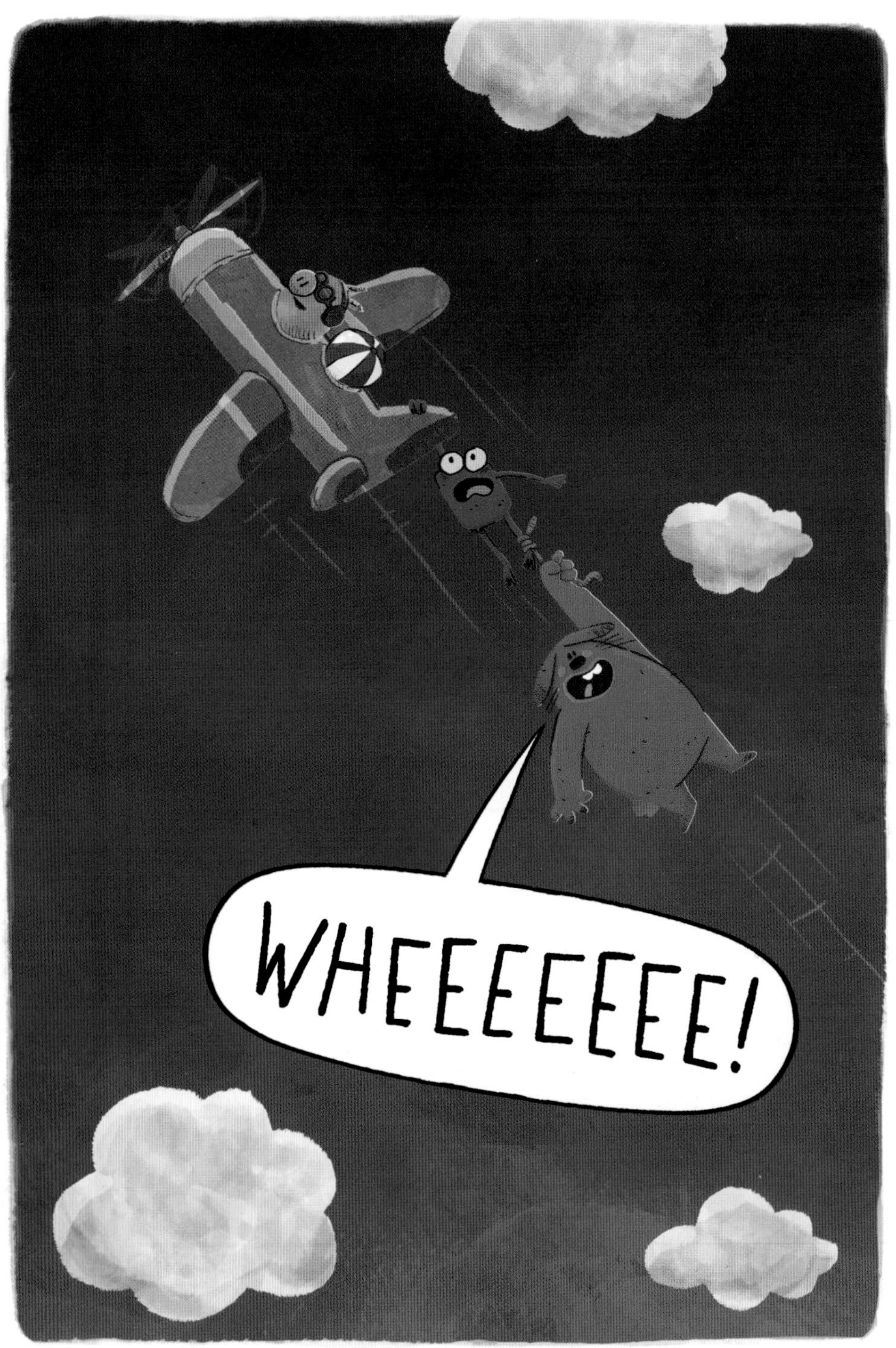
WHEEEEEEEE!

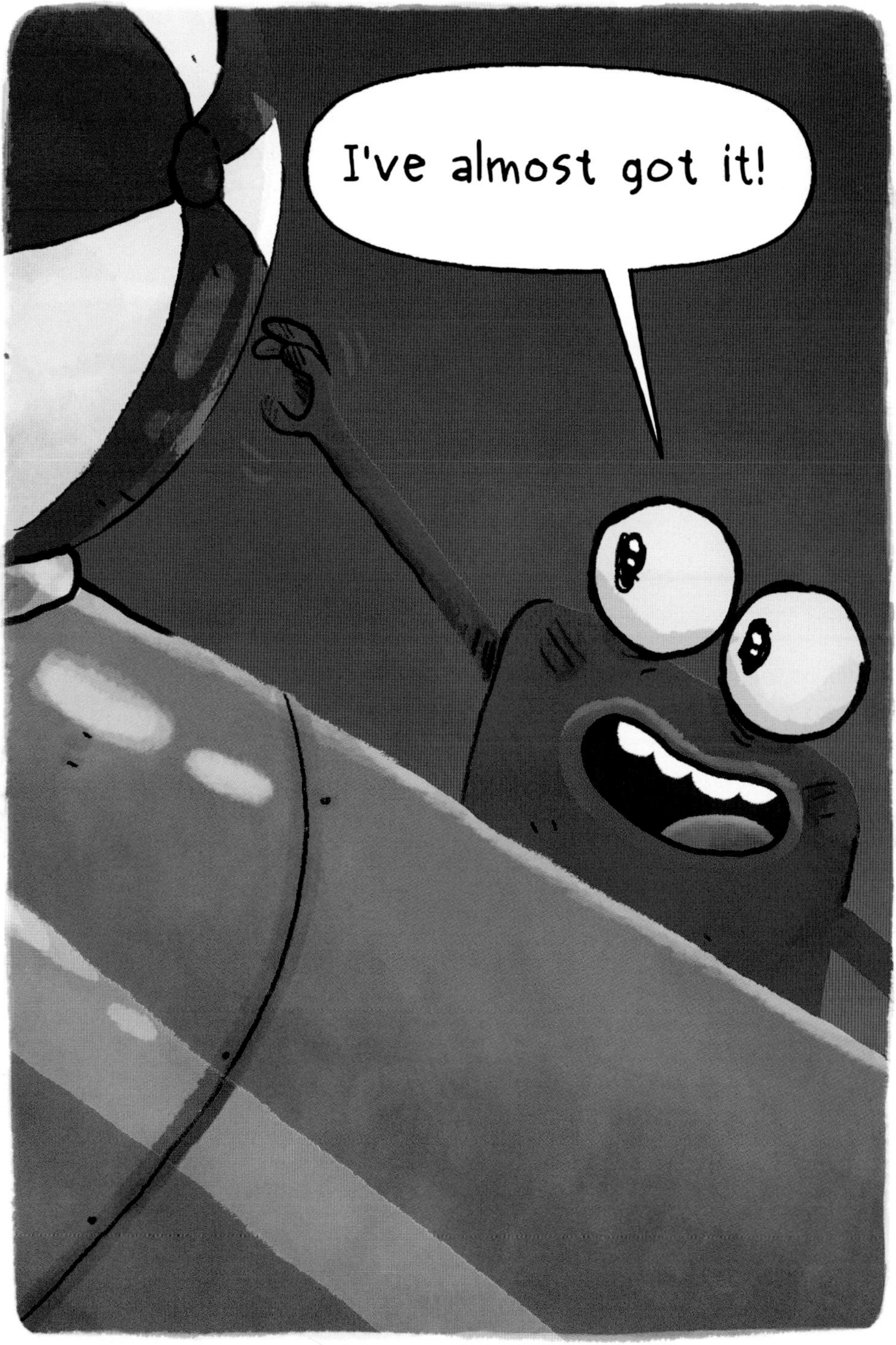
I've almost got it!

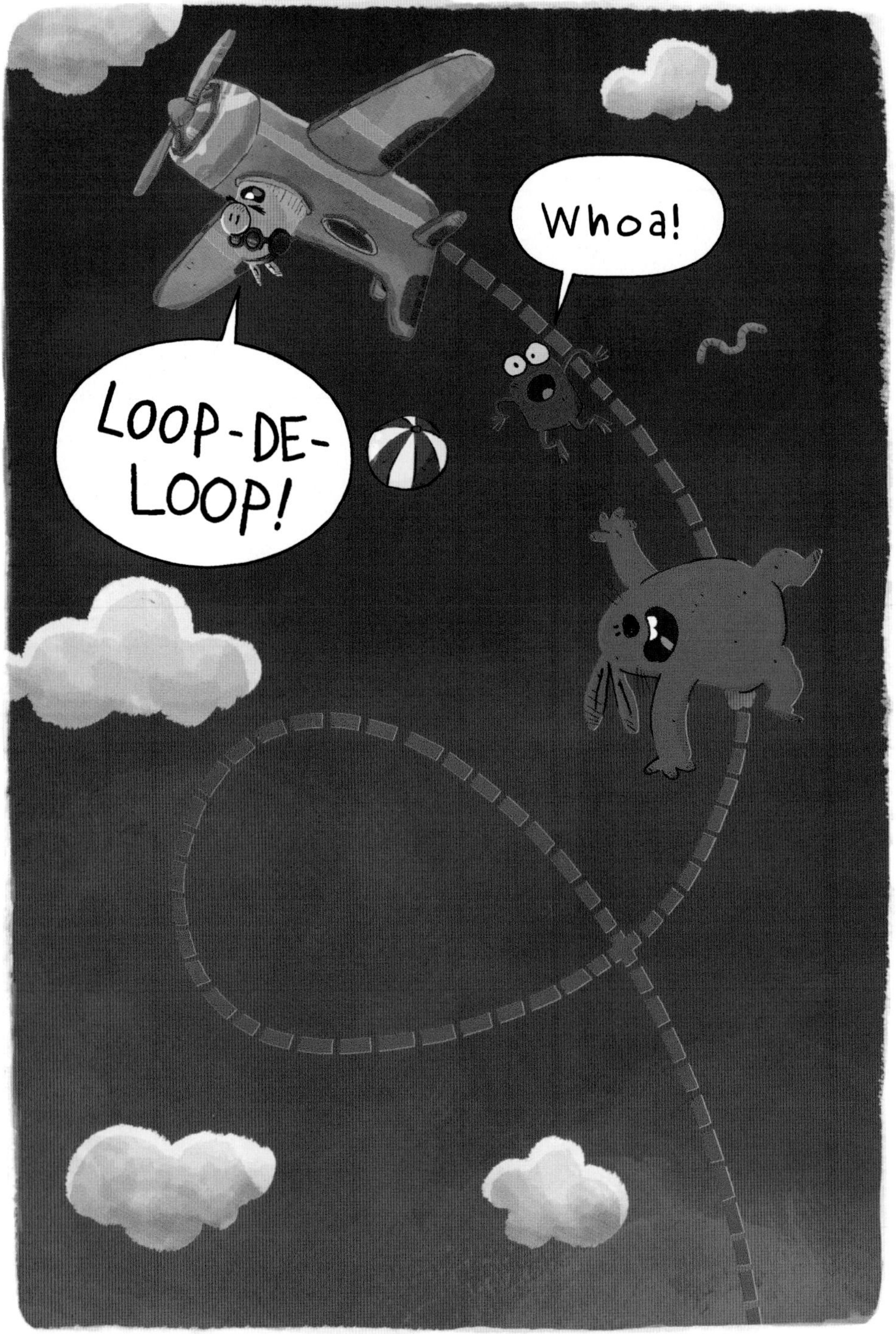
LOOP-DE-LOOP!
Whoa!

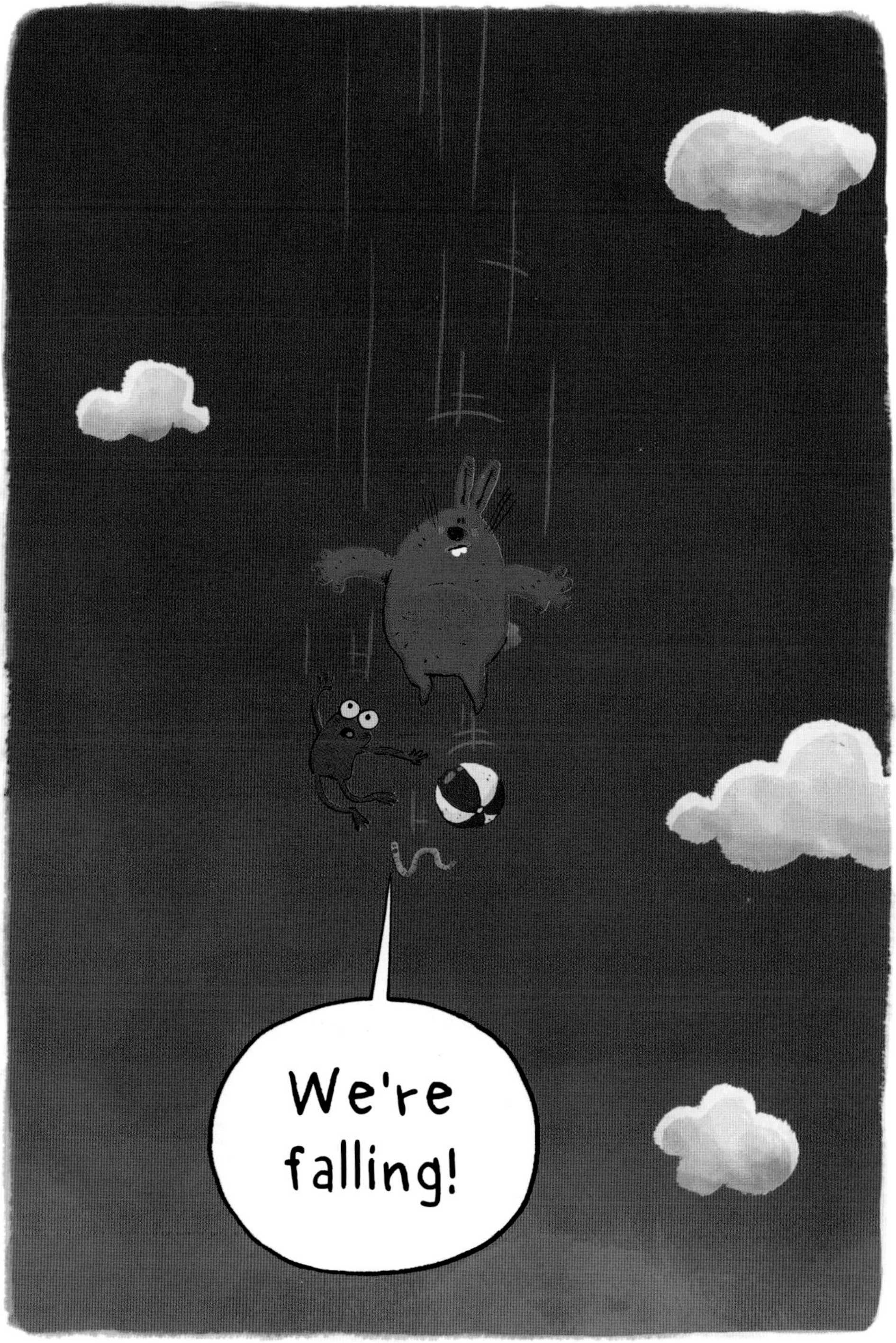
We're falling!

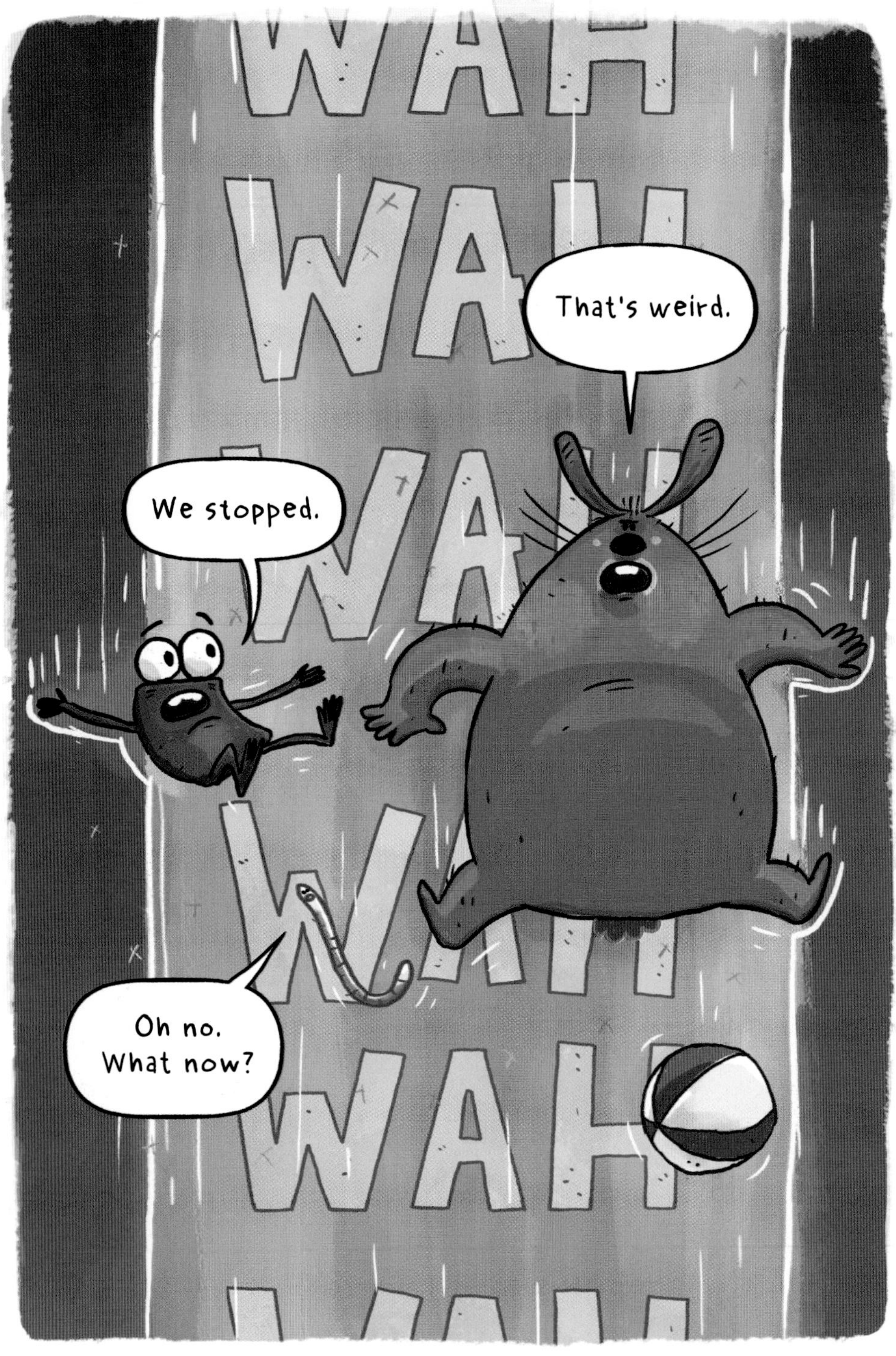
WAH
WAH
WAH
That's weird.
We stopped.
WAH
Oh no.
What now?
WAH

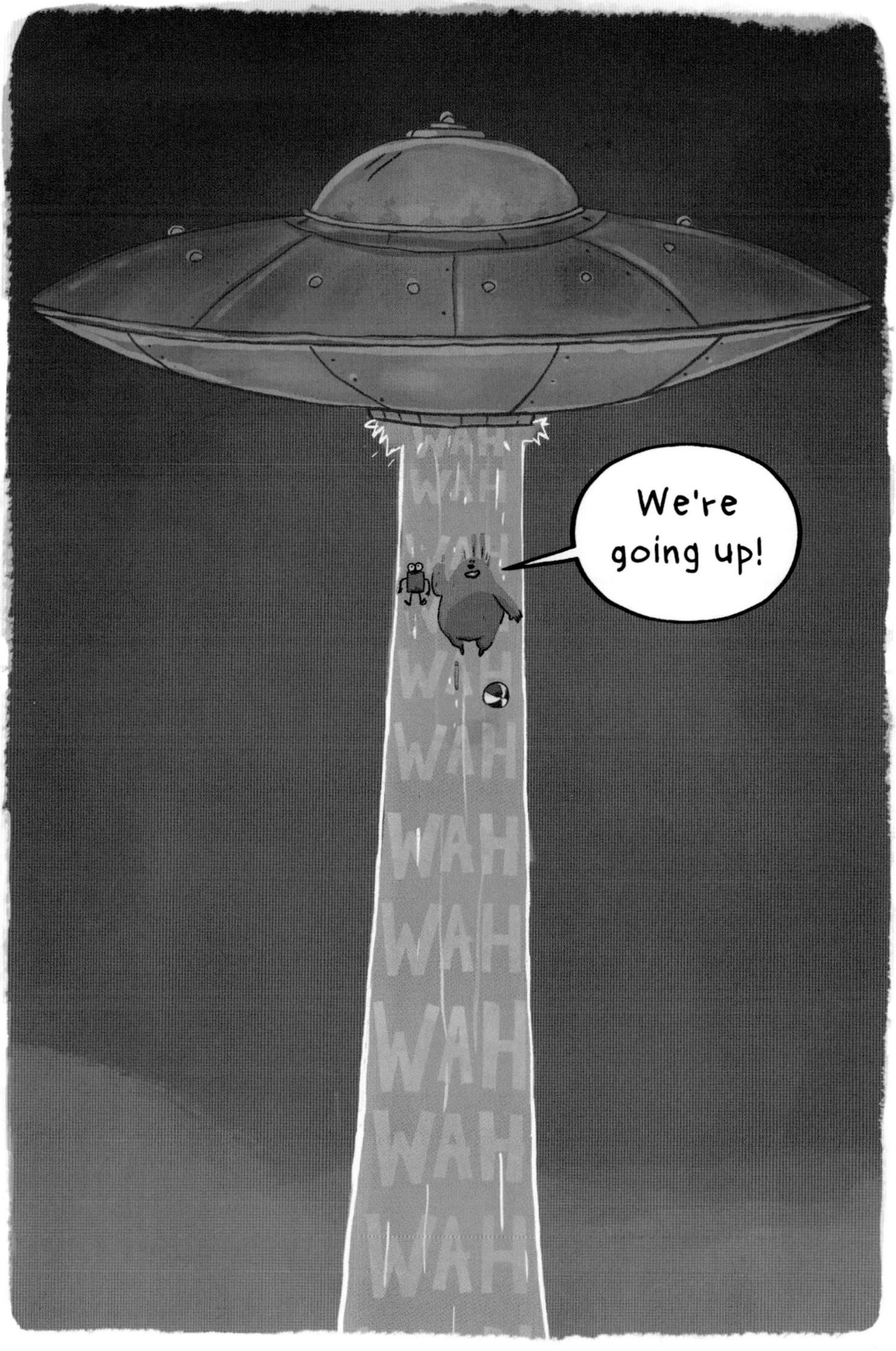
WAH WAH WAH WAH WAH WAH WAH WAH WAH WAH
We're going up!

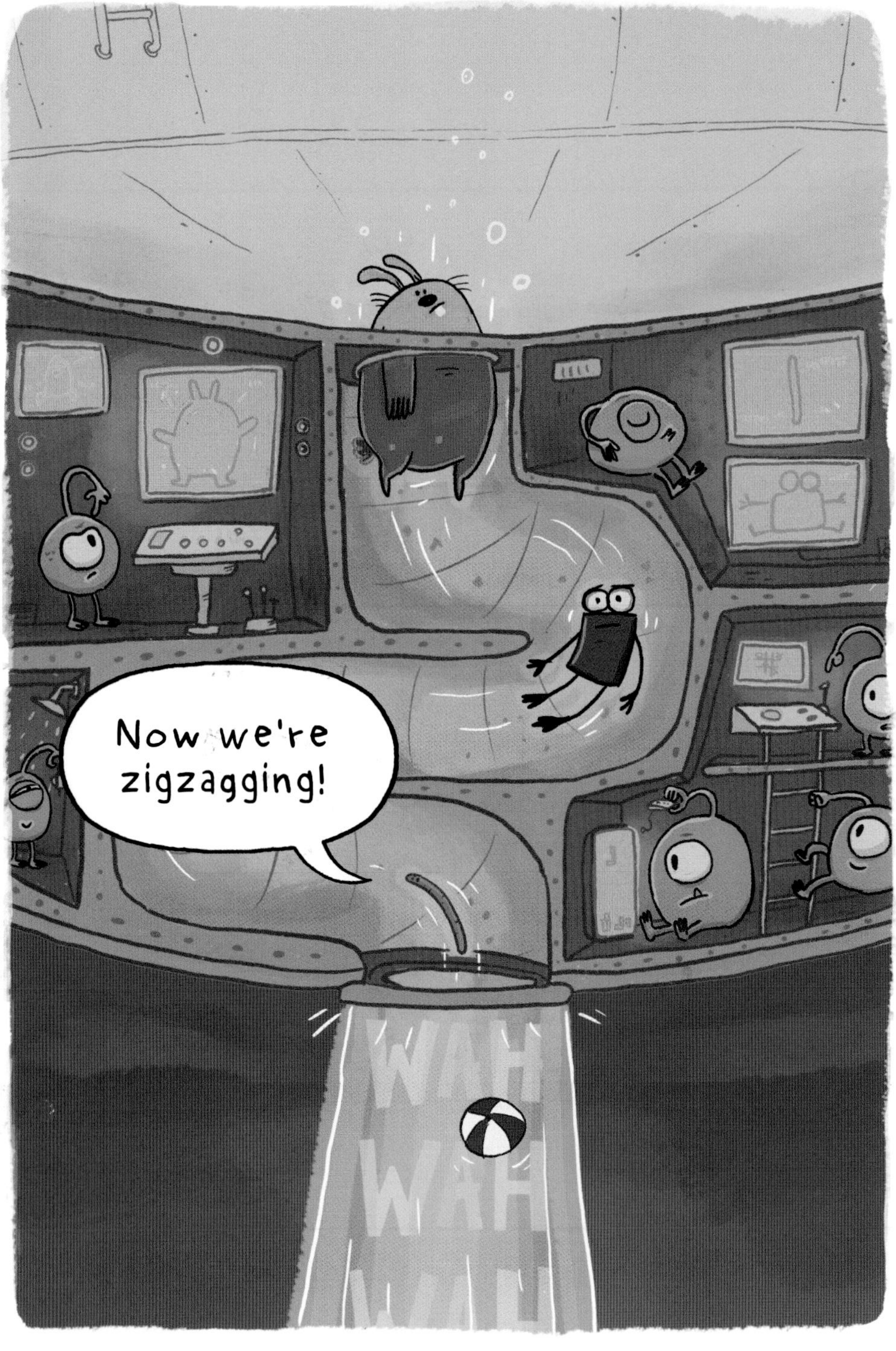
Now we're zigzagging!
WAH
WAH

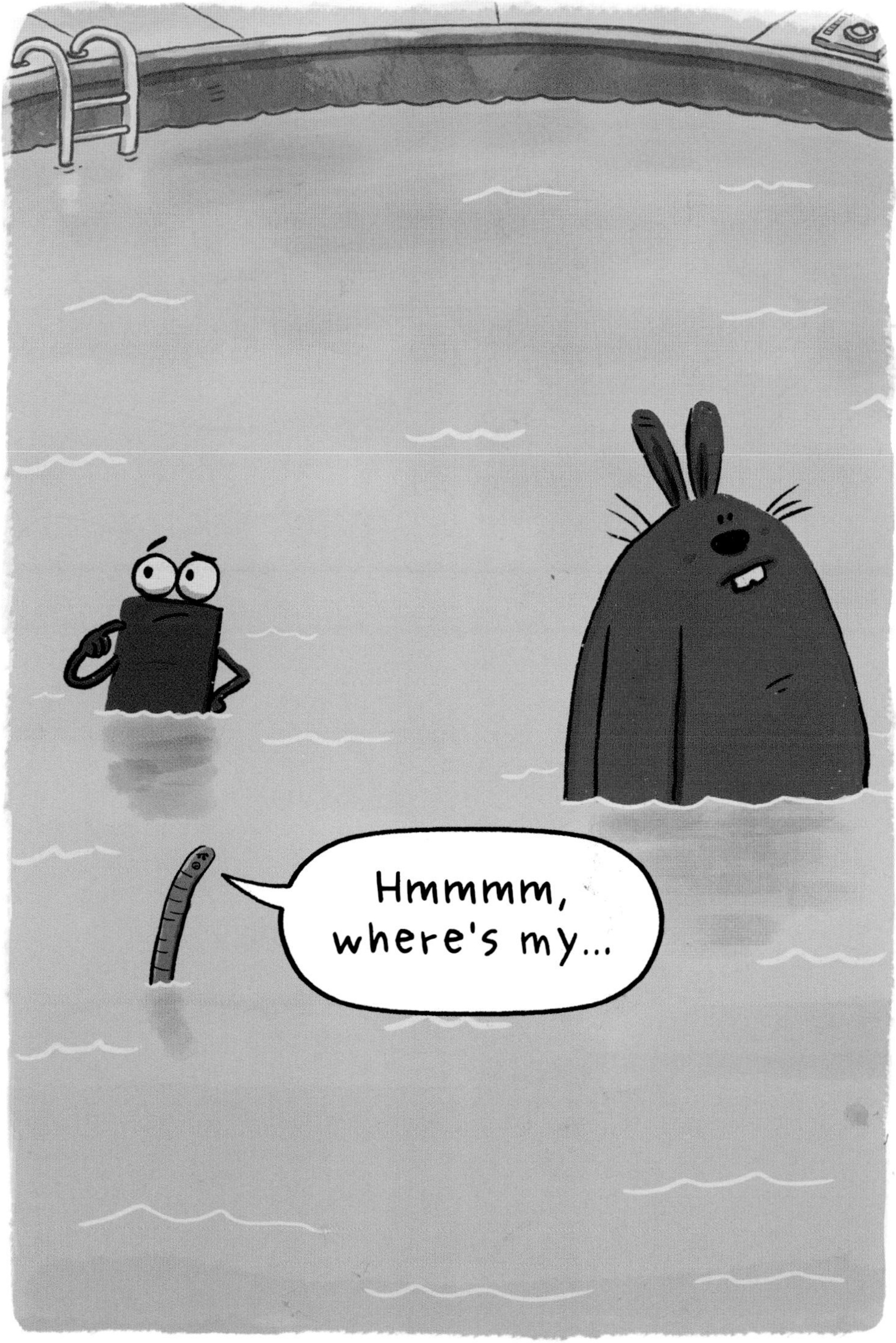
Hmmmm, where's my...

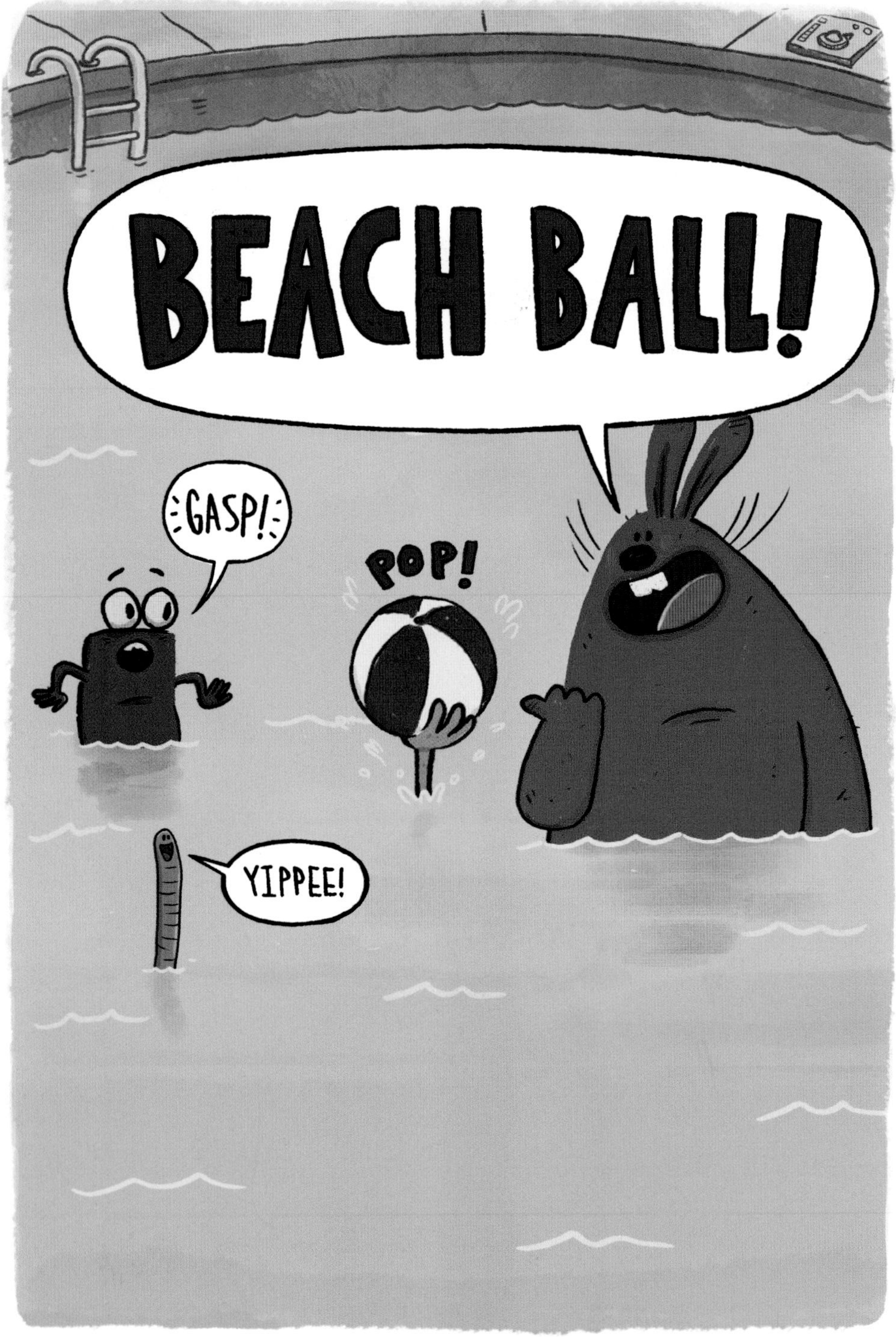
BEACH BALL!
GASP!
POP!
YIPPEE!

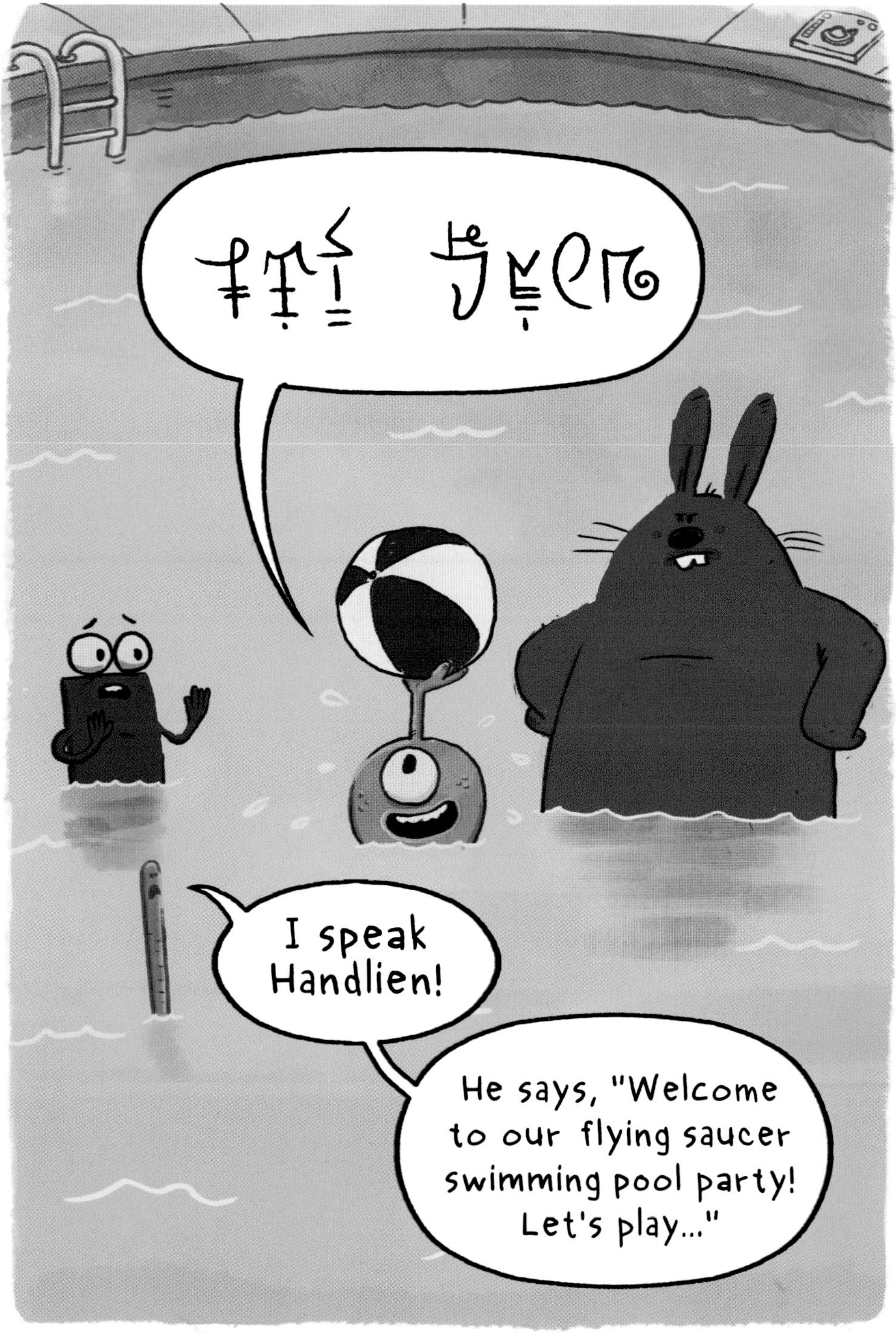
I speak Handlien!
He says, "Welcome to our flying saucer swimming pool party! Let's play..."

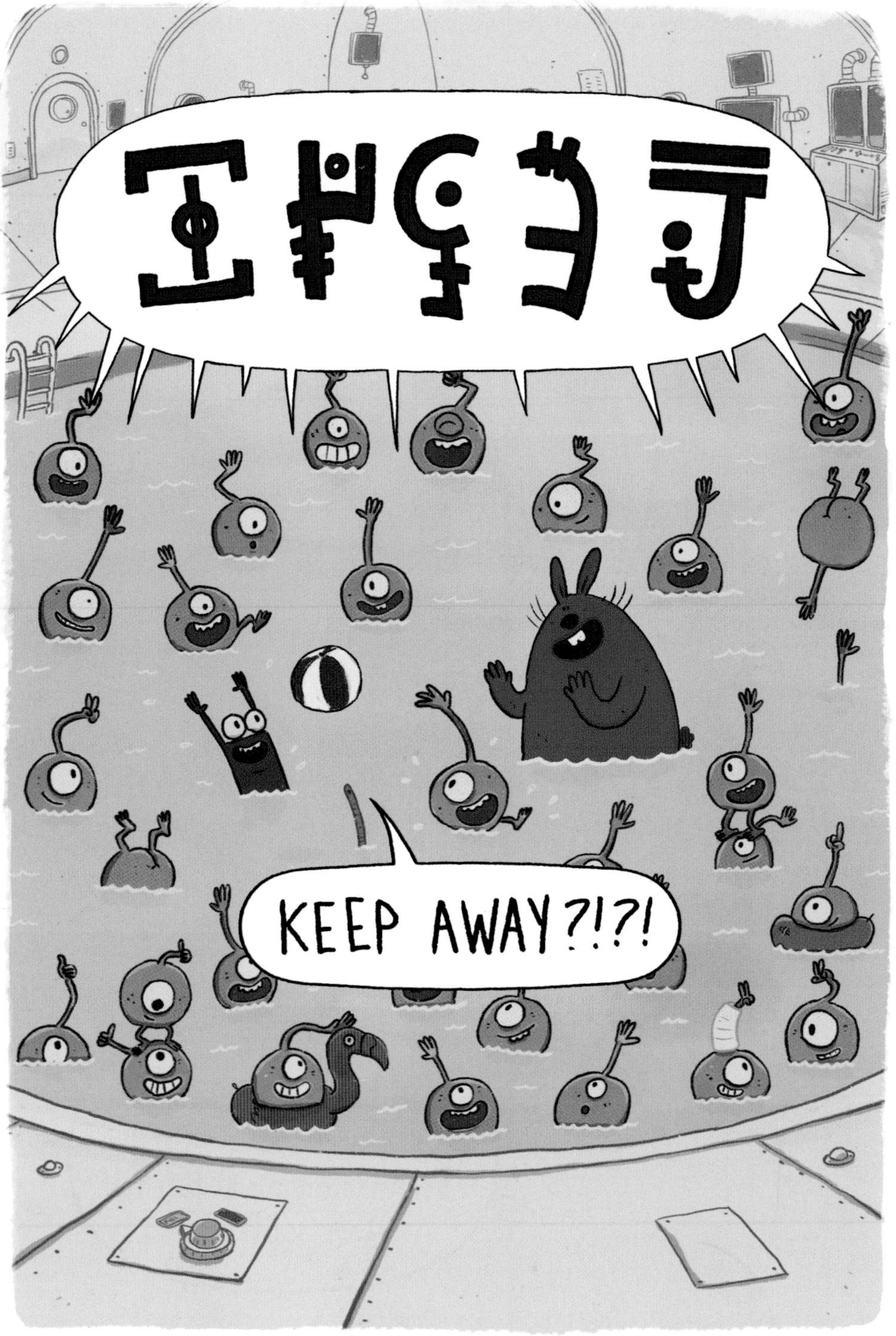
KEEP AWAY?!?!

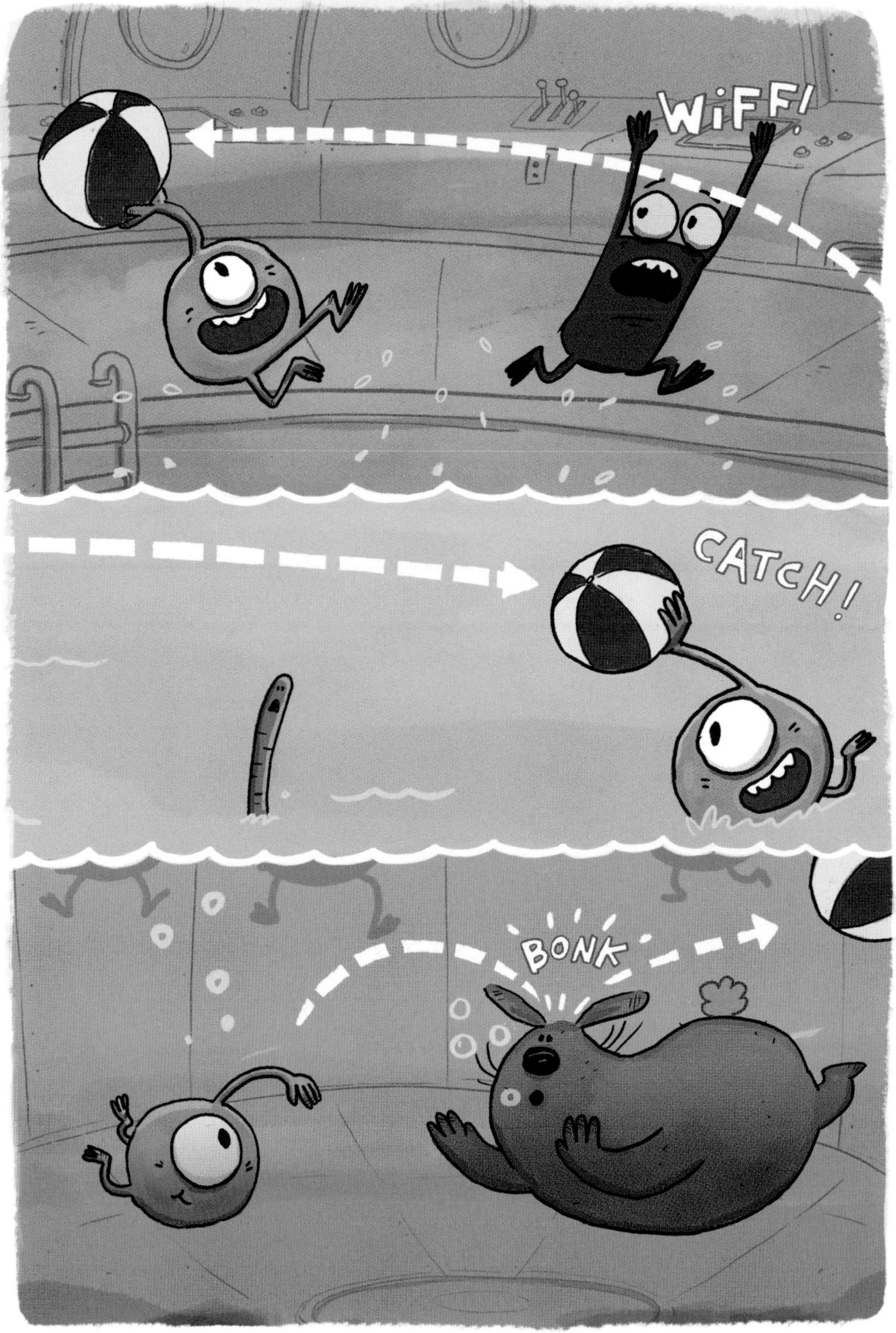
WIFF!
CATCH!
BONK

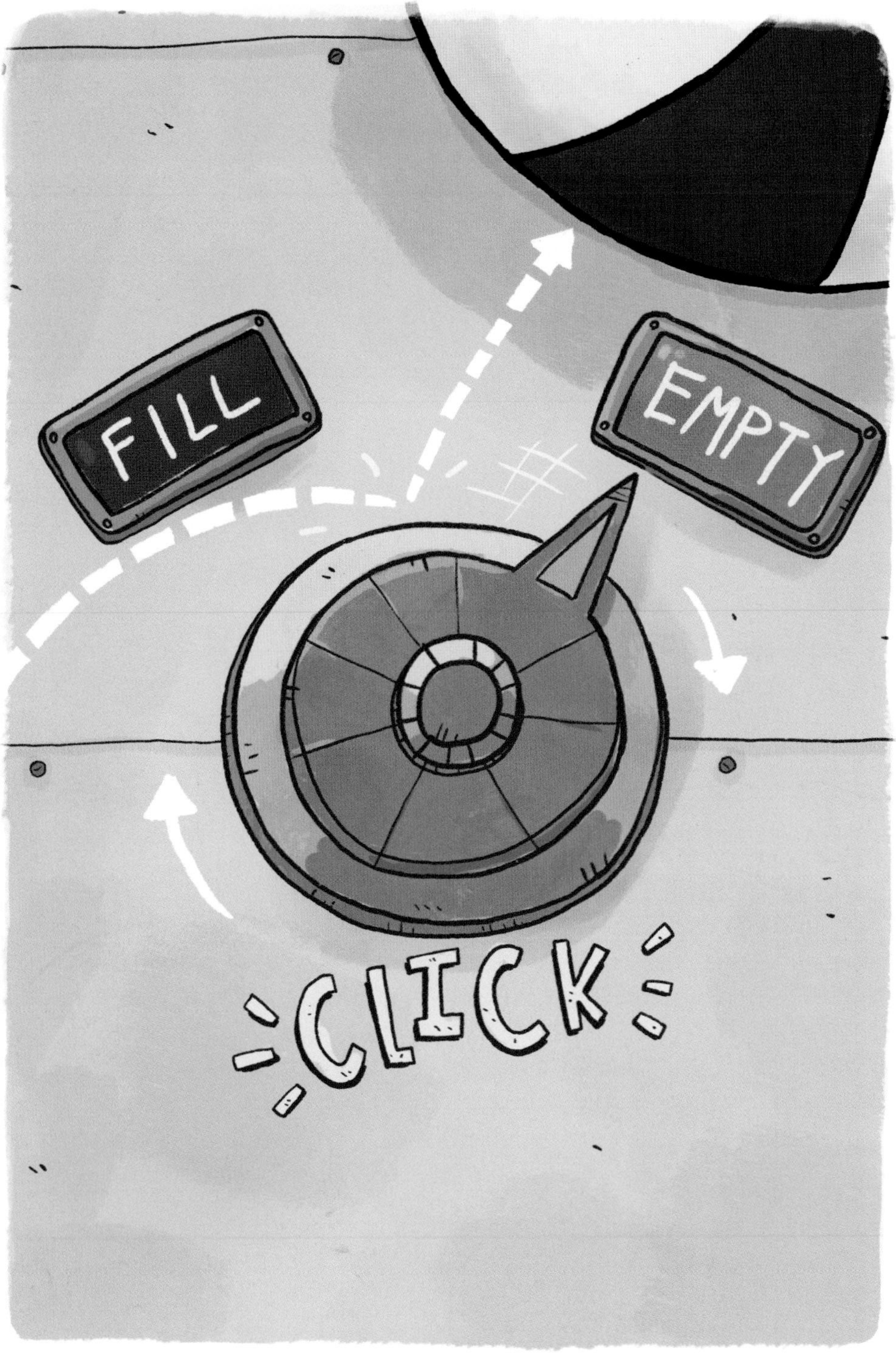
FILL
EMPTY
CLICK

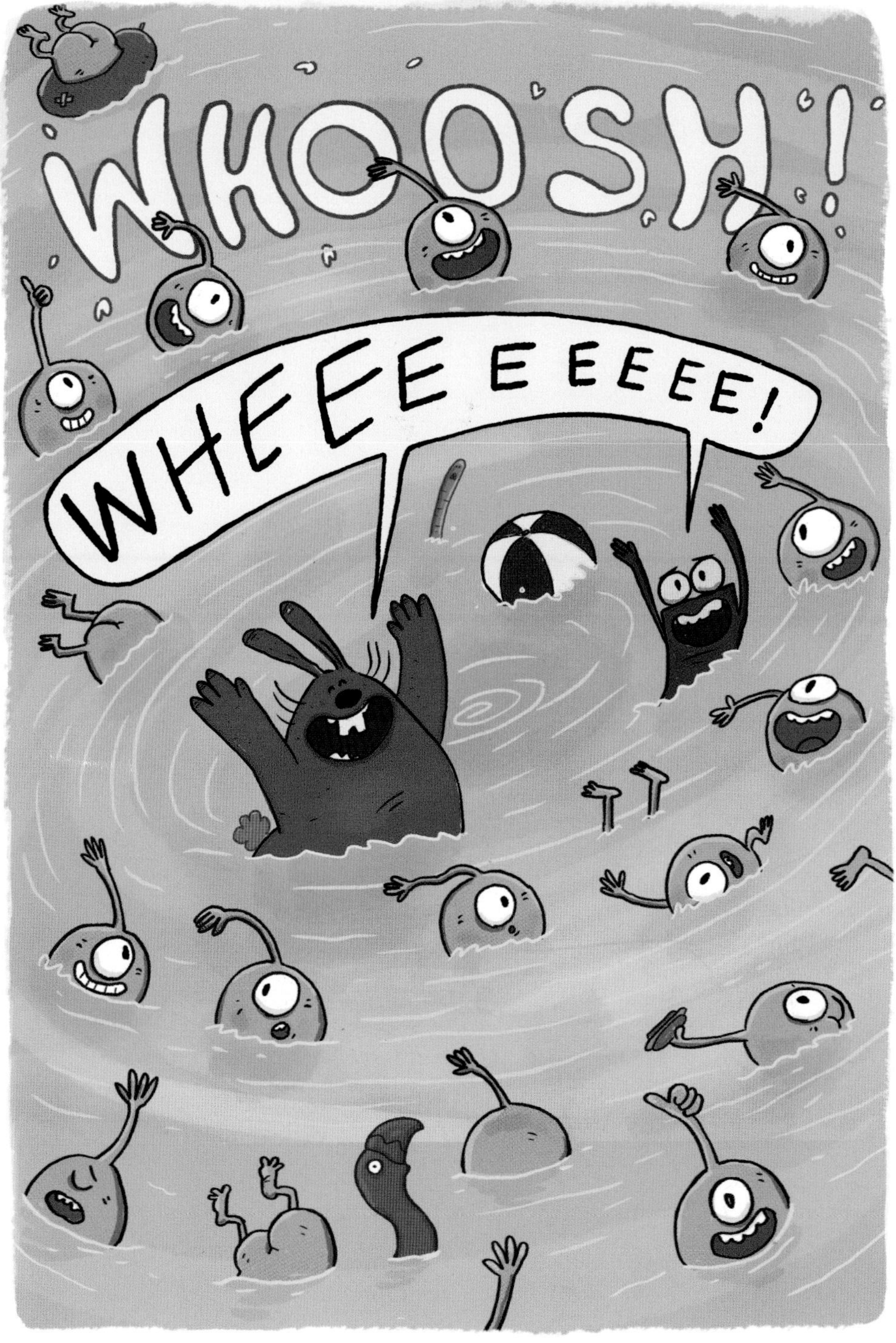
WHOOSH!
WHEEEEEEEE!

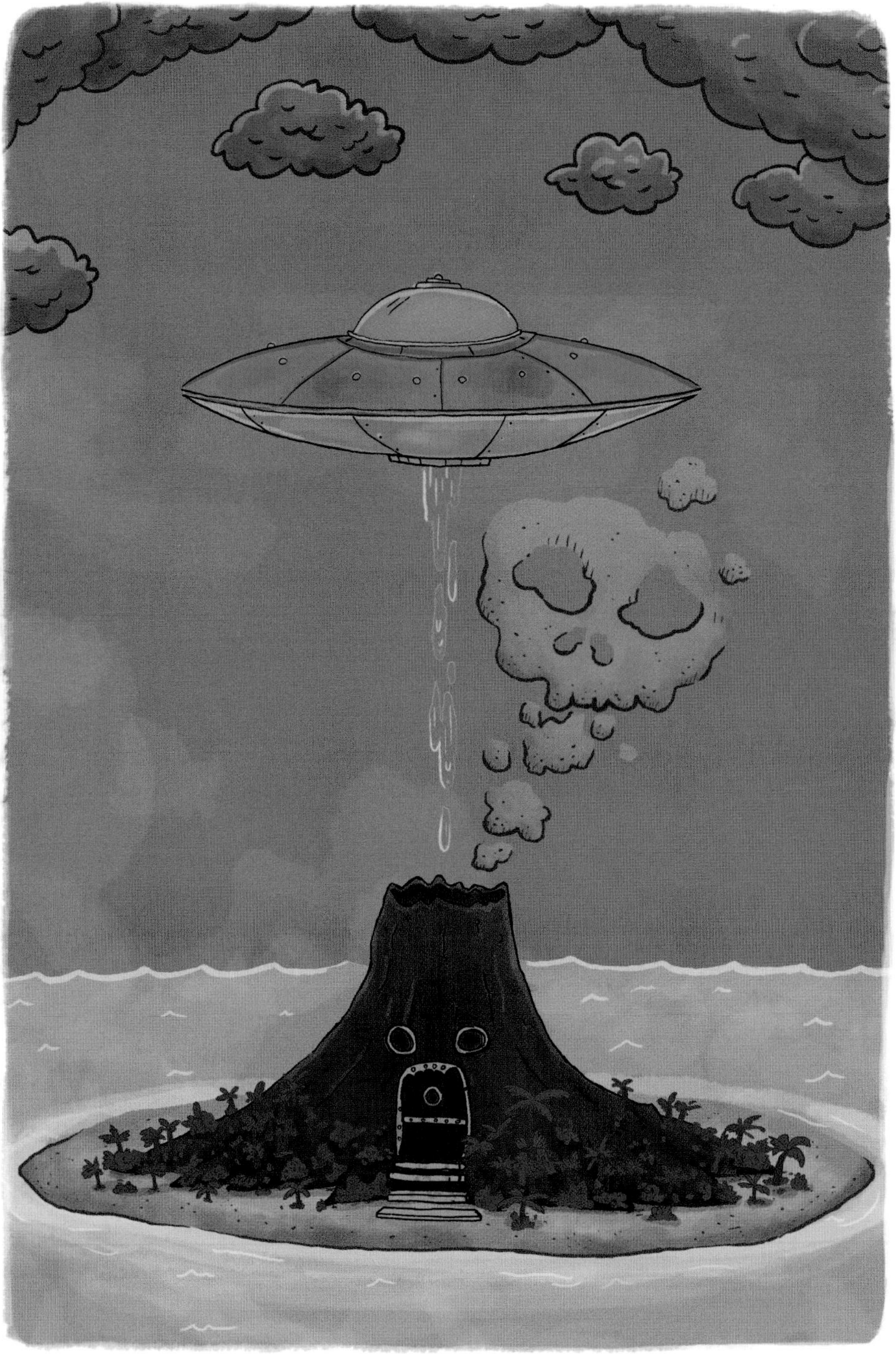

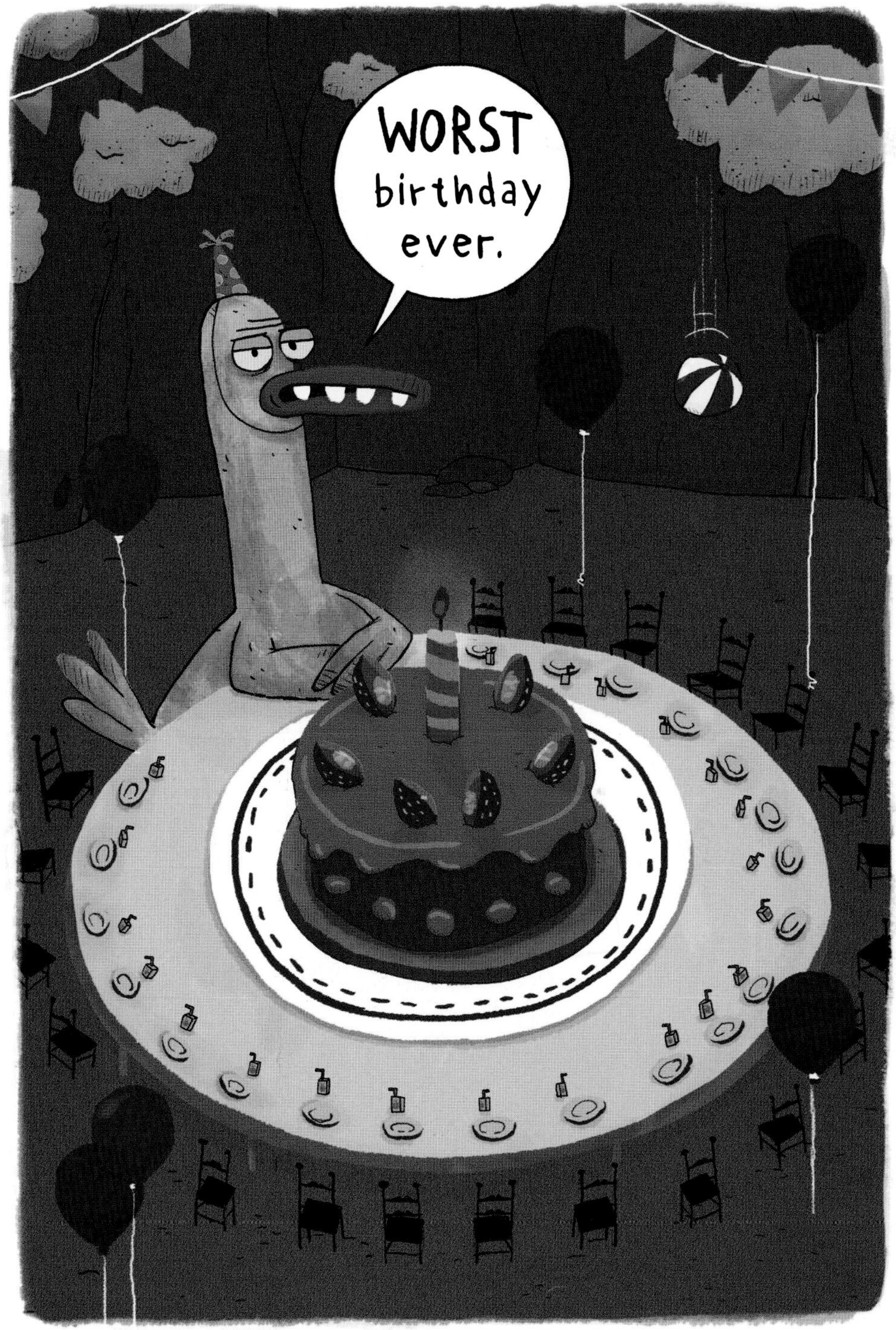
WORST birthday ever.

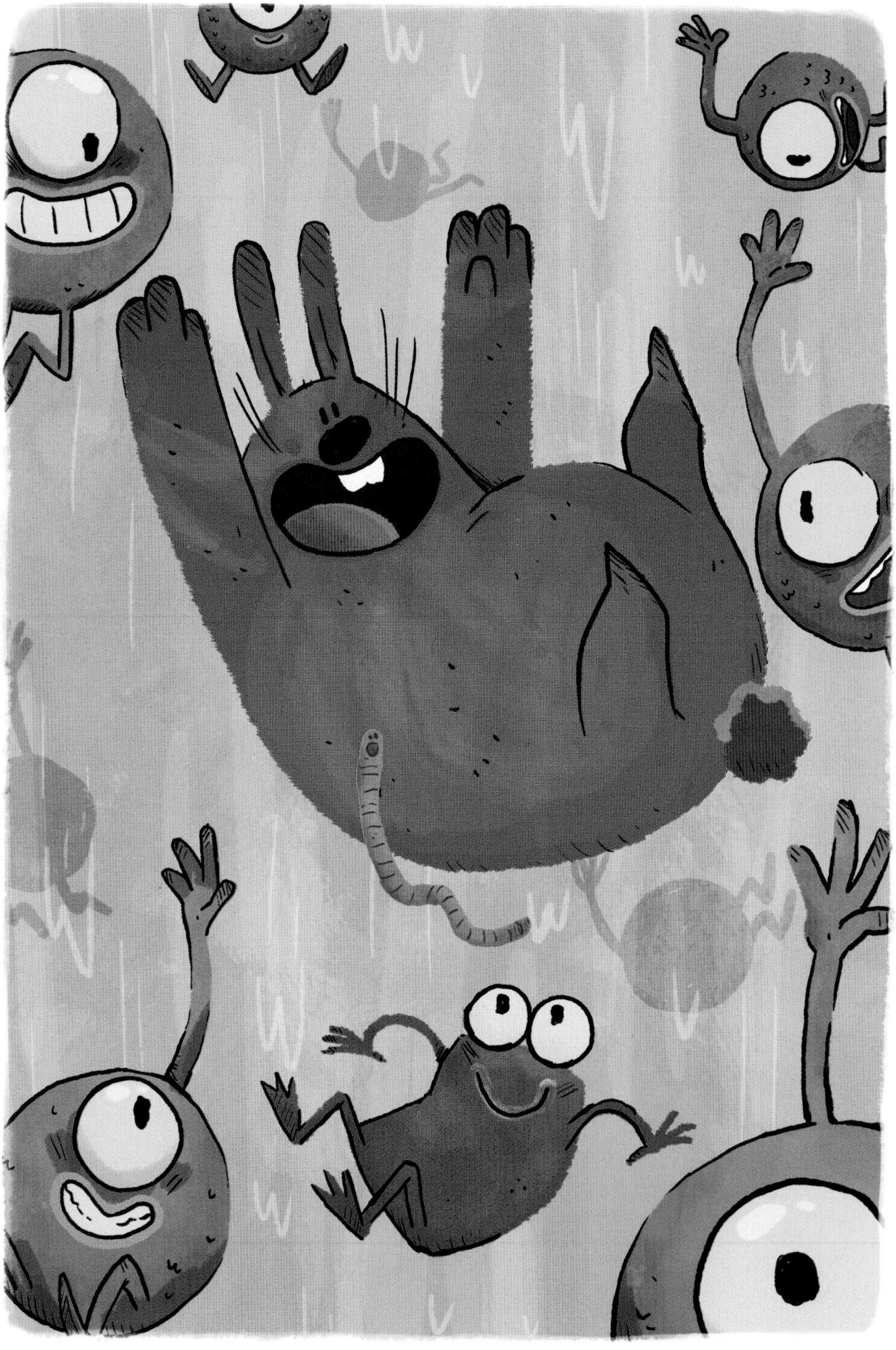

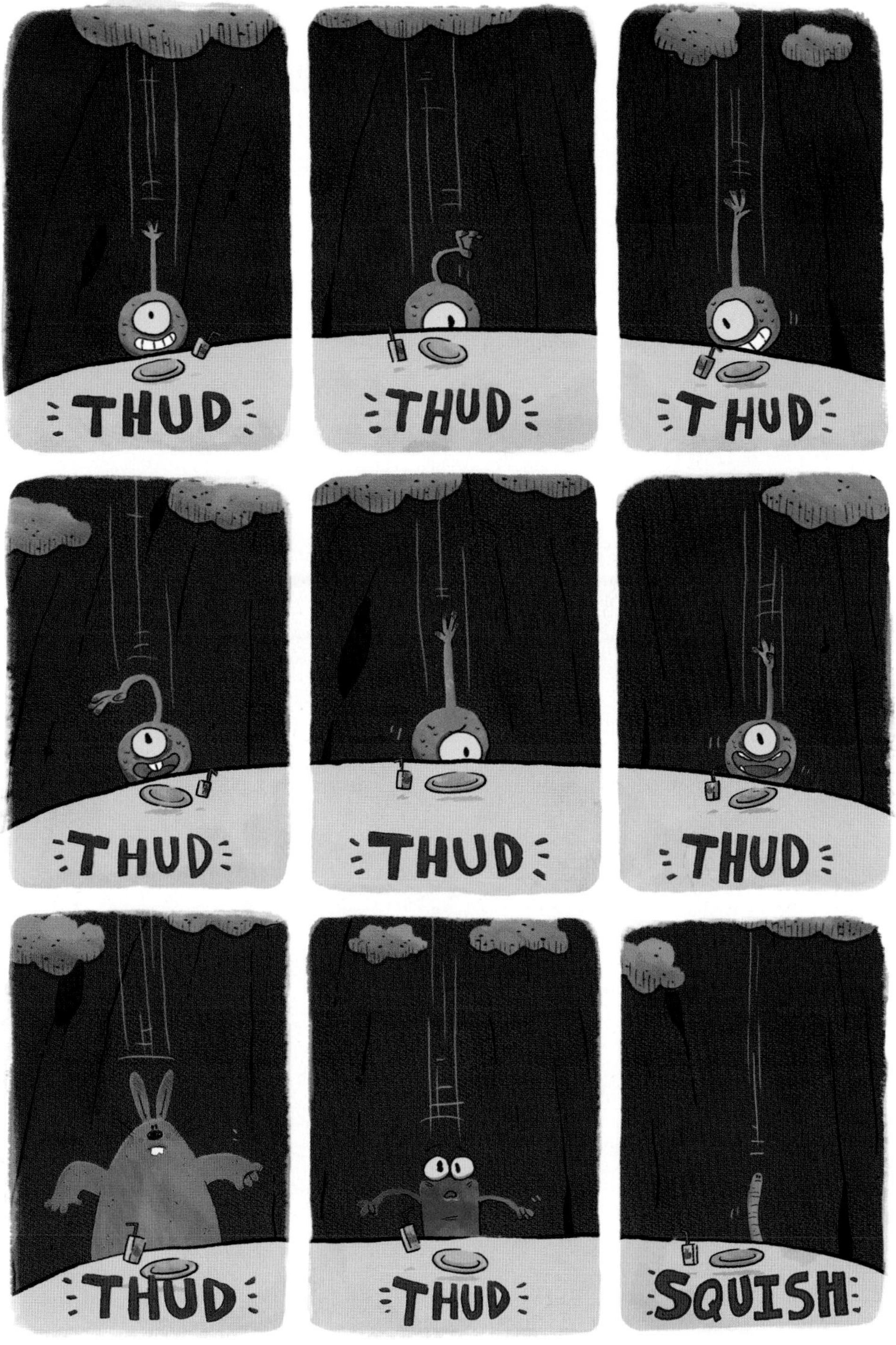
THUD
THUD
THUD
THUD
THUD
THUD
THUD
THUD
SQUISH

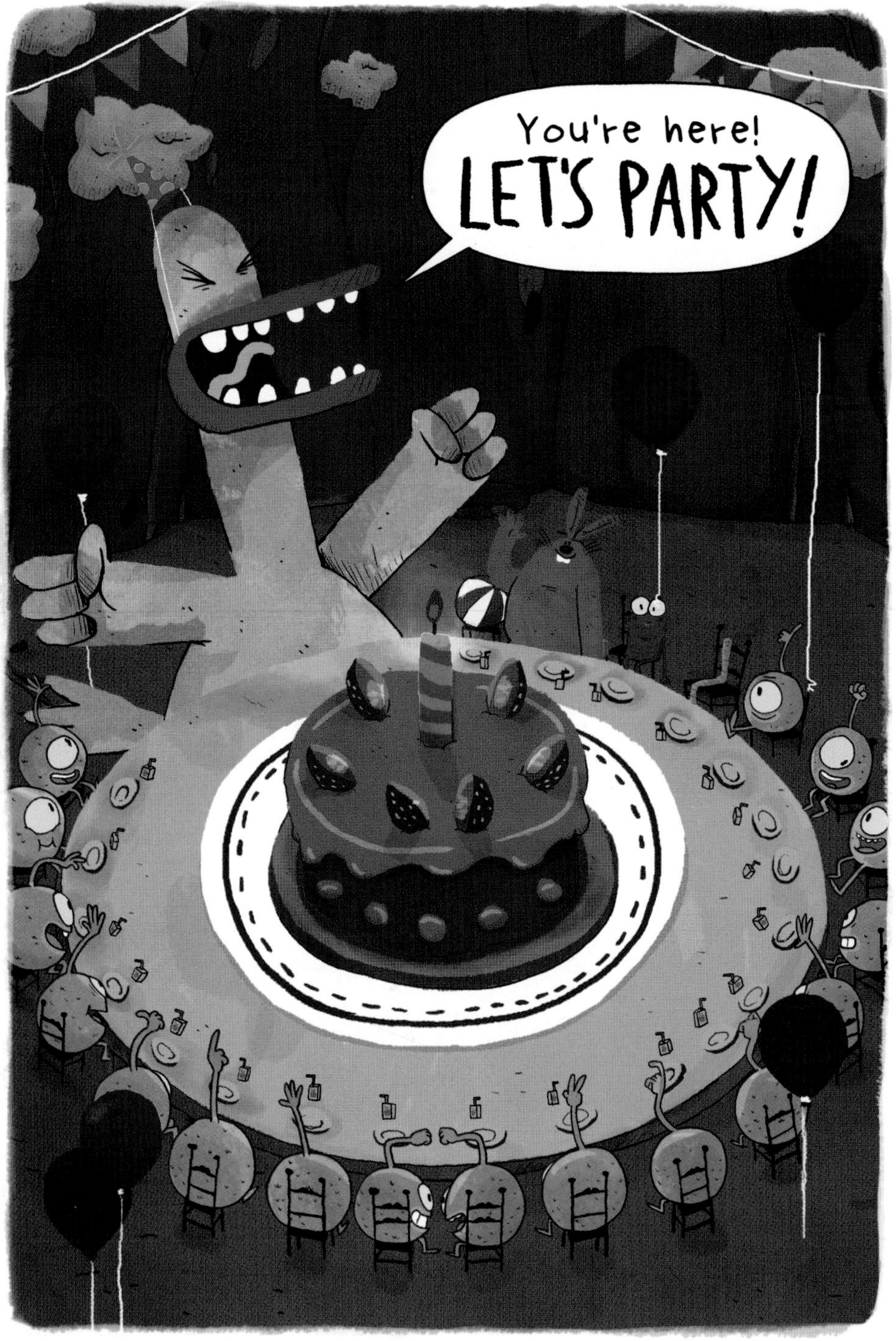
You're here!
LET'S PARTY!

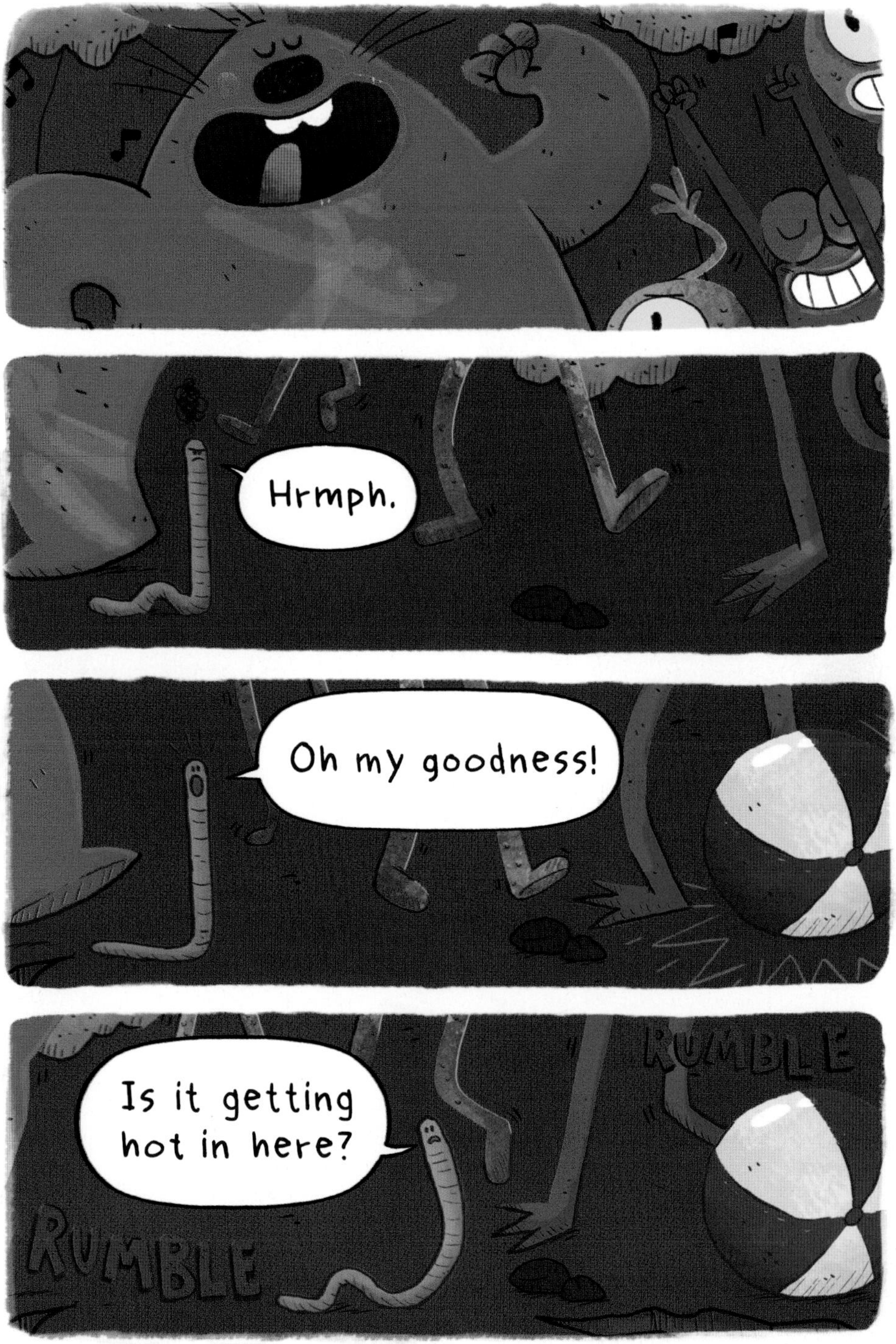

Hrmph.
Oh my goodness!
Is it getting hot in here?
RUMBLE
RUMBLE

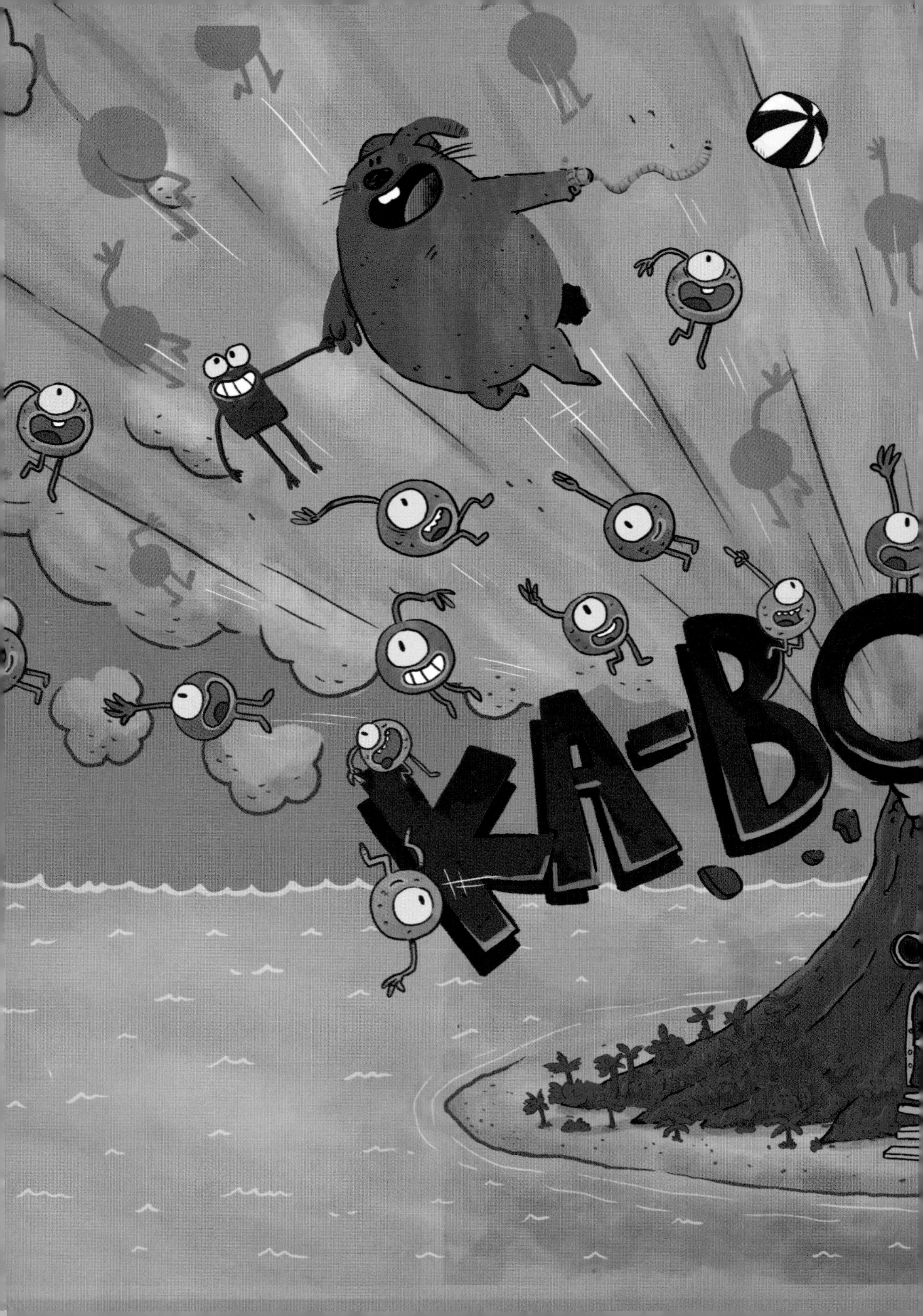
KA-BO

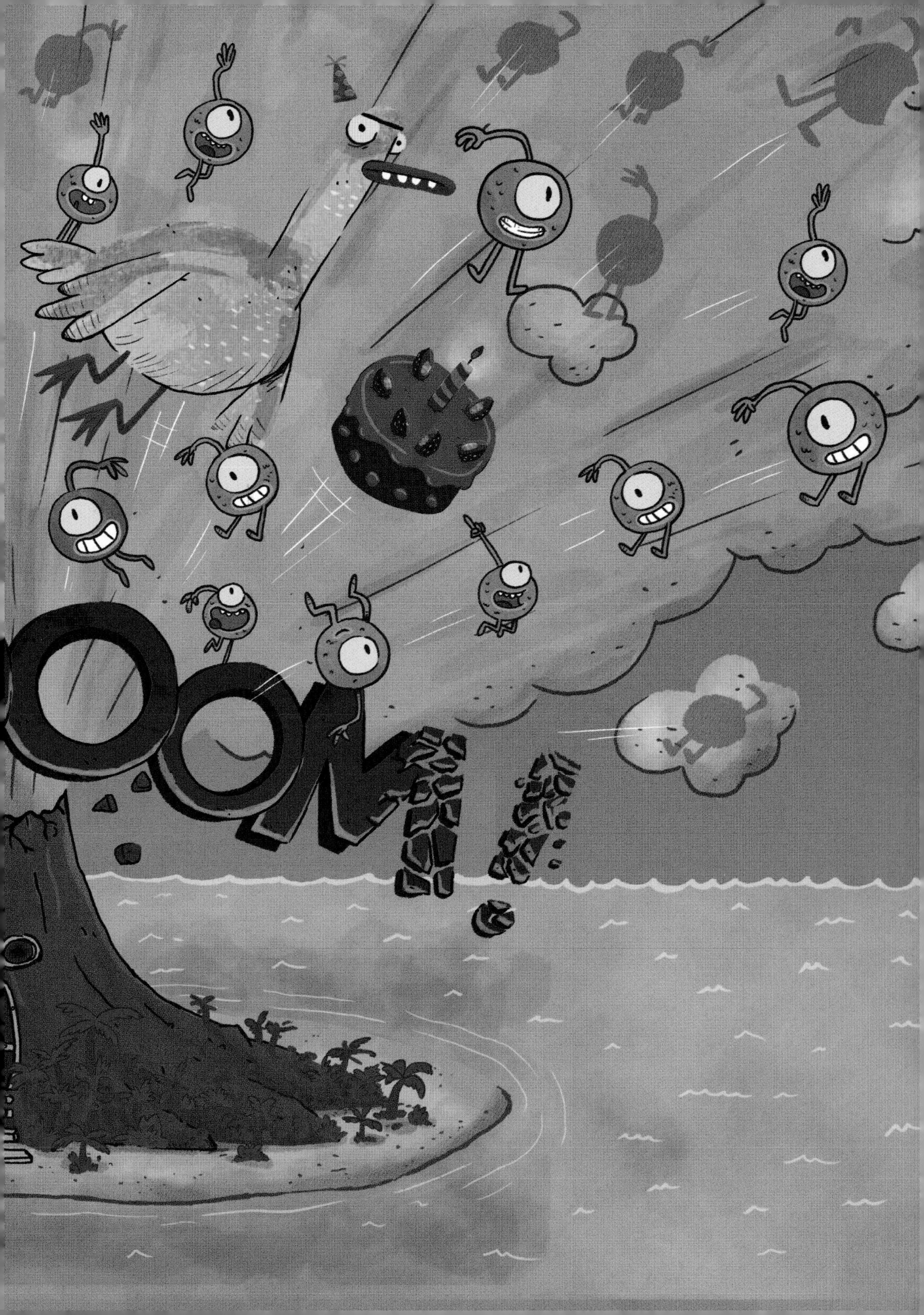
OOM!

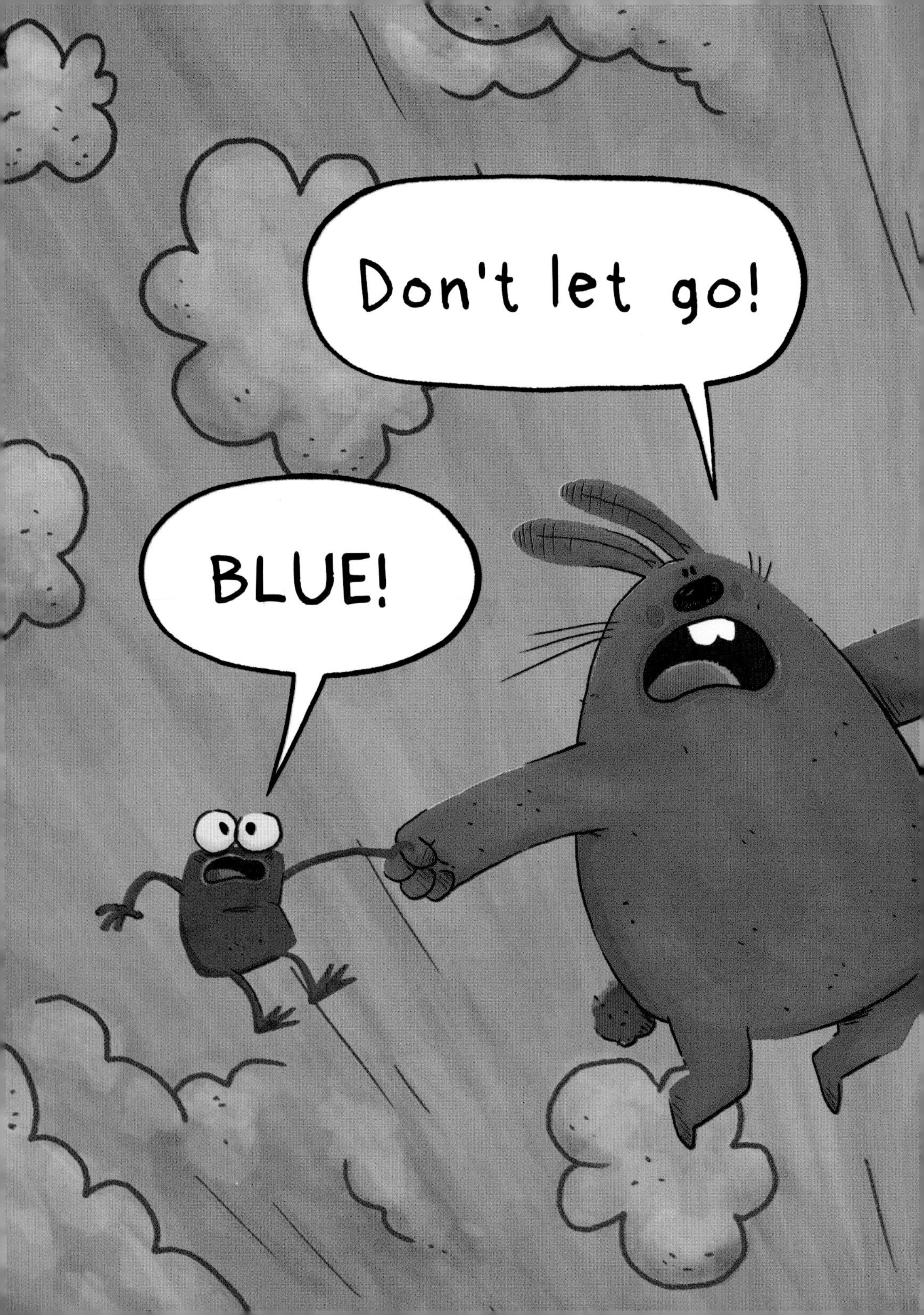
Don't let go!
BLUE!

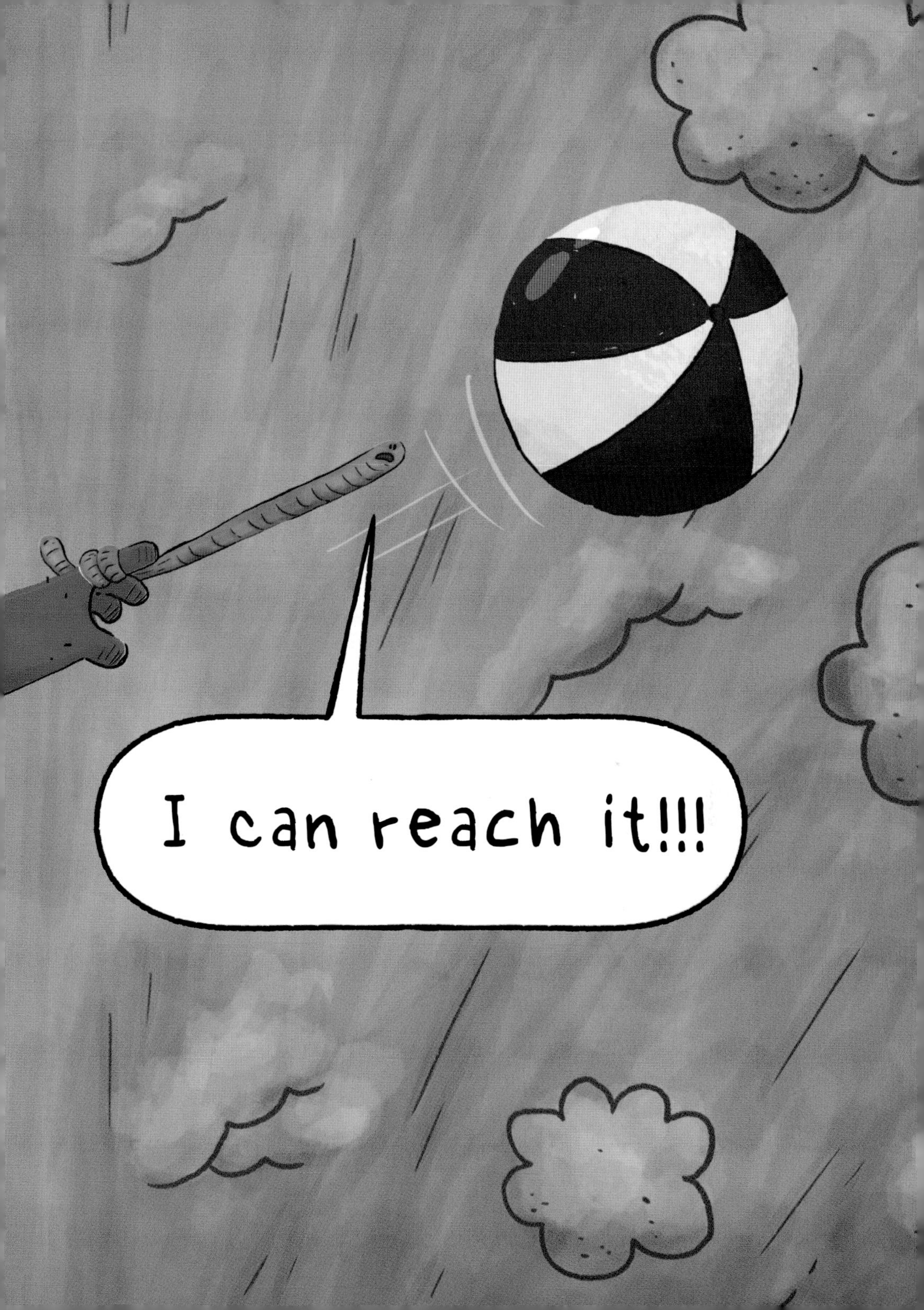
I can reach it!!!

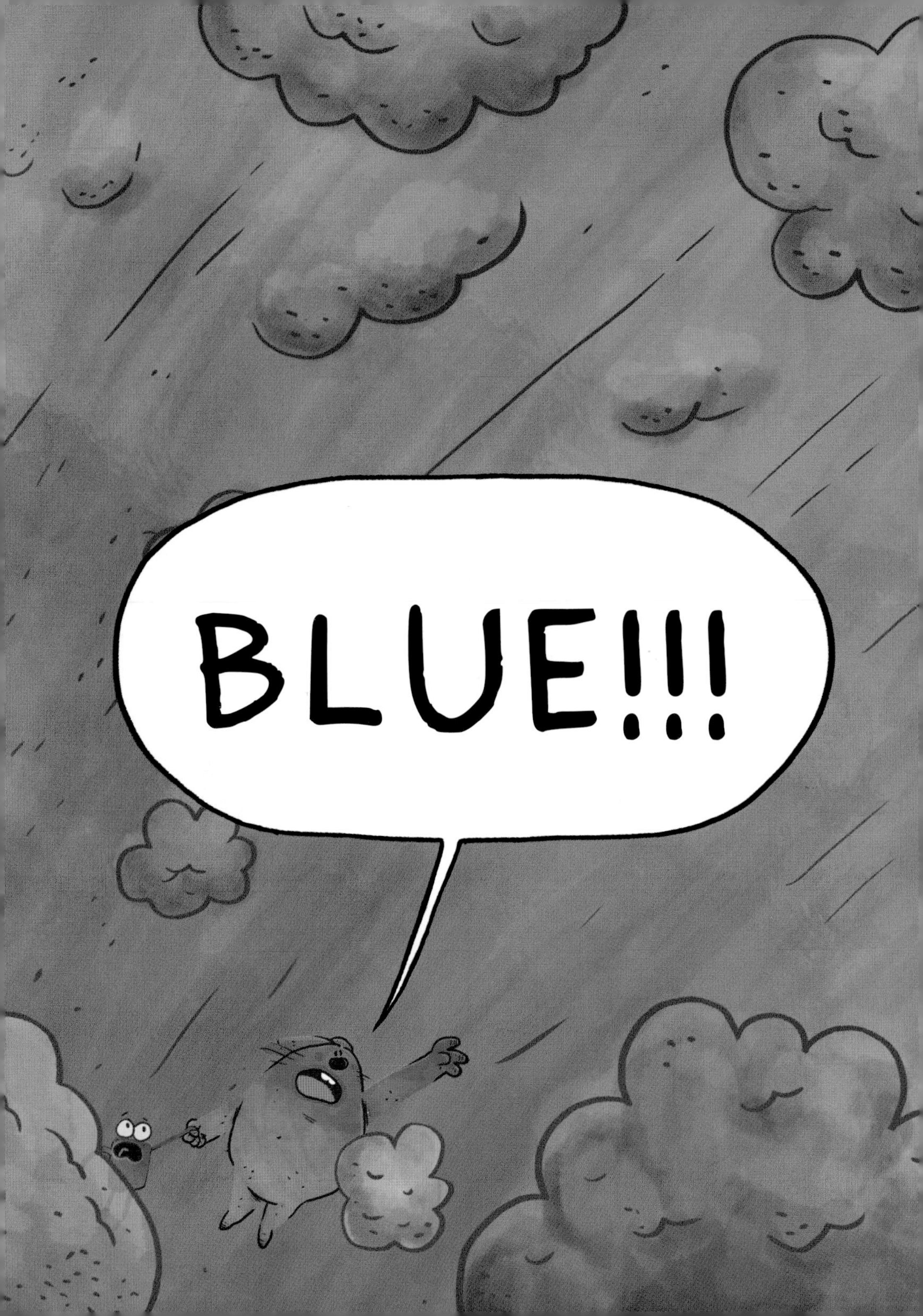
BLUE!!!

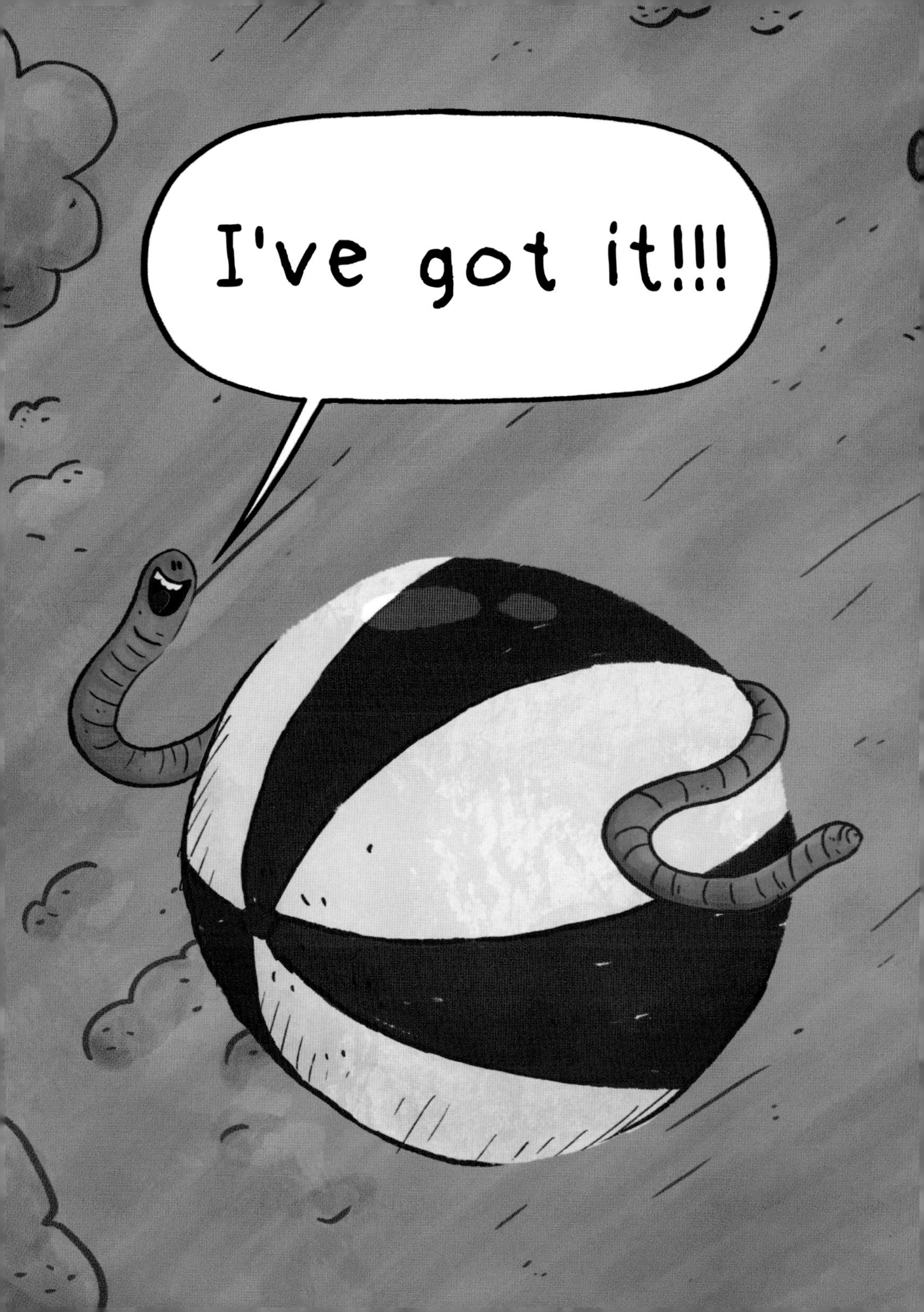
I've got it!!!

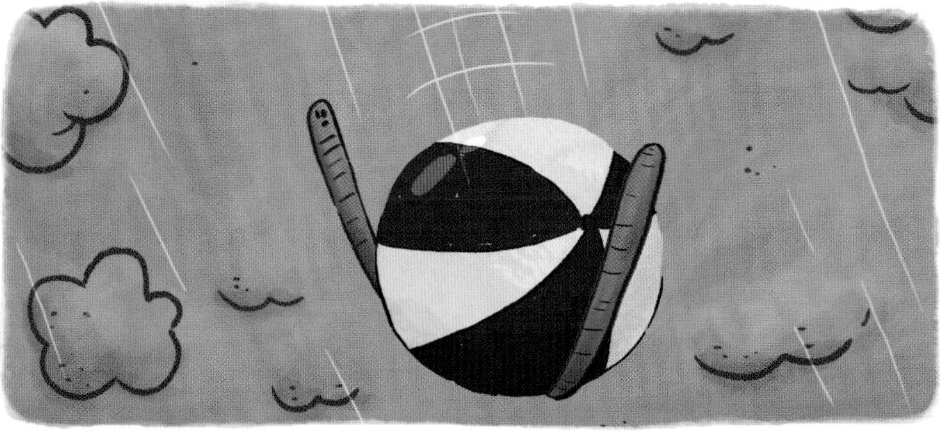

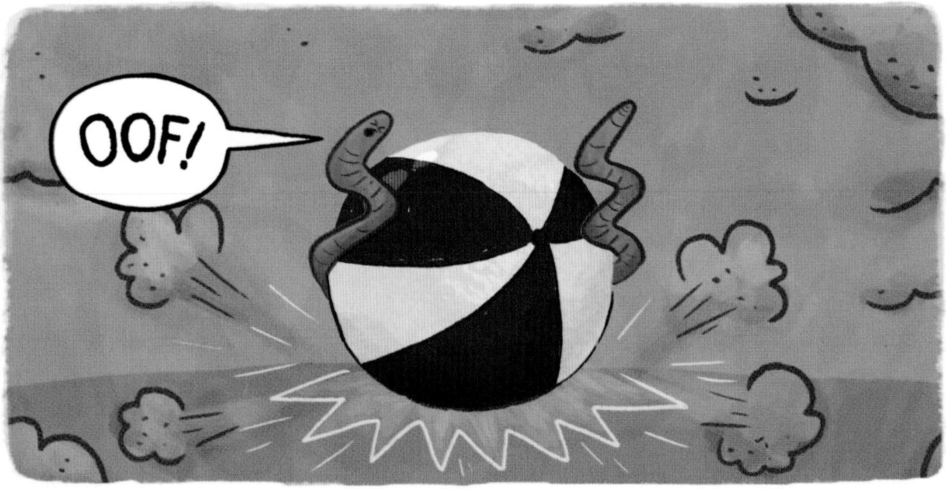
OOF!

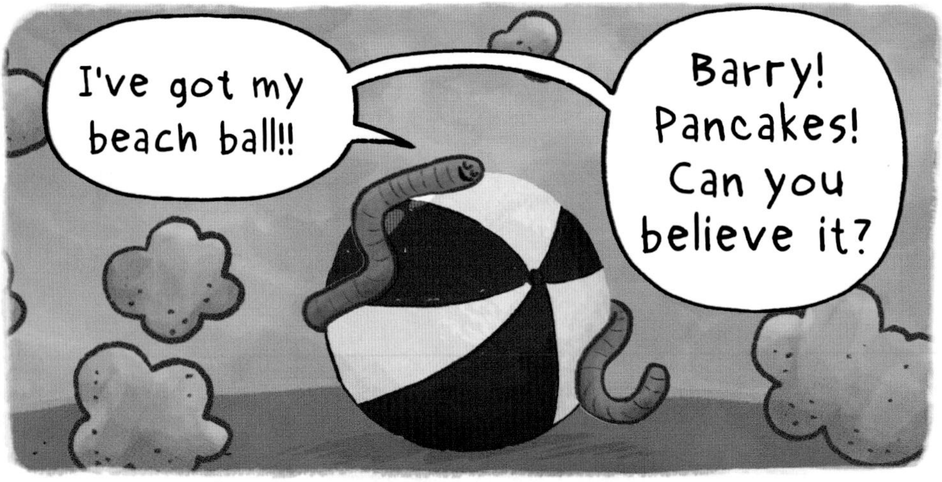
I've got my beach ball!!
Barry! Pancakes! Can you believe it?

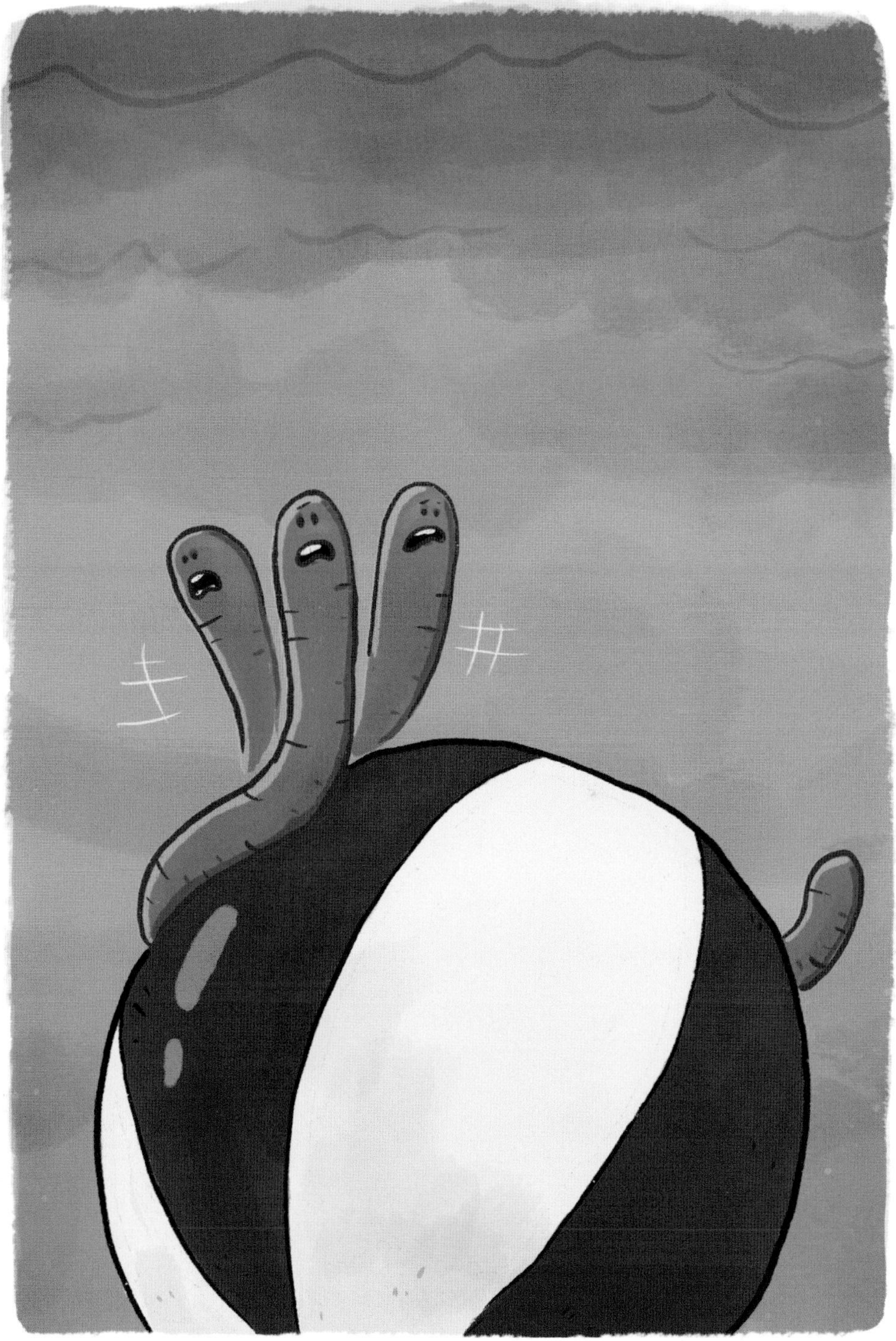

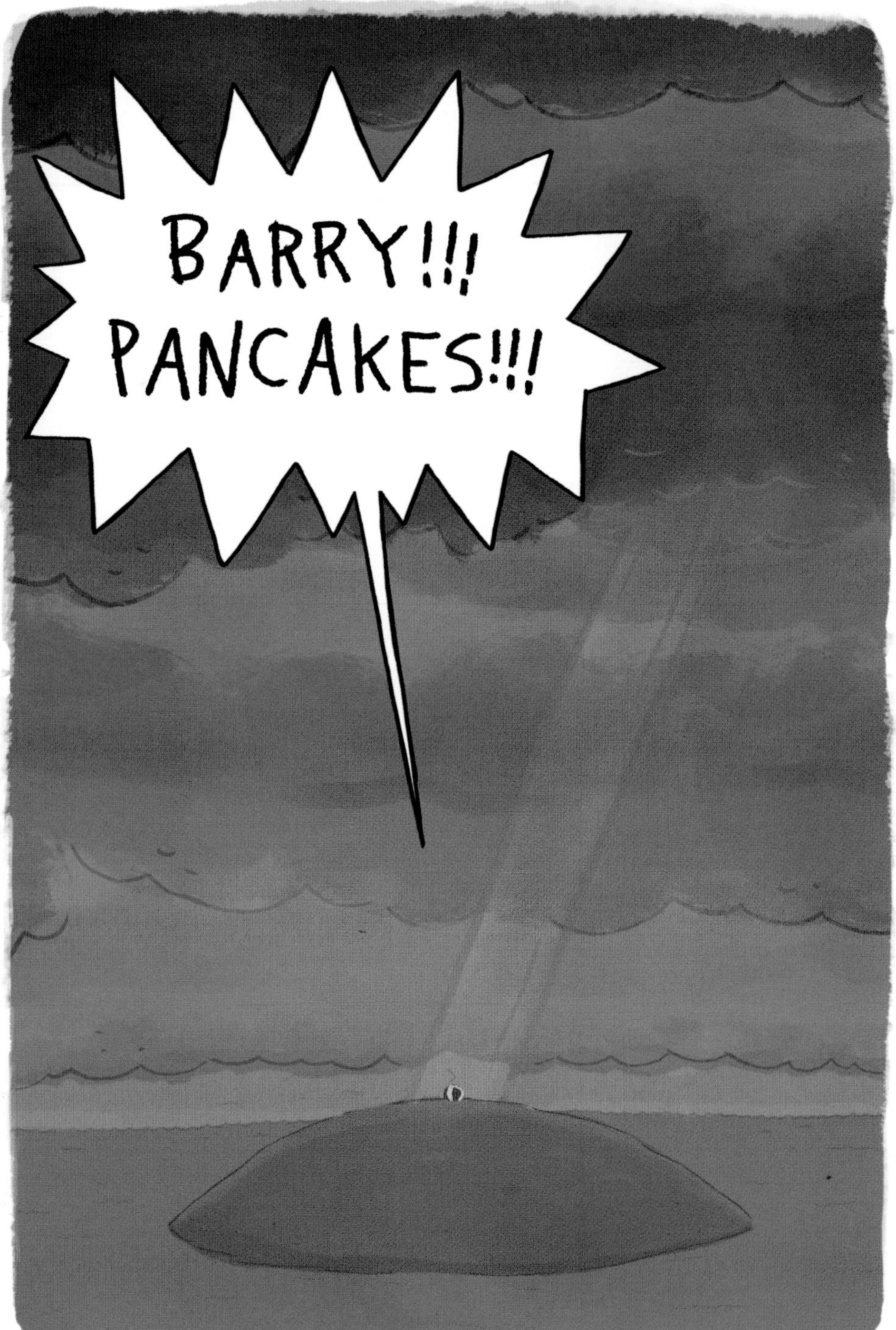
BARRY!!! PANCAKES!!!

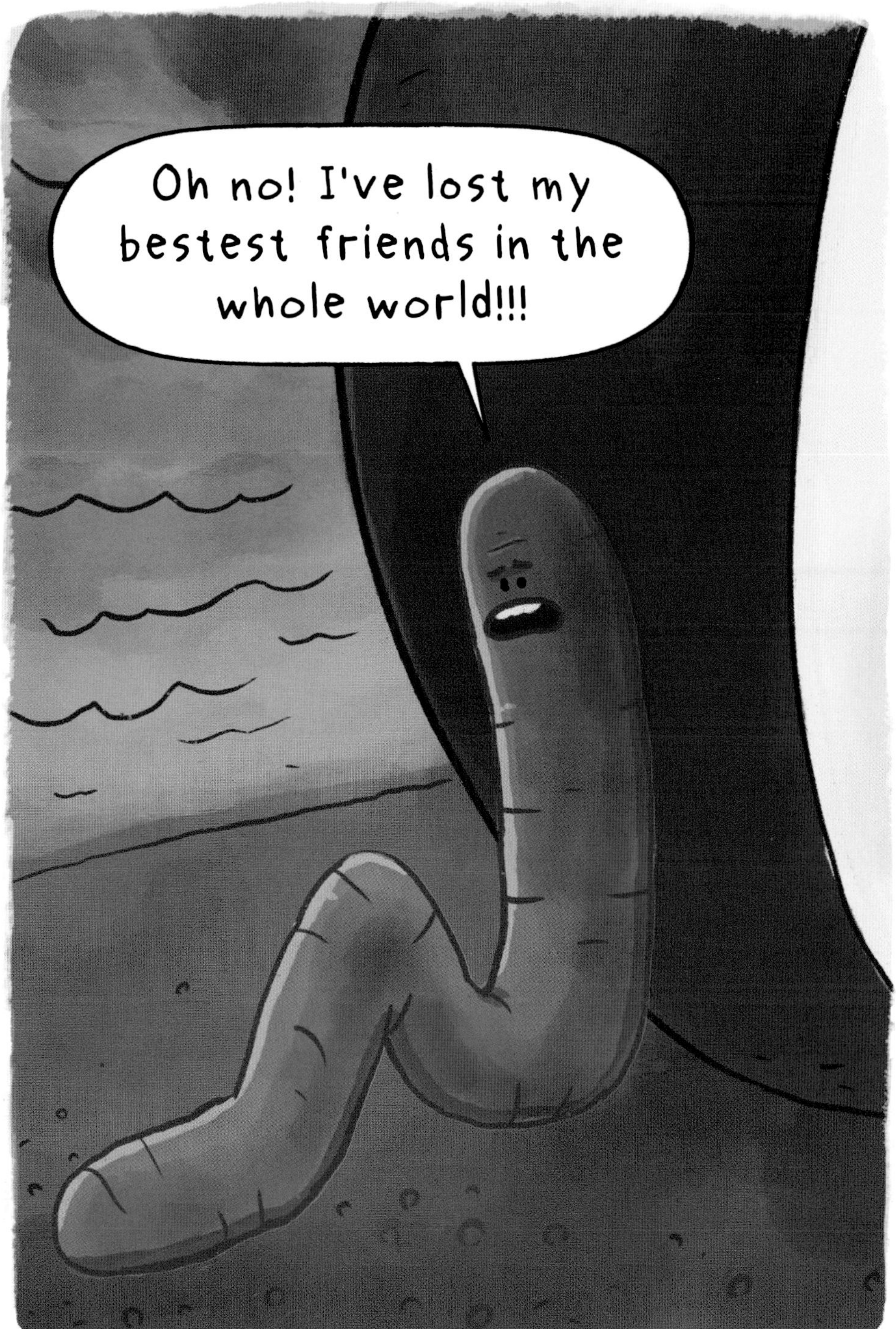
Oh no! I've lost my bestest friends in the whole world!!!

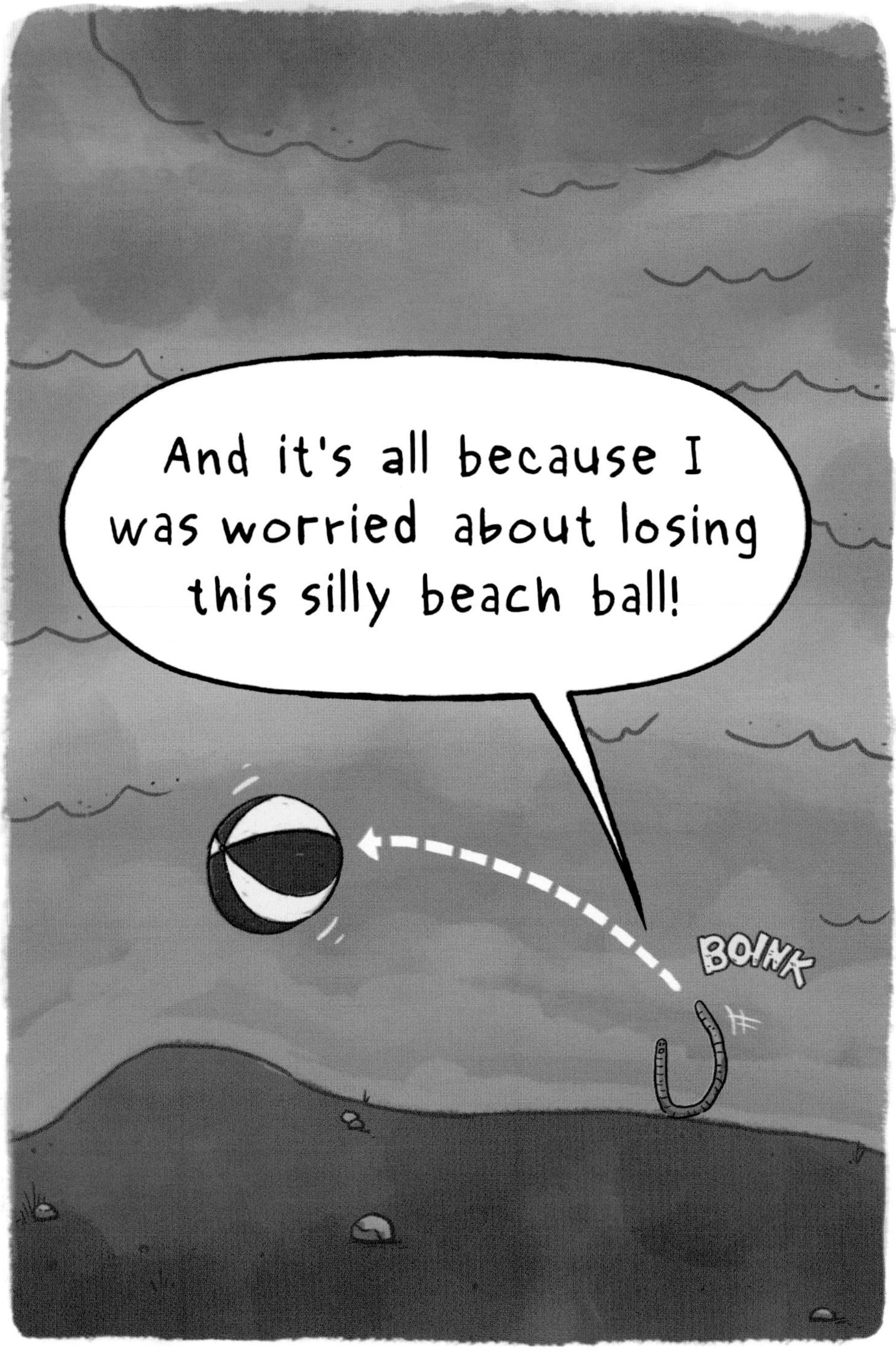
And it's all because I was worried about losing this silly beach ball!
BOINK

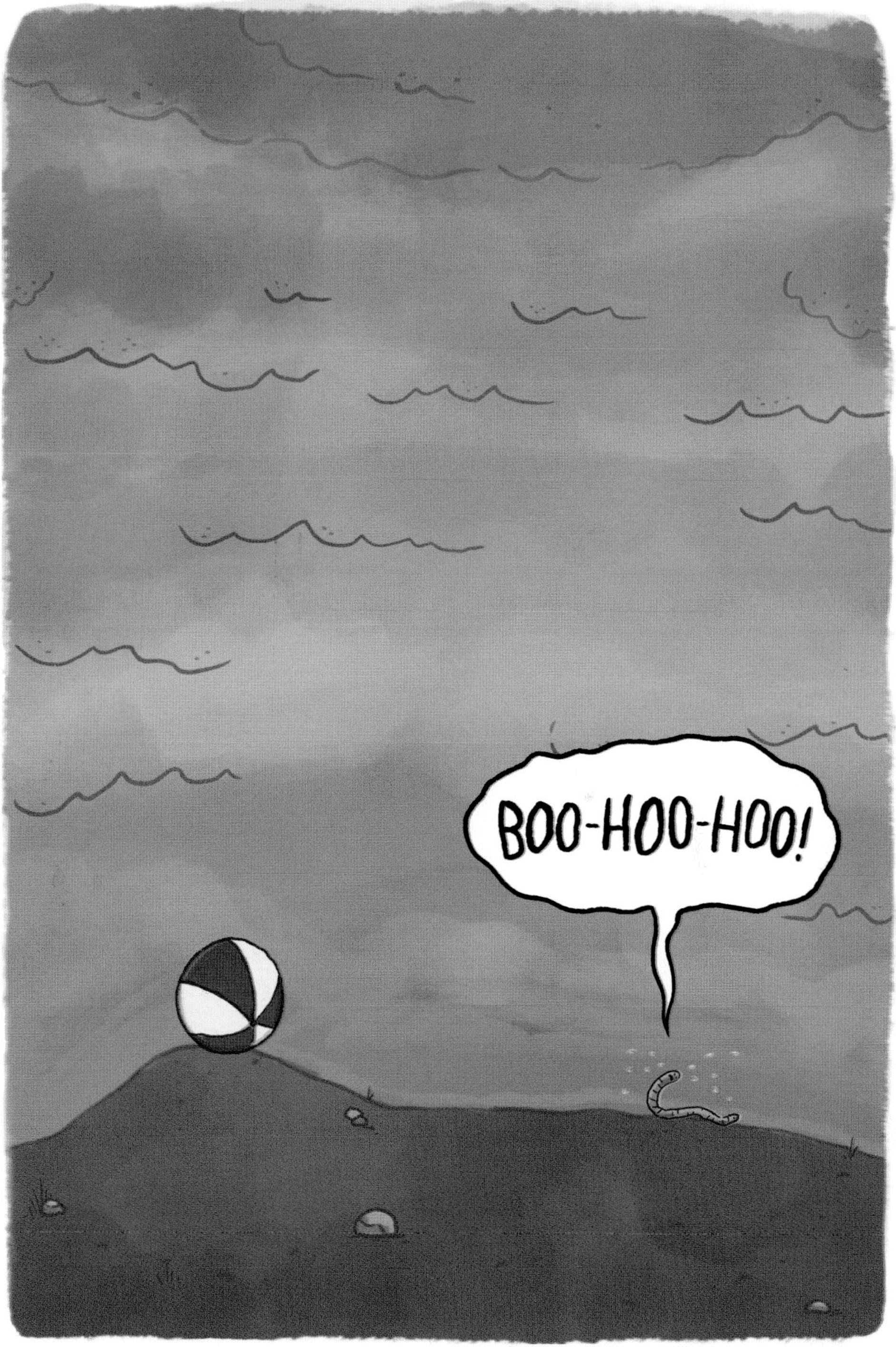
BOO-HOO-HOO!

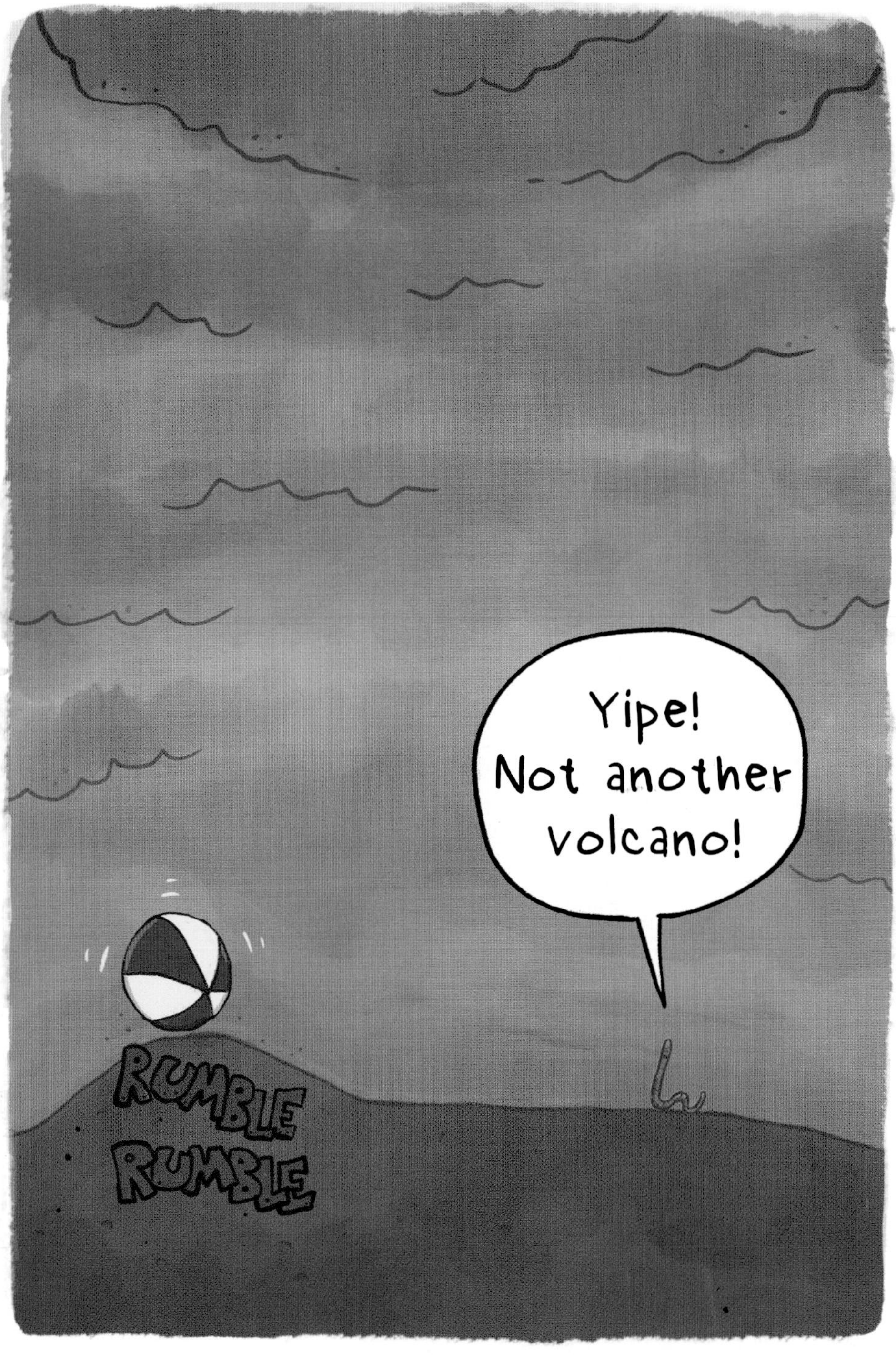
Yipe!
Not another volcano!
RUMBLE RUMBLE

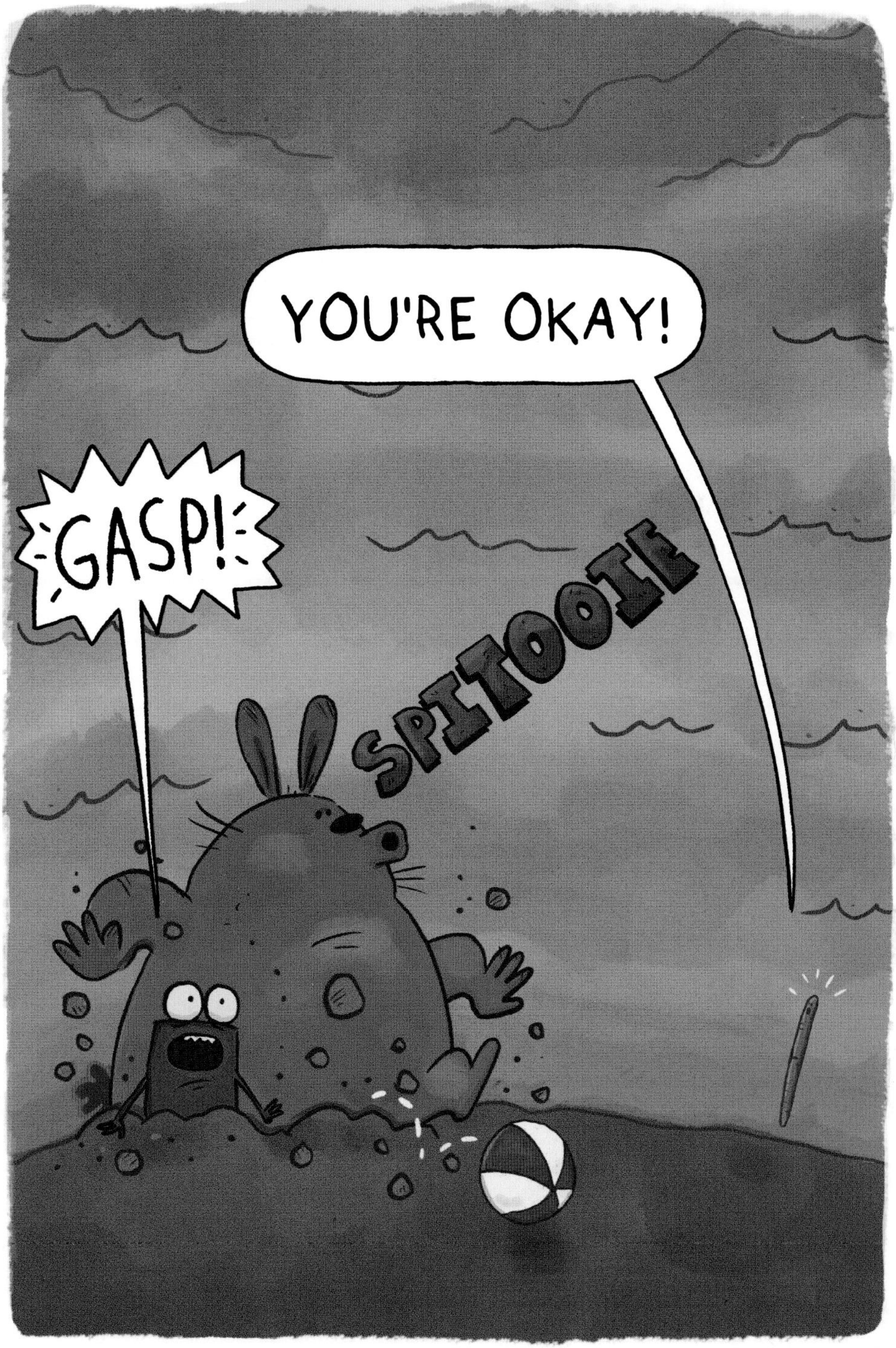
GASP!
YOU'RE OKAY!
SPITOOIE

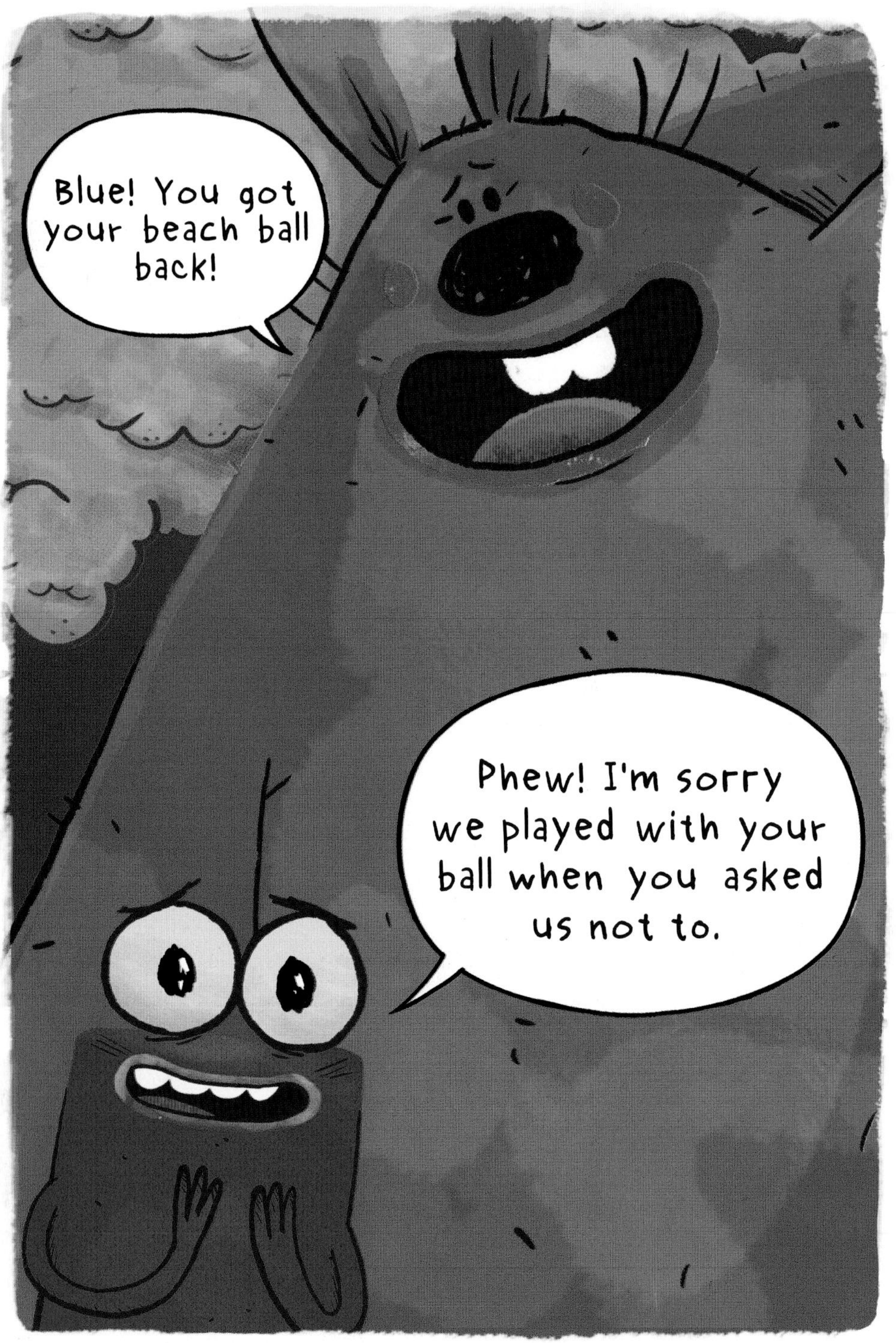
Blue! You got your beach ball back!
Phew! I'm sorry we played with your ball when you asked us not to.

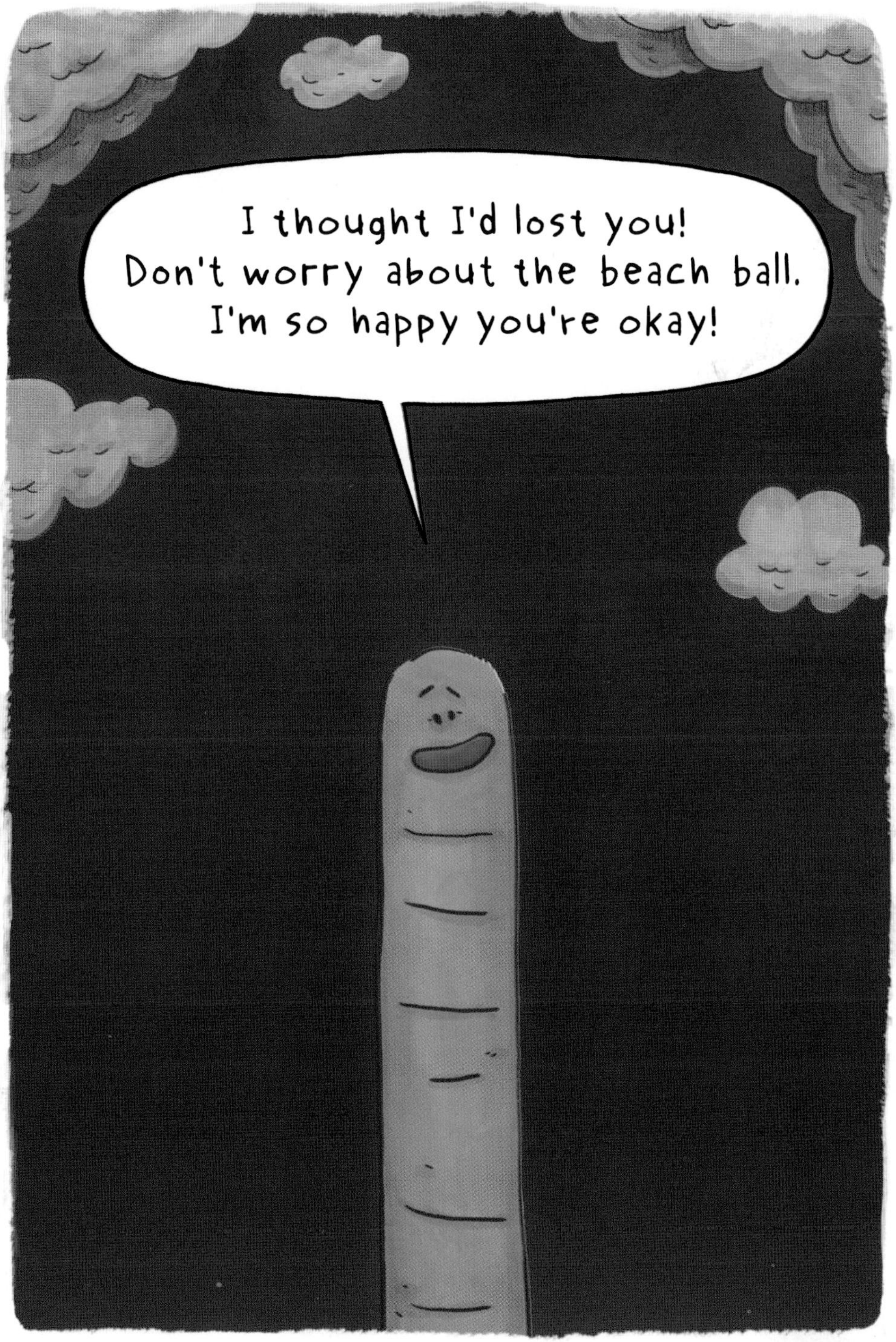
I thought I'd lost you! Don't worry about the beach ball. I'm so happy you're okay!

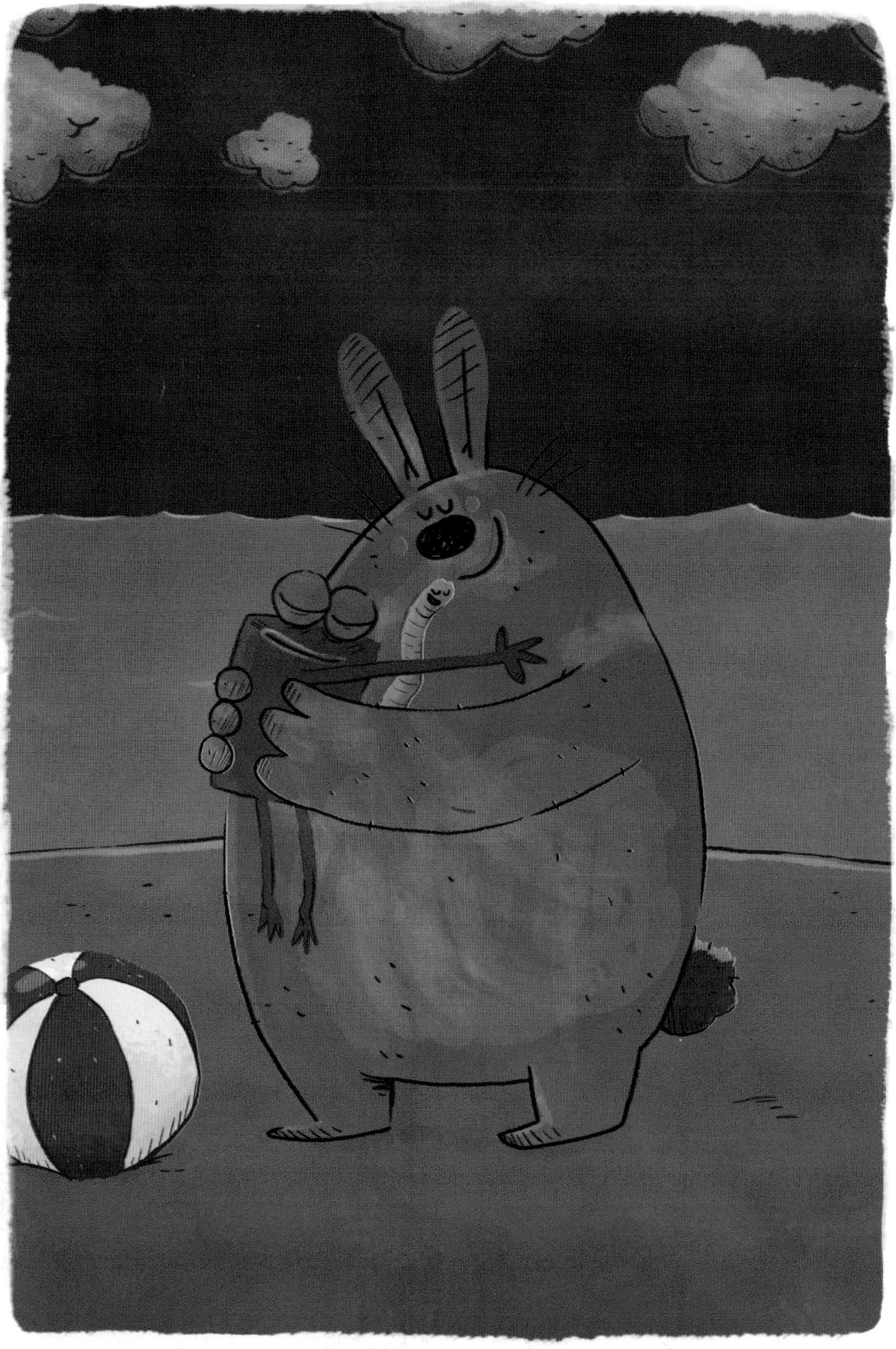

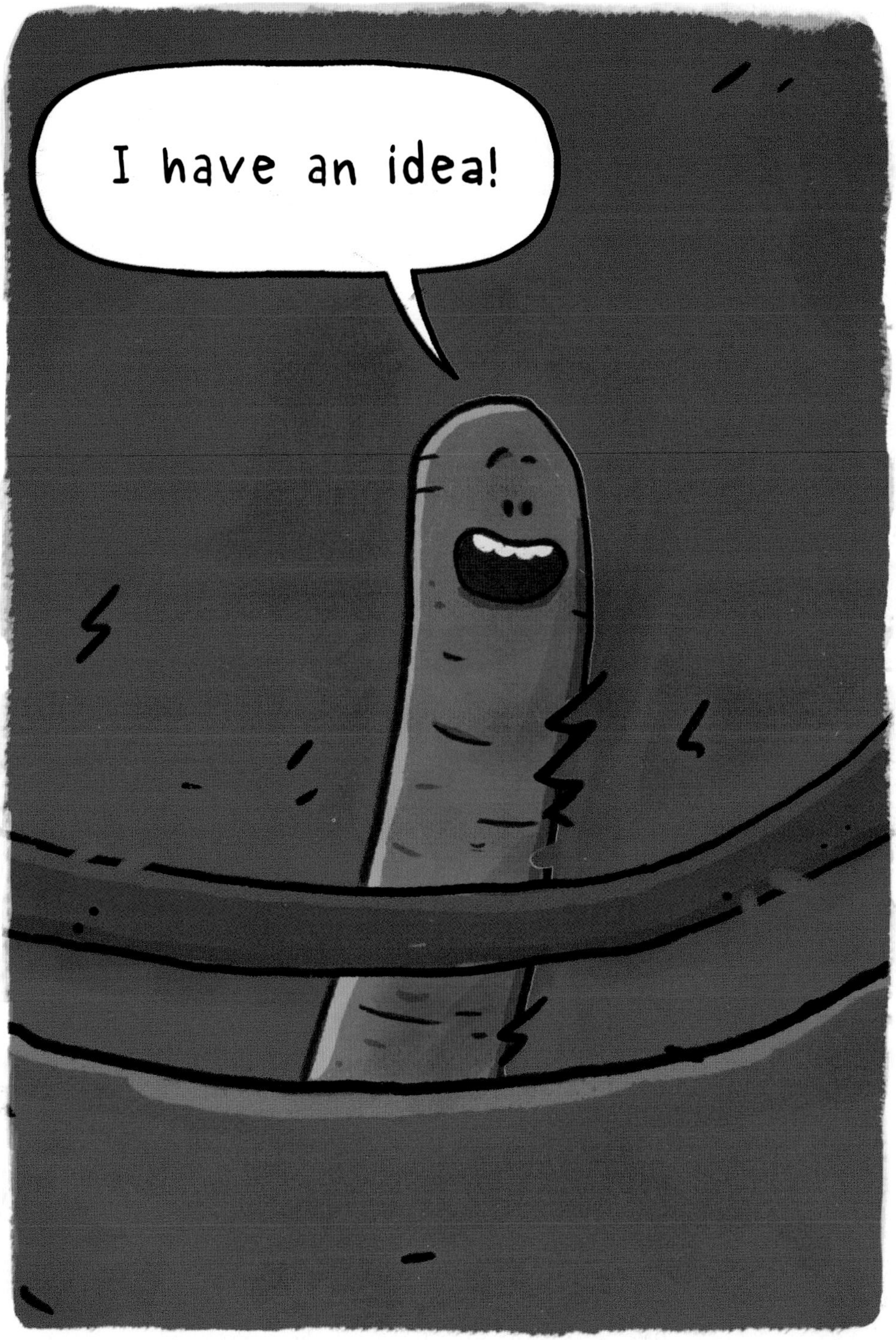
I have an idea!

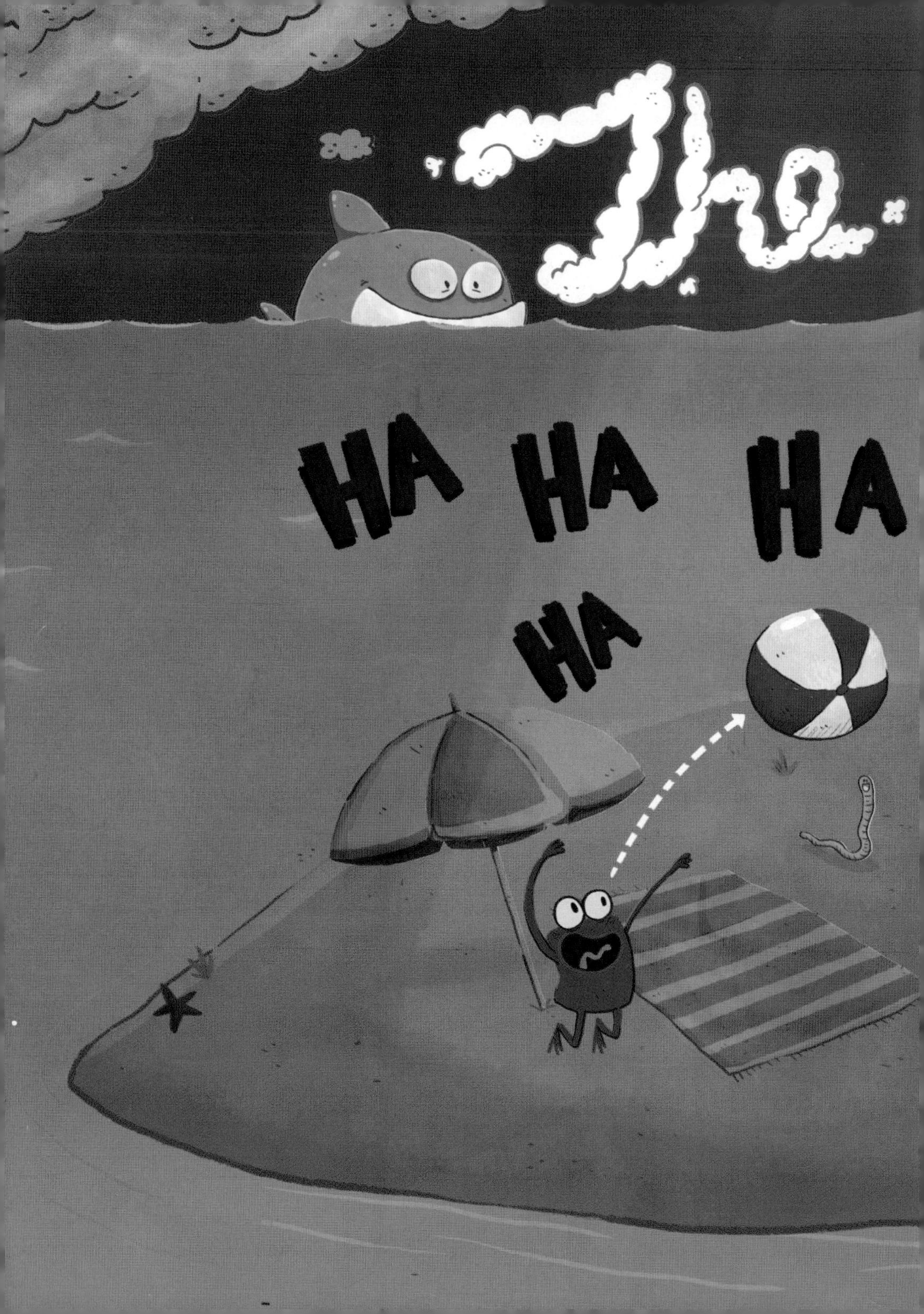
HA HA HA
HA

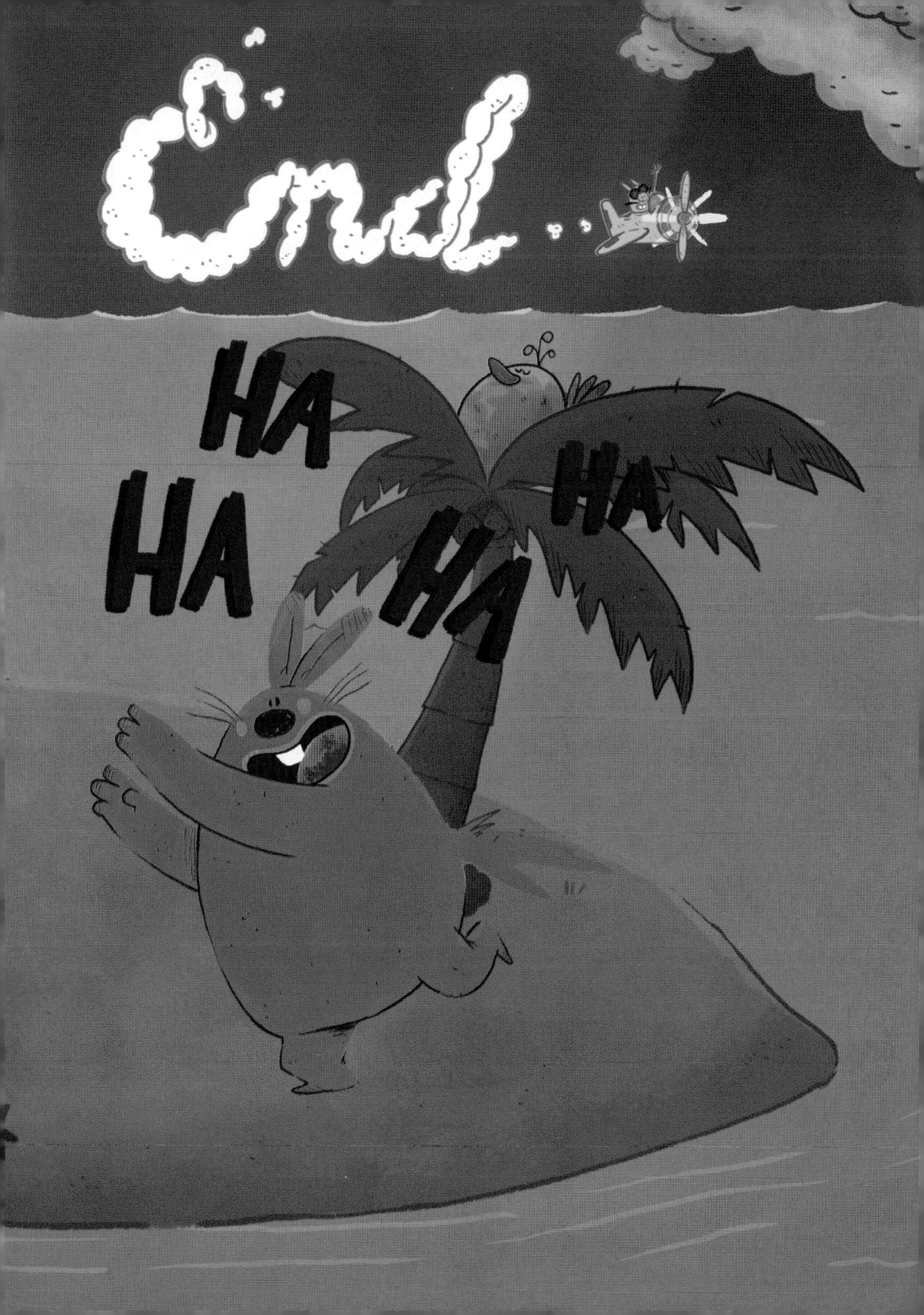

End
HA
HA
HA
HA

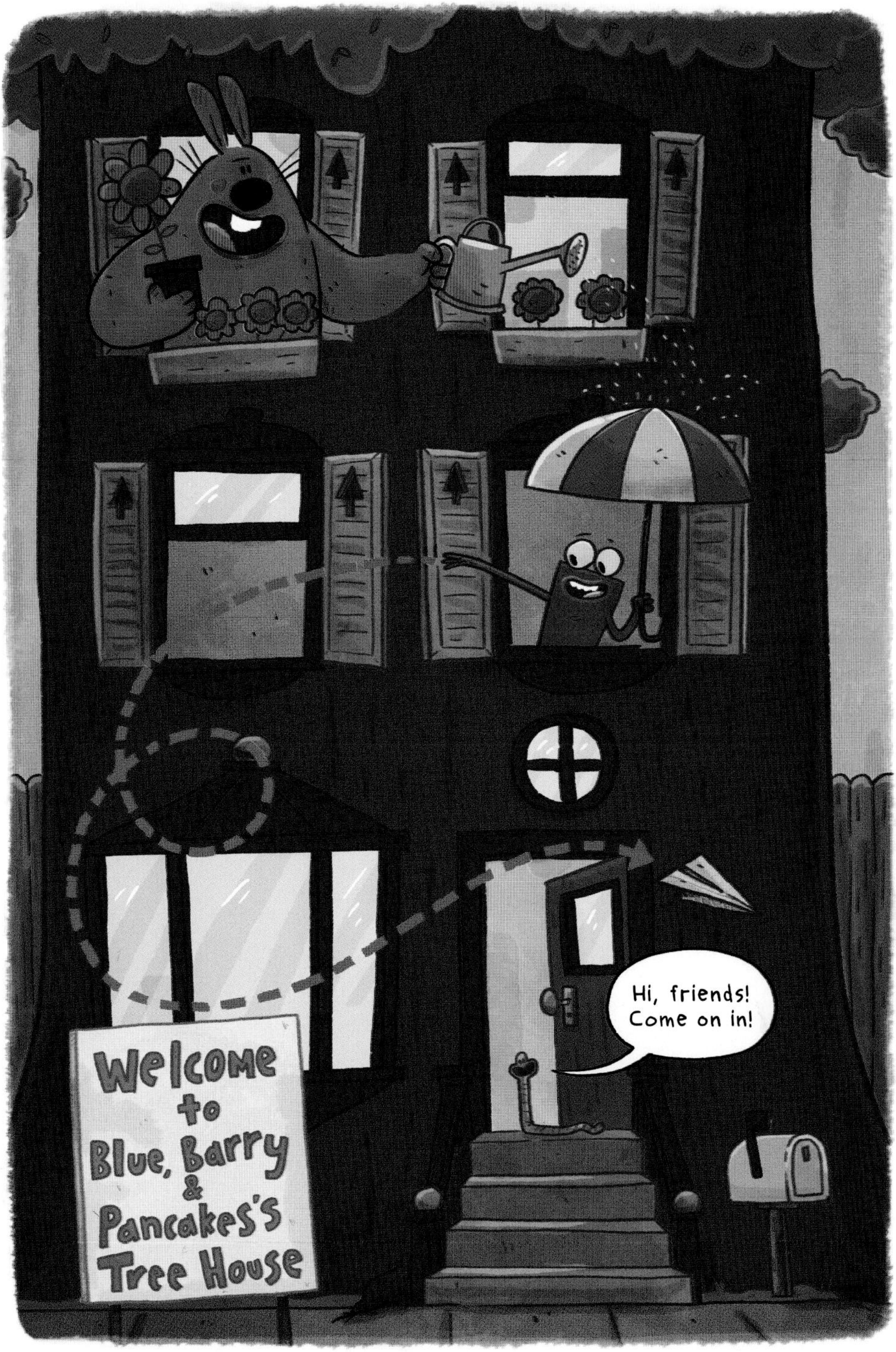
Hi, friends! Come on in!
Welcome to Blue, Barry & Pancakes's Tree House

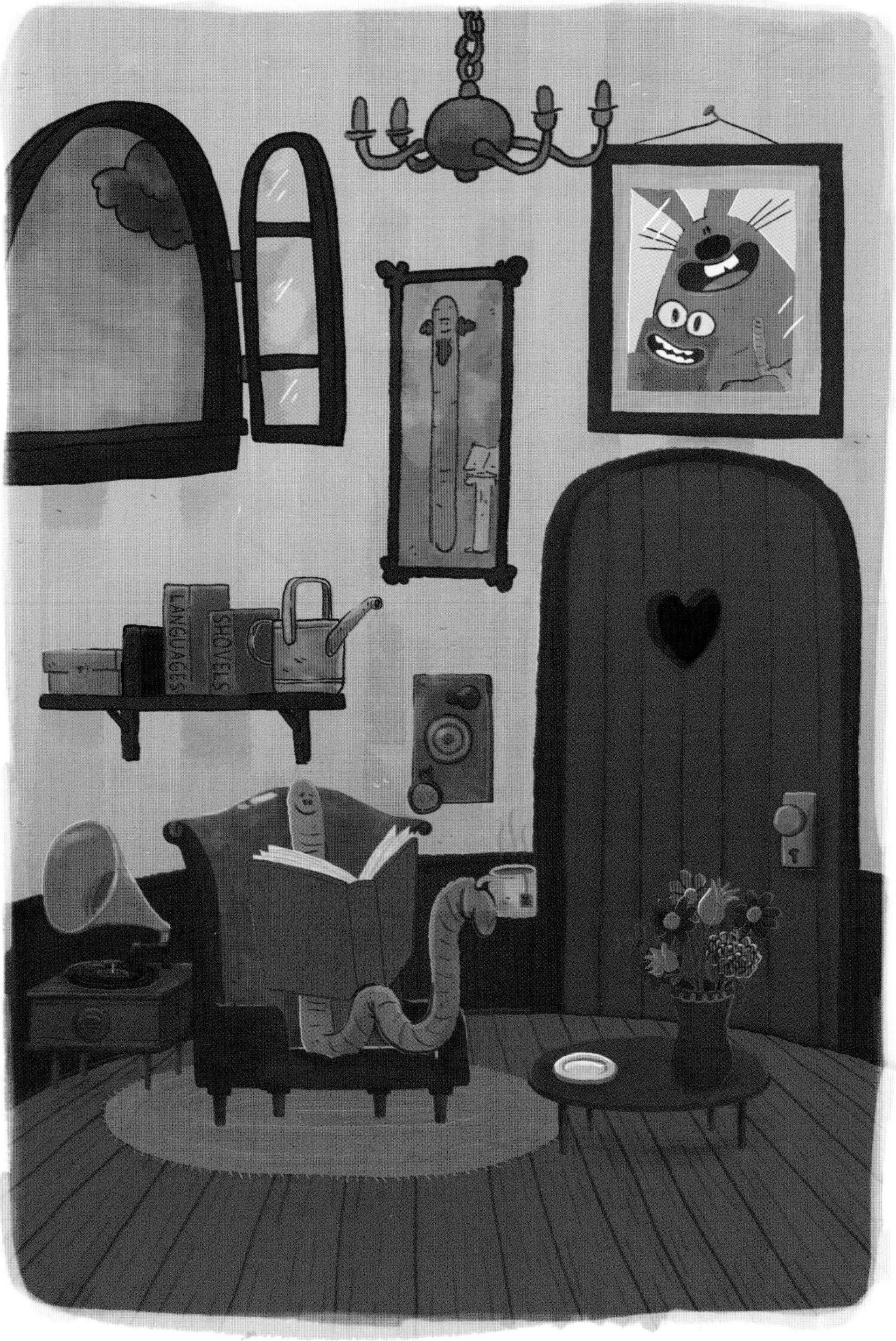
LANGUAGES
SHOVELS

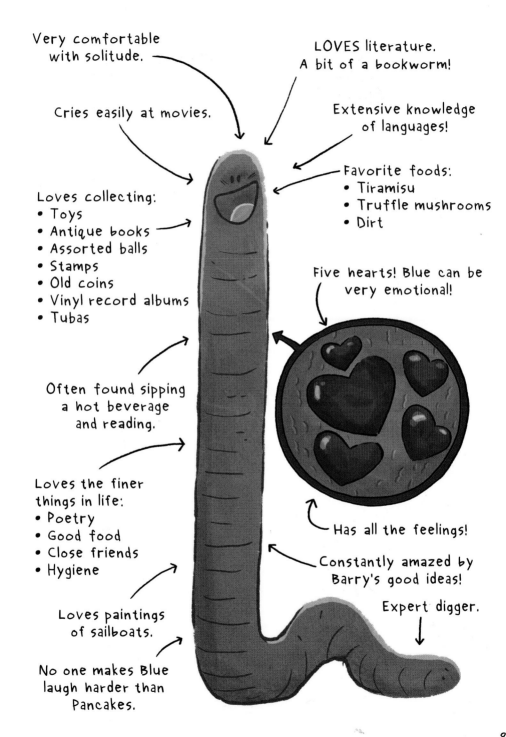

Very comfortable with solitude.

LOVES literature. A bit of a bookworm!

Cries easily at movies.

Extensive knowledge of languages!

Favorite foods:
• Tiramisu
• Truffle mushrooms
• Dirt

Loves collecting:
• Toys
• Antique books
• Assorted balls
• Stamps
• Old coins
• Vinyl record albums
• Tubas

Five hearts! Blue can be very emotional!

Often found sipping a hot beverage and reading.

Loves the finer things in life:
• Poetry
• Good food
• Close friends
• Hygiene

Has all the feelings!

Constantly amazed by Barry's good ideas!

Expert digger.

Loves paintings of sailboats.

No one makes Blue laugh harder than Pancakes.

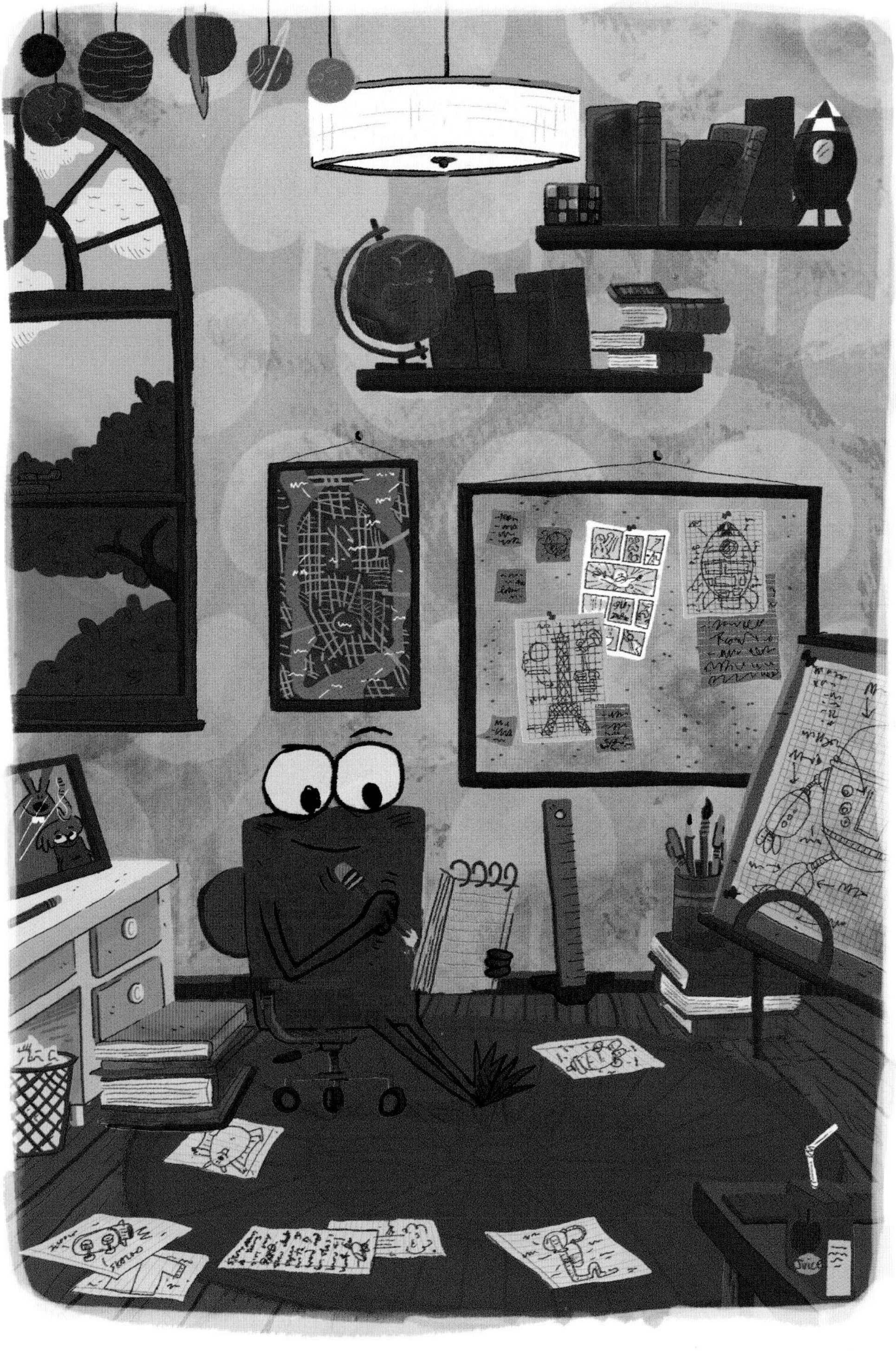

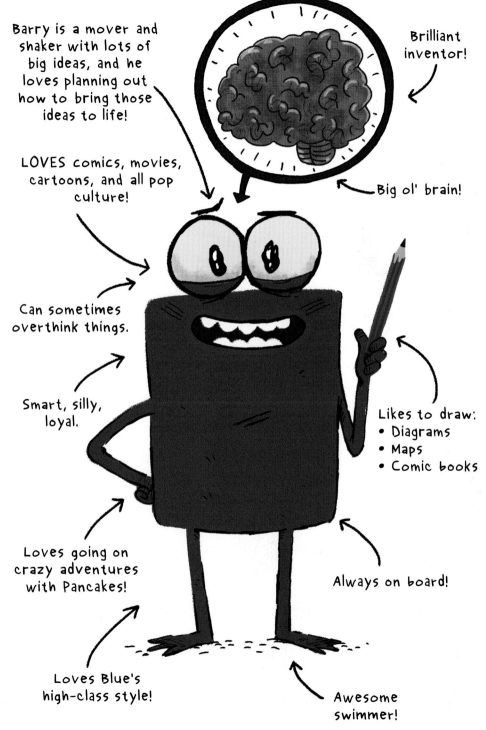

Barry is a mover and shaker with lots of big ideas, and he loves planning out how to bring those ideas to life!

Brilliant inventor!

LOVES comics, movies, cartoons, and all pop culture!

Big ol' brain!

Can sometimes overthink things.

Smart, silly, loyal.

Likes to draw:
• Diagrams
• Maps
• Comic books

Loves going on crazy adventures with Pancakes!

Always on board!

Loves Blue's high-class style!

Awesome swimmer!

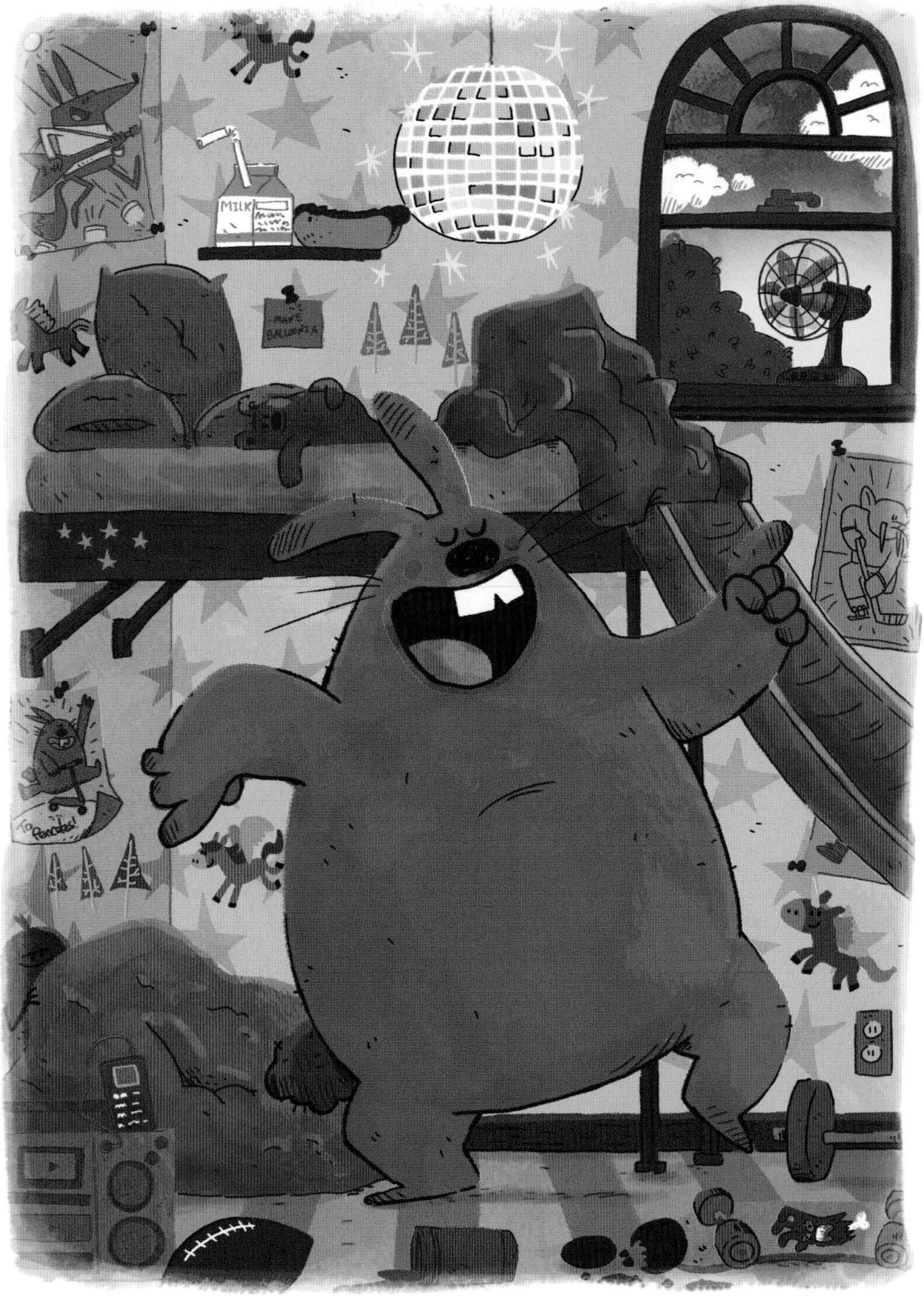
MILK
To Pancakes!

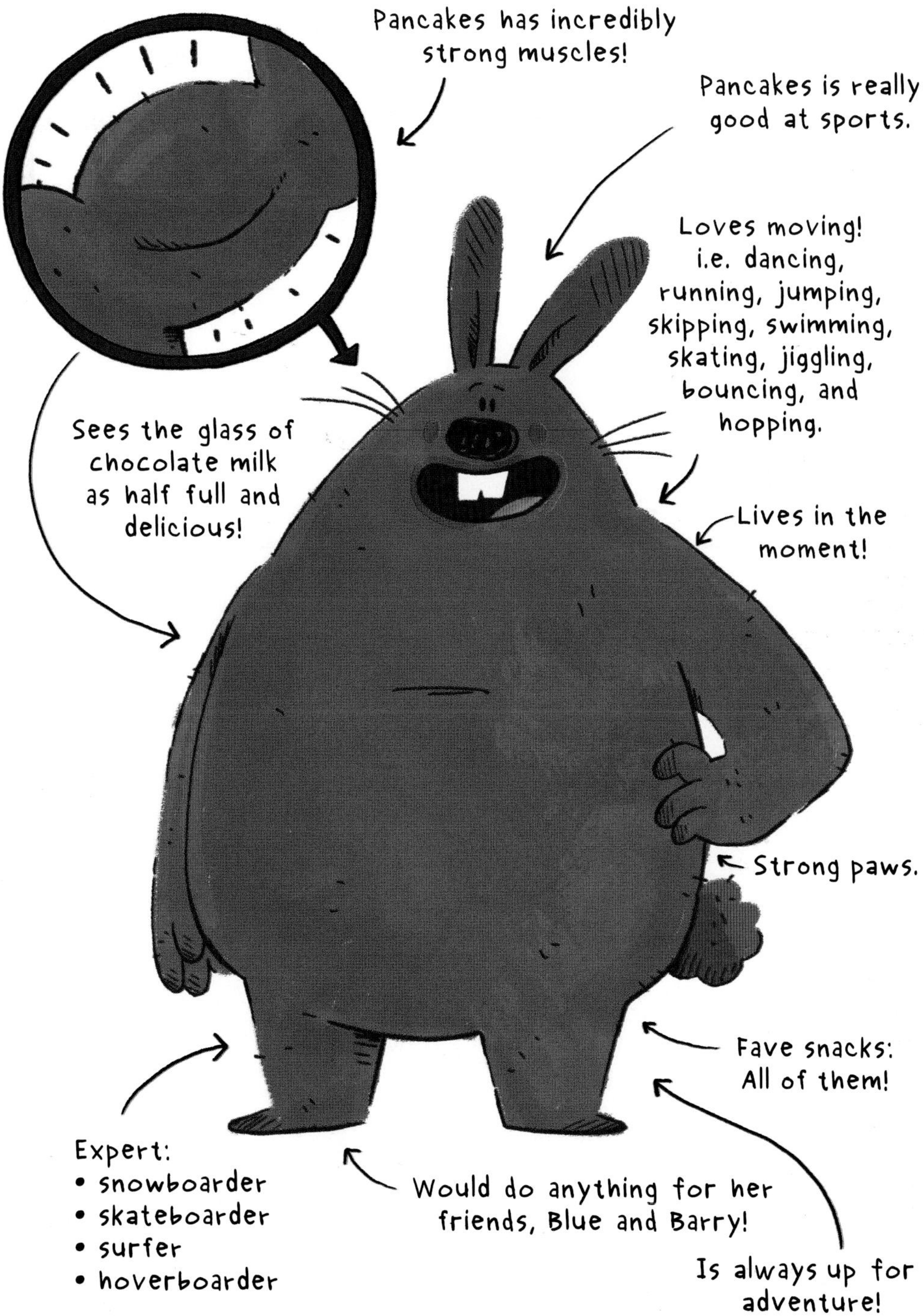

Pancakes has incredibly strong muscles!
Pancakes is really good at sports.
Loves moving! i.e. dancing, running, jumping, skipping, swimming, skating, jiggling, bouncing, and hopping.
Sees the glass of chocolate milk as half full and delicious!
Lives in the moment!
Strong paws.
Fave snacks: All of them!
Expert:
• snowboarder
• skateboarder
• surfer
• hoverboarder
Would do anything for her friends, Blue and Barry!
Is always up for adventure!

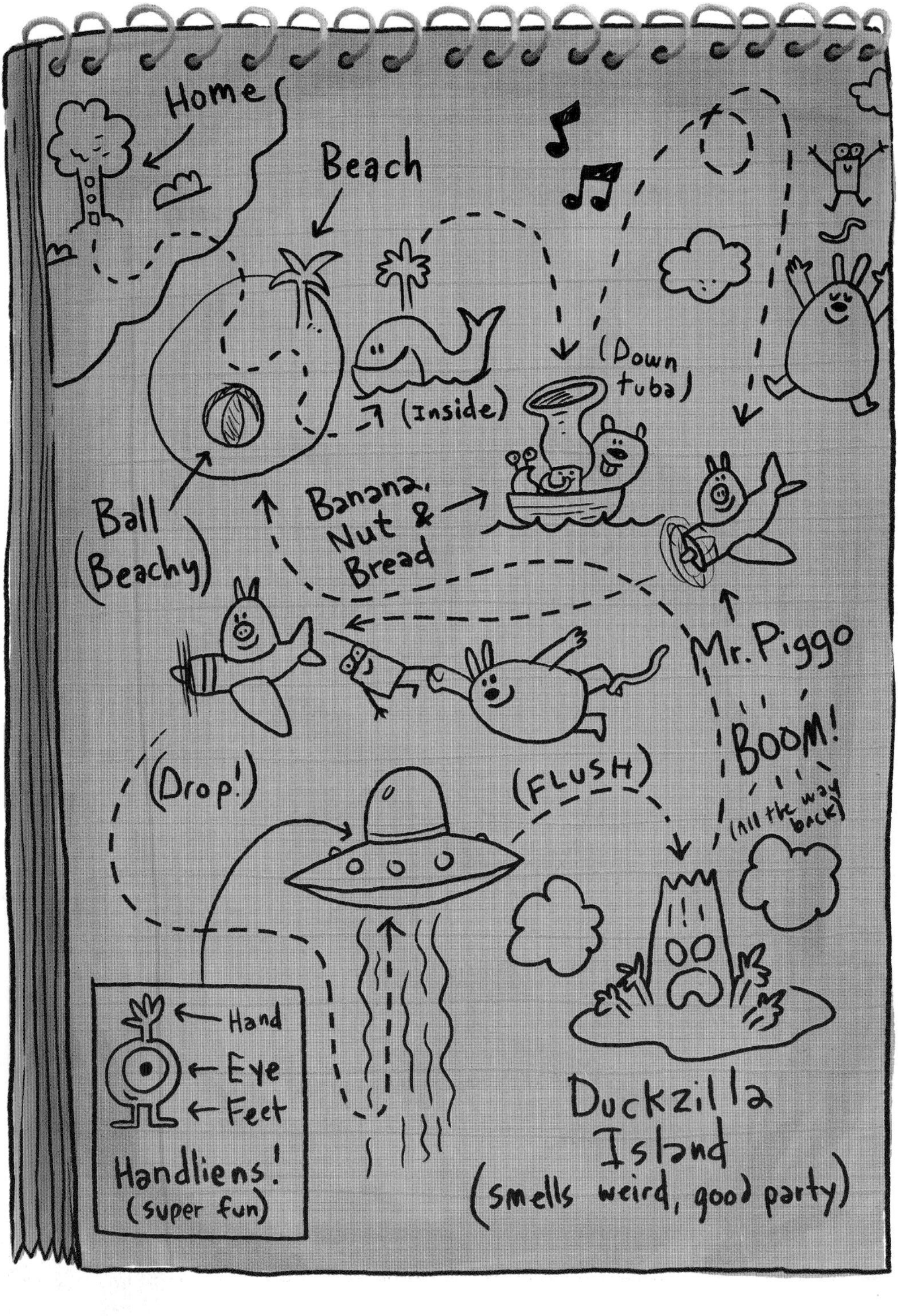
Home
Beach
(Inside)
(Down tuba)
Ball (Beachy)
Banana, Nut & Bread
Mr. Piggo
BOOM!
(All the way back)
(Drop!)
(FLUSH)
Hand
Eye
Feet
Handliens!
(super fun)
Duckzilla Island
(smells weird, good party)

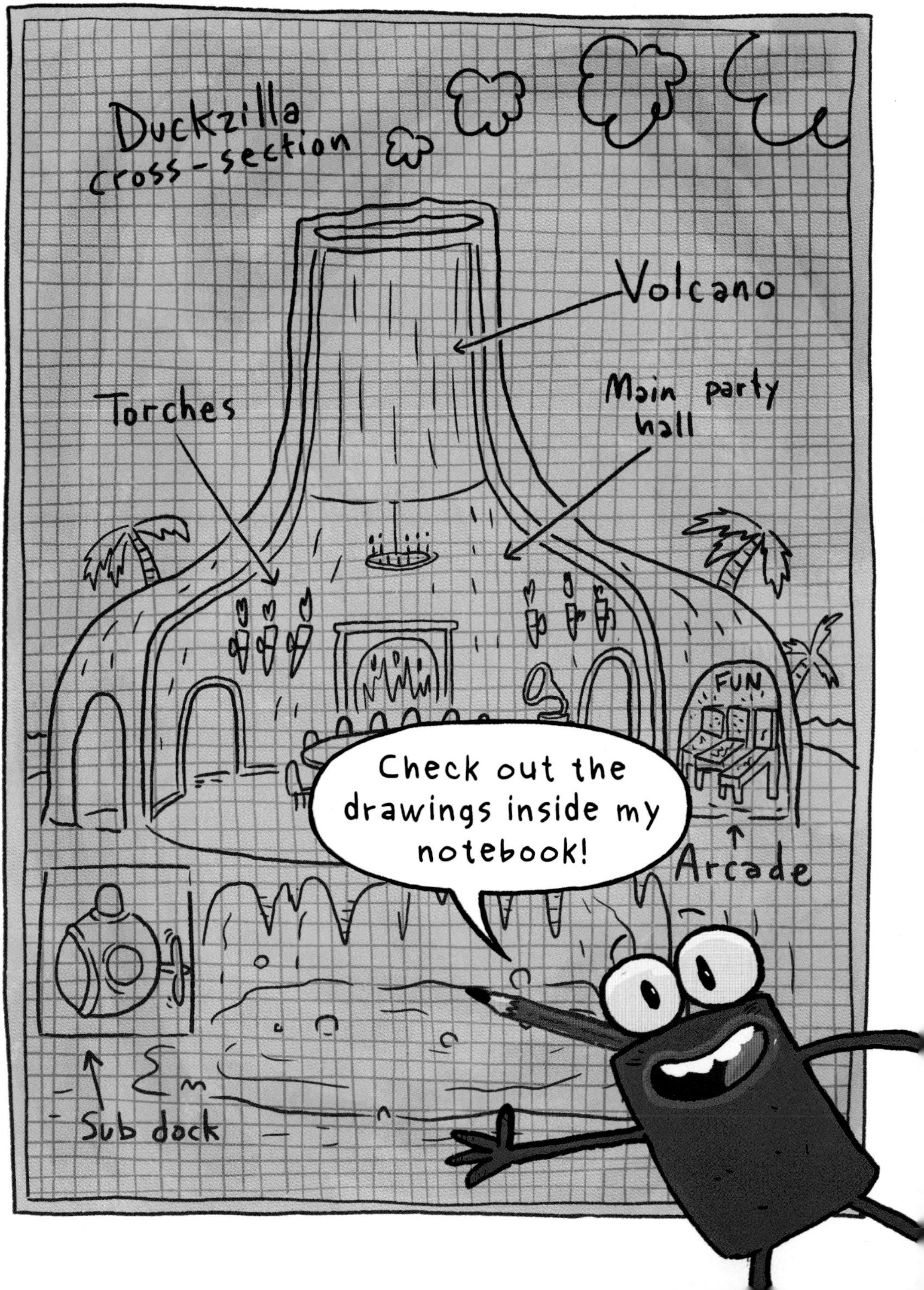
Duckzilla cross-section
Volcano
Torches
Main party hall
FUN
Check out the drawings inside my notebook!
Arcade
Sub dock

About the Authors

Jason

Dan

Dan & Jason go back. Waaaaay back. They got their start drawing and writing stories in what feels like the early Jurassic period, also known as the '90s, when they were making comics in the back of their high school art room. Annnnnd they never stopped!

Dan & Jason have directed award-winning commercials, created hit cartoon shows, and even sold a feature-film concept, but nothing has prepared them for this... the pinnacle of their storied career: publishing the hilarious and heartwarming comic tales of *Blue, Barry & Pancakes*! Dan & Jason have packed it with everything they know about drawing, writing, and the enduring power of friendship. Please enjoy their comic book debut! They make everything together. They think it, draw it, write it, mix it, bake it, and serve it together. Teamwork!

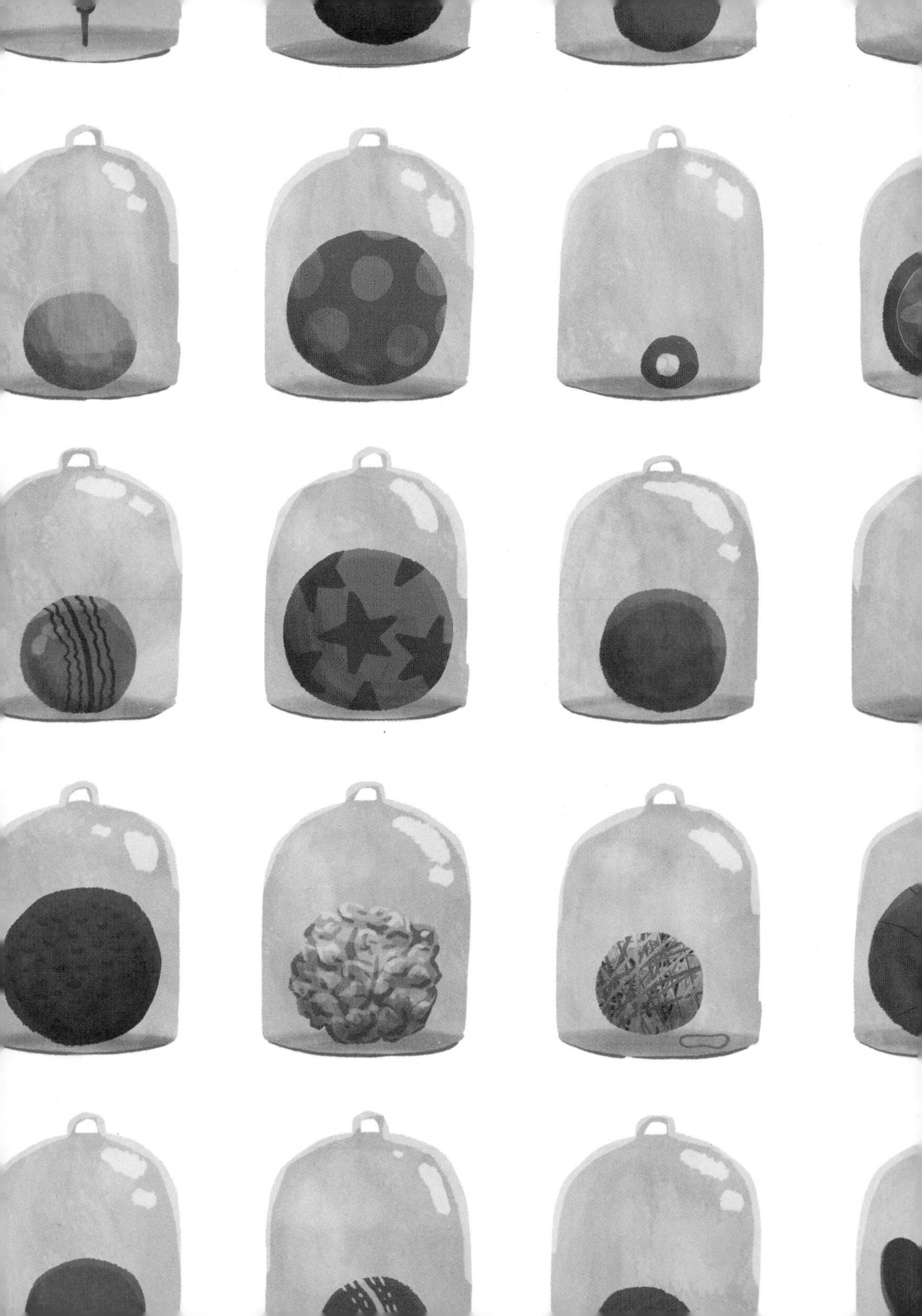